CONTENTS

CHAPTER 1:

SCARLET WIDOW

The Arrival

The door opened with hesitation, as though she had practiced the movement in her mind but was still unsure if she wanted to let it happen.

She stood framed in the warm light of her apartment, a robe the color of dried blood cinched tight at her waist. Her makeup was careful, a defense she hadn't worn in months, maybe years. Her hair was pinned as if she expected company, but her eyes gave her away—sharp at first glance but restless underneath, unable to hide that she'd been alone too long. Her heels sank into the rug as if they were unfamiliar shoes pulled from the back of the closet for this one night.

"I'm Iya," said the woman at her door. No business card. No explanation. She stepped inside before the widow could change her mind, laying a dark coat across a chair. She carried a small black tote that seemed too structured, too intentional, to belong to someone casual.

The widow's voice came out lower than she intended. "You're not what I expected."

"No one ever says I am." Iya did not try to fill the silence, letting the room adjust to her instead. In the background, a record player faintly turned jazz—something smoky, familiar, but too soft to take up the space that grief had claimed.

The widow's throat tightened. "I don't even know where to start."

"That's fine," Iya said. Her tone was even, steady. "We start where you are. Have you eaten?"

The widow blinked. "I... I do not remember."

"Then no," Iya said, already moving toward the kitchen. She opened the refrigerator without asking. Inside was the collection of someone with good intentions to cook, but not yet up to the task: a few chicken thighs wrapped in clear film, half a zucchini, a jar of olives, butter, wine, and a lemon that had waited too long for purpose. On the pantry shelf—garlic, stale bread, canned tomatoes.

Iya set the items out with quiet precision, as though they were enough. "This will do."

"You don't have to cook," the widow said, hugging her arms across her chest.

"You didn't call me to cook," Iya agreed, rolling up her sleeves. "But you called me to care. Tonight, that begins here."

Oil warmed in the pan. Garlic met the heat with a sharp sizzle. The widow startled at the sound, the way the silence shattered and filled with something alive. She sank onto a stool at the counter, robe slipping slightly at her collarbone. "You move like you've done this before," she said, watching.

"I know what to do with hunger," Iya answered simply. She

salted the chicken and laid it skin-side down. The hiss filled the apartment. Fat crackled, releasing a smell the widow had not felt in her chest for years. She looked away, embarrassed by the sudden sting of tears.

"You make it look easy," she said, clearing her throat.

"It isn't," Iya said, turning the meat. "It is just deliberate. That is different."

The widow gave a small, helpless laugh. "Everything feels deliberate with you."

"That's because nothing should feel accidental," Iya replied, sliding zucchini ribbons into the pan, spooning in tomatoes, adding brine from the olive jar. She moved with a rhythm—practiced, assured, never rushed.

Dinner came together in minutes: golden chicken resting on a bed of zucchini, olives scattered like small secrets, sauce spooned carefully, shavings of Parmesan falling in thin curls. She placed a plate in front of the widow and another for herself.

The widow hesitated, fork poised, as though the food itself might accuse her. Then she tasted. It spread across her tongue, savory and sharp, pulling breath from her lungs she hadn't known she was holding.

"There," Iya said quietly.

The widow set her fork down too quickly, then picked it up again. "I haven't tasted anything in so long."

"You stopped asking food to matter," Iya said. "Tonight, it does."

The widow studied her plate. "You talk like you know me."

"I don't," Iya said evenly. "But I know what forgetting looks like."

The widow chewed slowly, shoulders easing without her permission. Her robe slipped looser. The wine on the counter waited, untouched.

"I haven't had someone cook for me in years," she murmured.

"Then remember this," Iya said. Her gaze held steady. "This is what being cared for tastes like."

The widow's eyes darted away, as if the words burned hotter than the food. She forced a small laugh. "You're quite sure of yourself."

"Not *quite* sure," Iya corrected. "Certain."

The silence that followed was not empty. It hummed. Steam

rose between them from their plates, softening the air. The widow's fork slowed, each bite less about filling hunger and more about stretching the moment.

"You haven't asked me about the weather," she said finally. "Or the news. Or anything safe.""I don't want to," Iya said. "Safe is what you have had too much of. Tonight, you do not need safe."

The widow's lips parted, but no words came. She reached for her wineglass, then set it down untouched.

Iya leaned slightly forward, not reaching, just letting the space between them close by degrees. "You don't have to explain anything. You just have to be here."

The widow's breath caught. Her robe had slipped from one shoulder now, the fabric heavy against her arm. She didn't pull it back up.

Dinner became secondary. The conversation, the silences, the looks—they were already undoing her.

"Tell me something," Iya said, casual as passing the bread. "If life were a flavor, what would it taste like to you right now?" The widow's mouth twitched.

"That's not... a normal question."

"Then it's perfect," Iya said.

The widow looked at her plate, then at the window, where the city threw its own light back on itself. She considered being clever. She considered being false. She did neither. "Burnt," she said finally. "Not inedible. Just... like someone forgot to turn off the heat and only noticed when the smoke smelled like yesterday."

Iya did not rush to fill the space. "And before?"

"Sweet," the widow said. A brief, helpless smile. "Too sweet, maybe, but I didn't know that at the time."

"Most sweetness works that way," Iya said. "It's not a sin to have liked it."

The widow's eyes flashed with gratitude. She took another bite, and the sauce moved across her tongue with a conviction that felt, briefly, like certainty about something again. The widow's chest rose, fell. She swallowed.

"So... what happens now?"

Iya turned to her fully, calm, and unhurried. "Now," she said, "we stop pretending this is only dinner." She did not move closer. She did not need to. The invitation was in the steadiness of her voice, in the way her gaze held without pressing, in the weight of silence that made the air itself lean forward. The widow stood slowly. Her heel caught in the rug for half a second, then freed itself. She let her robe hang open just a fraction more than it had before. Her hands shook, but not enough to stop her.

"Leave the lights as they are," she whispered.

"Good," Iya said, her approval quiet and steady. They walked toward the bedroom. The door remained slightly ajar, as though even the walls knew to breathe. The lamp inside glowed a low, forgiving gold.

Iya reached for nothing—not the robe, not the light, not the woman's hand. She only looked at her, and the looking was enough.

"The first touch isn't skin," Iya murmured. "It's deciding."

The widow let her robe slip from her shoulders. She had decided.

The night had begun.

The First Night

The lamp held its warm glow. The door stayed open by an inch, as if the air itself needed passage.

Iya did not rush. She set a folded throw on the chair, placed two towels within reach, slid a small bowl of lemon water onto the nightstand. No ceremony—just readiness. The widow stood in the center of the room, the robe a red pool on the floor, her arms at her sides as if any gesture might break the spell.

"Anything you don't want," Iya said, voice softened by the lamp's light, "say so. If you want more, ask. If you want less, ask. You don't have to be brave. Only honest."

The widow nodded. Honesty felt heavier than courage, yet kinder.

"Breathe," Iya murmured. "Slow in. Slower out."

The widow inhaled, the breath catching before it found a longer path. The room began to breathe with her.

Iya stepped close enough that heat crossed the last inch. She didn't touch, she looked—face, throat, the soft line of jaw, the old map of years along the shoulder, the strength in the legs, the subtle tremor that had nothing to do with cold. Not appraisal—attention. The steady kind that settles a room.

"Still with me?" Iya asked.

"Yes." She wavered and stood anyway.

A single touch, back of the fingers along the jaw. A pause. Then a kiss to the inside of the wrist where pulse met skin. The widow startled at the temperature of it—soft heat over a quick drum.

"Slow," Iya hummed.

She traced the places that wake without argument: hollow of the throat, the curve behind the ear, the slope where shoulder becomes neck. Not downward yet—outward, like drawing the outline of a continent before stepping onto it. When her lips grazed the collarbone, the widow shivered in a way that had nothing to do with the night.

"Don't hide your breath," Iya said. "Let it leave you."

It left the widow in a long exhale, the sound of a seam loosening.

Guided to the bed, the widow sat; Iya's palms warmed her knees, then slid slow along her thighs and stopped a finger's width before expectation. The widow gave a small, helpless laugh at the near-miss—how an almost-touch could be an ache.

"That ache," Iya said, mouth close enough to count as warmth, "is your body remembering it wants."

"It... almost hurts," the widow whispered.

"Good," Iya said. "We'll keep it where it hurts just enough to feel alive."

Oil warmed in Iya's hands turned to a soft sheen. She pressed her palms to the widow's ribs and moved up, not down—long, patient strokes asking the breath to widen, to trust itself. The widow's shoulders learned—slowly—how not to grip. "Don't hold your own weight," Iya murmured. "Let me."

The widow lowered her head, a small surrender. A sound escaped her, not performed, not polite—simply true.

"Lie back," Iya whispered.

The sheets were cool, the air over bare skin cooler still. Iya's hand rested briefly on the widow's sternum to measure the rise and fall, then her mouth pressed there—light as punctuation at the end of a sentence that had taken years to say.

"Here," Iya said, as if naming a place on a map.

Her hands mapped the neglected commons: sternum to shoulder, shoulder to elbow, elbow to palm—working the base of each finger until the tiny hoards of tension gave up their store. The widow's eyes flickered. She had not known how much grief lived in her hands.

Iya's mouth followed, a beat behind her palms: warmth where space had just been made, heat where the press had softened. Press. Heat. Release. The pattern repeated until the body believed in patterns again. The ache sharpened into want. The wanting made the widow brave.

"Please," the widow said, surprised by how steady it sounded.

"Say it plain," Iya murmured.

"I want more."

"Good," Iya said, and answered without talk. One knee braced beside the widow's hip; weight, yes, but not heavy presence. The widow arched into it, as honest as breath. Iya's lips found the place just below the breastbone, then lower and lower in a path the body recognized before the mind did. First with breath, then with focused warmth that sent a current through the widow from spine to heels. The first sound that left her was small and astonished; the second was need.

The widow's hand rose to cover her mouth; Iya paused only long enough to catch it and lower it gently. "No hiding."

The widow trembled, determined to let sound be sound. A tremor ran along her thighs. The breath she had been taught to swallow came out longer, richer.

"Stay with your breath," Iya said. "When it climbs, do not choke it. Let it go."

She obeyed. Each exhale made more room for the next touch. Iya lingered at places that had been ignored: the inside of the knee, the soft notch beside the lowest rib, the curve of hip where wanting settles before it declares itself. A kiss to each, then the next, and the next, a simple logic the body understood and welcomed. When Iya finally gave her what she had been circling—patience, mouth, that devastating steadiness—the world narrowed to pulse and heat and the old name for relief.

The ache became an edge. The edge became a tremor. The tremor rose.

"Let it," Iya said, voice low against her. "Don't hold."

She did not. It took her like a storm—lifting, breaking, rushing. The startled cry of it was not punished by silence afterward. Air returned to her lungs as if they had been relearning a lost word. She lay open-mouthed, eyes wet, body shaking with the kind of weakness that arrives with strength.

Iya didn't move away. She softened the pressure, steady hands resting warm to ground the aftershocks until they weakened into quiet.

"Here," Iya said when the widow's gaze drifted.

"I'm here," the widow breathed—and it was true.

Water. The glass steadied in Iya's hand while the widow drank; a drop slid to her chin, caught by Iya's thumb in a gesture so ordinary and tender it made the widow's throat tighten. "You're shaking," Iya noted, not worried, just seeing.

"I don't know what to do with my hands," the widow said, half laughing, half undone.

"Give me one." Iya guided it to her shoulder. "Hold. If you want closer, ask."

The widow's fingers curled, then flattened. "Closer."

Iya settled beside her, not on her. They lay in a shared warmth that made the world smaller and kinder. The widow felt Iya's breath at her temple; she realized there was a quiet hum in Iya's throat, not a melody, just focus-made sound. She matched her breathing to it until their chests rose together and the thin wire inside her loosened another inch.

Iya eventually rose to look at her properly. The forehead had smoothed. The mouth was softer. Grief's grip had eased.

"Again?" Iya asked, a question, not a dare.

"I didn't think—" The widow laughed at herself. "Yes."

"Different, then," Iya said. "Slower. Higher. Let breath lead."

She began with breath alone—warm drafts over chest and ribs, the almost-touch that feels like a promise. The widow's body moved before her mind could, back arching to meet what was not quite there, thighs trembling at the suggestion of contact. "Stay," Iya murmured, and the word pinned her in the gentlest way.

When Iya touched her again, it was a thinner line of sensation, less pressure, and more intent—like writing with a finer nib. The widow gasped at how it changed everything— the way less could lead to more. This was not a breaking wave; it was a tide pulling through every part of her until edges blurred and her center warmed. When it came, it came from a deeper place, a quiet surrender she met with her mouth open and eyes wet for a different reason. The sound was low and full, and afterward she laughed into Iya's shoulder, astonished and grateful. "I thought that was a myth," she said, breathless. "The kind that feels like it belongs to me."

"It does," Iya said, matter-of-factly, as if naming the sky's color.

They lay in the soft hum of the lamp, the room enlarged by

quiet. The widow's breathing, once ragged, had settled to a calm tide. Then something changed—not in Iya, but in the widow. It was small at first: the way she lifted her hand from Iya's shoulder to the line of her neck; the way her fingers paused—not asking, not claiming—simply resting where warmth pooled.

Iya stilled.

The widow's voice was a whisper that dared itself. "May I?"

Iya's breath paused in her chest. A boundary lived in that pause, old and well-kept. "That isn't what tonight was meant for," she said, gentle but true.

The widow's hand began to retreat, apology blooming too quickly.

Iya caught her wrist—not to push away, but to keep the moment from leaving. "But it doesn't mean it can't be," she added, quieter. "If you ask for it."

"Iya," the widow said, saying her name like a decision, "please."

A long beat. Then Iya nodded once, a surrender shaped like consent more than yield. Control did not fall away; it re-arranged, made room. "Then be slow," she said. "And keep your eyes open."

The widow did as she was told. She watched Iya watch her as she drew her fingers along the tendon of the neck, the curve where shoulder meets collarbone, the length of an arm that had done so much careful work tonight. Iya's breath changed —barely, but the widow felt it. She traced the back of Iya's hand, the lines of palm, the pulse at the wrist. She lifted, kissed that pulse once. Iya's eyes closed, then opened again as if that was the rule.

"Here," the widow said softly, echoing earlier.

"Here," Iya answered, a faint smile in it she rarely let anyone see.

The widow's mouth found the quietest places—the corner of a jaw, the slope beneath, the hollow where breath gathers before speaking. She didn't rush down; she learned what she had been taught: outward before inward, permission before pressure. When she finally drew Iya close and their bodies met—curves aligning, heat answering heat—the widow felt Iya do something she hadn't expected: lean into her, not to be held up, but to be held.

"Tell me if—" the widow began.

"You'll know," Iya said.

They moved with fewer words. The widow learned the pace that made Iya's breath catch, the angle that softened her mouth, the pressure that turned focus into shiver. Iya's hand, which had been steady all night, tightened in the sheet, then relaxed, then tightened again. The widow pressed her forehead to Iya's temple and understood without language that this was rare—a place not many had been allowed to see.

"Stay with me," Iya murmured.

"I am," the widow said.

There was no choreography; there was responsiveness. A shift of hips. A change of rhythm. The kind of honest sound you cannot manufacture. The widow felt when Iya's composure thinned—not vanished, never that—but enough to reveal heat underneath. She realized they were breathing the same way—short, then long, then short again, the cadence of a breaking tide.

"Now," Iya said, not a command, a recognition.

It happened together, not identical but aligned—two bodies answering the same call at the same time. The widow's cry and Iya's low exhale braided in the small space between their mouths. Tremors ran through them in unison and out of phase, continuing until the room felt wider than the bed could explain. When the shaking turned to warmth, they did not speak. The silence after was not the earlier kind, not absence. It was full.

The widow's hand, which had learned what to do, found the

back of Iya's head and held—not to keep her, not to claim her —but to thank the moment without a word. Iya let herself be held, just long enough to be human, then eased her breath back to even.

Eventually, Iya reached for the throw and covered them both. The widow tucked in close to her, drowsy in the clean way sleep arrives when the body stops bargaining. She was almost gone when she stirred and asked, "I hope you're satisfied too?"

Iya didn't answer right away. She shifted slightly, her hand trailing slowly across the widow's ribcage, leaving goosebumps in its wake. Her mouth was close enough for her breath to warm the widow's ear.

"Satisfied… isn't the word."

The widow swallowed, a small tremor in her chest.

"Then what is?"

Iya let the silence stretch, her lips grazing the corner of the widow's mouth without fully kissing her. "Maybe you'll spend the night trying to guess," she whispered, as if she was telling a secret but pulled it back at the last second.

The widow let out a shaky laugh, half-embarrassed, half-aroused again. Her body shifted closer as if reaching for the answer.

Iya pulled away just enough to reassert control, brushing her thumb along the widow's jaw.

"You wanted me to feel it too," she said softly. "I did. But what I felt..."—her smile flickered, unreadable—"...that stays with me."

The widow laid back, flushed and smiling, unsure if she'd given Iya release or if Iya had turned the moment into another layer of mystery. Either way, she felt powerful—not just relieved, but like she had touched something rare.

The widow made the sound of someone who had finally gotten the answer they did not know they needed. Sleep took her with efficiency.

The Departure

The room smelled of sweat and candle wax. Not heavy, not dirty—just lived-in, charged with what had passed between them. The widow lay curled on her side, chest rising and falling in slow waves, the red robe tangled around her legs like a flag of surrender.

Iya sat at the edge of the bed for a moment longer, her back straight, breathing already returned to its calm rhythm. She reached for her jumper, pulling the soft black fabric over her skin. The ritual of dressing grounded her. She smoothed her hair into place and slid her earrings back in. It was not vanity.

It was armor.

The widow's voice was drowsy, almost childlike.

"Already?"

Iya looked at her, just briefly. The woman's cheeks were still flushed, her lips parted as if she wanted to say more but didn't know how.

"That's not what I do," Iya said softly.

The widow shifted, hugging a pillow to her chest. "Stay anyway."

Iya walked to the sideboard, gathering empty glasses, straightening the folded throw the woman had kicked aside. She didn't answer right away. Instead, she busied her hands, restoring small bits of order to the disrupted room. It was habit. A final gesture of care that was never spoken, never requested.

When she did speak, it was with a kind firmness.

"You're stronger when I leave."

The widow pressed her face into the pillow, hiding whatever

expression threatened to escape.

Iya bent down, placing the folded throw neatly at the foot of the bed. Then she stood, smoothed her jumper once more, and glanced at the woman—at the freckles scattered across her bare shoulder, at the faint shadow of grief still stubborn in her eyes.

"Sleep," Iya murmured. "You'll need it."

She left the bedroom without another touch.

The kitchen light was still on. On the counter, the remnants of their simple dinner sat waiting: two plates, one with only a scrap of vegetable left, the other with half a piece of bread untouched.

Iya moved with quiet efficiency. She stacked the plates, rinsed them in the sink, wiped down the counter. She even refolded the dishtowel, hanging it over the oven handle.

It wasn't part of the service, not really. But in Iya's mind, it was essential. She didn't just leave bodies behind—she left stillness, order, the illusion that nothing had happened except the righting of something unbalanced.

When the dishes were done, she took her coat from the hook by the door, buttoning it slowly. A final glance around: everything tidy, the air still faintly humming from what had passed upstairs. Then she stepped into the hallway.

The night met her like a cool cloth against warm skin. The air was crisp, carrying the faint tang of exhaust and the sweetness of damp pavement. Streetlights pooled yellow onto the sidewalk, halos stretching around each post like soft crowns. Somewhere nearby, a radio played muffled oldies through an open window.

Her phone buzzed once. The car had arrived.

The black sedan idled at the curb, headlights low, engine steady. Iya descended the steps without rush. Her heels clicked against the pavement, measured and calm. The driver —a man in his fifties with a neat gray beard—stepped out to open the back door. He didn't look at her longer than necessary. Discretion was part of the job, both theirs.

"Good evening. Iya?" he said simply.

She nodded yes, slipping inside.

The car was warm, faintly scented with pine from the air freshener clipped to the vent. The door closed with a muted thud, sealing her into a quiet bubble.

For several blocks, neither spoke. The city blurred outside: neon buzzing over corner diners, laughter spilling from a late-night bar, a cyclist cutting across the street with a red light blinking on his back.

"Good night for fresh air. Streets are calm. World feels lighter when it's like this," the driver said casually.

Iya's gaze stayed on the window, but her voice was steady, touched with something close to agreement.

"Yes. Quiet makes room for things to settle."

The driver nodded, satisfied. He did not say more.

The city passed in quiet blurs outside the window. Neon signs flickered over late-night diners. A group of students stumbled out of a bar, laughing too loudly. A woman in a yellow coat hurried across the street with a bag of takeout swinging from her wrist. Life moving, loud and messy. Inside the car, Iya sat in silence, a self-contained world.

Her apartment was dark, except for the faint glow of the television in the living room. Her roommate sat curled on the couch, half-asleep with a blanket and a rerun murmuring on the screen.

"Late night?" the roommate mumbled without looking away from the TV.

"Work," Iya said simply, setting her coat on the rack.

The roommate yawned. "At least you don't look like work. Good night, Iya."

"Good night," she replied, her voice even, carrying no trace of what had just passed hours earlier.

She poured herself a glass of water, then slipped quietly into her bedroom. Only there, with the door closed and the noise of the TV muted by the walls, did she open her black notebook.

She wrote with neat precision:

Client: Widow in Red

- *Entered tense, posture defensive.*

- *Anchored in grief, reluctant speech.*

- *First release: sudden, emotional, tears followed.*

- *Second release: deeper, restorative; body softened.*

- *Third release: shared, client initiated, sought to reciprocate. Tears + smile simultaneous.*

-     *Post-session prediction: relief will hold. Likely weeks before another call, if ever.*

Notes: Client attempted to give back. Significant. Suggests readiness to re-enter her own agency.

Closing the notebook, she slid it into the drawer, switched off the lamp, and lay back against the pillow. The widow's face lingered in her thoughts—not the trembling or the moans, but the look of release.

That was what Iya offered. Not fantasy. Not love. Relief.

Her last thought before sleep was simple:

Tomorrow, I will care again. Just not in the same way.

CHAPTER2:

THE DOCTOR'S REQUEST

The Caregiver

Before she became a name passed in whispers, Iya was just a caregiver.

Well—not just. Never just.

She was the kind of woman who could walk into a room and change the air without saying a word. Even in plain navy scrubs, she moved differently. Not hurried, not sluggish— just... composed. She wore them like silk. Her hair was always neat, her faint scent clean, citrus with a trace of something floral no one could name but everyone remembered.

She was not the youngest in the ward, and that was part of her power. She carried herself with a kind of quiet poise that made even new nurses instinctively straighten when she passed. She did not try to stand out. She simply refused to blend.

Patients noticed. Families noticed. Staff noticed.

"Morning, Iya," one of the nurses said as they passed in the corridor, juggling a stack of charts. "How do you manage to look like you slept eight hours?"

Iya smiled without stopping. "Who said I did?"

Her voice had that effect—dry humor, but gentle enough to soften the edges of a long shift.

She entered Mrs. Chen's room, where the ninety-two-year-old sat by the window, wringing the same handkerchief she'd been holding all week. "My daughter's coming, right? She said she would visit today."

It was the fifth time she'd asked this morning. Iya felt the familiar tug—the part of her that wanted to sigh, to remind the woman she had already explained. Instead, she crouched to eye level, softened her tone, and nodded.

"Maybe not today, Mrs. Chen. But she will come. And until then, you have me."

The old woman's clouded eyes watered. She clutched Iya's hand like it was an anchor.

As Iya helped her back into bed, a heaviness settled in her chest—the quiet grief of watching people wait for love that rarely arrived. Some days it stung. Some days it made her angry on their behalf. But most days, she bore it, one breath at a time.

Outside the room, a voice called: "I swear, girl, you got the patience of a saint."

It was Lorna, one of the senior aides—a Black woman in her fifties, sharp-eyed and quick-tongued, who had worked there long enough to have seen every kind of drama. She leaned against her cart, watching Iya smooth the sheets.

"Saint?" Iya gave a half-smile. "More like stubborn. I just do not like giving up."

Lorna chuckled. "Well, keep at it. Lord knows this place eats up the soft-hearted quick. But you? You got steel under that silk."

Iya didn't answer right away. She adjusted her badge, exhaled, and moved down the hall.

She was tired. She was human. But she would never let them see her crack. Not here.

The Storm

By late afternoon, the sky was the color of bruised fruit. Thunder rolled over the roof like furniture being dragged, and the fluorescent lights in the hall flickered once, twice— then died, plunging the corridor into darkness. A beat later the red EXIT signs glowed, the generator coughed awake, and the unit exhaled a nervous chorus: call bells, distant voices, the shuffle of rubber soles.

"Okay," Iya said to no one and everyone. "Simple things first."

She palmed a small penlight from her pocket and clicked it on. Not bright, just enough to make faces feel seen. Fear spiked her own pulse for a second—the quiet, practical kind she reserved for two things: wet floors and darkness. People fell in the dark. People panicked in the dark. And panic was contagious. But so was calm.

She started down the corridor, shoulders loose, smile tucked into the corner of her mouth like a secret.

Mr. Alvarez—who never liked to miss the weather—had pushed his walker half out of his door. "Storm's here," he announced, as if he had summoned it.

"Front-row seats for you," Iya said, steering him gently back. "But from the window, not the hallway. Deal?"

He squinted at her penlight and, after a beat, nodded. "You always make it sound like I have options."

"That's because you do." She angled his chair to the glass and pulled the blinds just enough for him to watch lightning stitch the sky.

Across the hall, a young nurse clutched a stack of charts like they might bolt. "Iya, the vitals machine is restarting and the medication room—"

"Take a breath," Iya said, soft. She tilted her chin toward the ceiling. "Listen? Everyone is loud right now. We do not add to it. You grab flashlights from the drawer. I will handle the folks who are up."

The nurse drew in a shaky breath, nodded, and moved.

In 214, Nora was twisting her bedsheet into a rope. She had good days and days when the memory fog rolled in thick. Storms made it worse.

Her eyes darted to Iya in the doorway. "Who are you? You are not supposed to be here," she said, voice sharp with fear. "Where is the other one? The nice one."

"It's me, Nora," Iya said gently, stepping closer. But the navy scrubs, the pinned-back hair—the picture did not match the one Nora's mind clung to. Her hands trembled harder, tugging the sheet tighter.

"Iya," Lorna whispered from behind, "you want me to try?"

"I got it," Iya murmured. "Two minutes."

She stepped into the hall, slipped into the staff closet, and in three practiced motions swapped her navy top for the pale rose scrub she kept folded on the shelf for nights like this. She loosened her bun, let a few strands fall, and drew in a breath.

Back in 214, she stood a step to the left of where she had been.

"It's me, Nora," she said softly.

Nora's eyes softened in recognition. Relief washed over her face like someone had finally switched the picture back to the right channel. "There you are. I was afraid that stranger was going to stay."

"You know I wouldn't leave you," Iya said, smoothing the sheet and resting her hand over Nora's. "The storm is loud, but we are safe. Let me fix this blanket—you always hated crooked corners."

Nora huffed a laugh, the fear already ebbing. "That is right. You fold them better than anyone."

"Good thing we prefer blankets." Iya smoothed the sheet, tucked it tight, and let her free hand rest over knuckles that had been wringing the weave. The tension in them melted slow as sugar.

From the doorway, Iya could see Lorna mouth, "you are a menace," and made a little halo with her fingers.

Iya flashed her a quick look—half warning, half thanks—and kept her voice steady for Nora until the woman's breath found a slower rhythm.

Down the hall, a call bell shrilled three times in quick succession. Mr. Rafi did not like bells. "Make it stop," he barked, thumping his fist at the air.

"On it," Iya said, already moving. She passed the nurses' station where the young nurse was distributing flashlights, every third one sputtering. "If one dies, switch hands," Iya told her. "It tricks your brain into thinking the light changed, not the room." A small smile—she made it rule number one: never joke at someone, only around them.

By the time she looped back toward the break room, rain was rattling the windows like someone tossing coins. She could feel sweat cooling at the base of her neck where the loose hair stuck. A thread of irritation pulled taut—at the storm, at the cheap bulbs, at the daughter who had not visited in months and the son who had promised to fix the remote and never did. She let herself feel it. Then she let it go.

The break room buzzed with the thin, insect hum of backup lights. The air smelled like coffee gone bitter and the sugar-free cookies no one wanted. Dr. Johansson was there, perched at the edge of a chair like she did not quite believe in sitting. Pearls. Perfect lipstick. Stethoscope looped on the table beside a tablet that had given up mid-sync.

"Generator's slow today," she said, watching Iya enter with her rose scrubs and looser hair. Her tone was even, but her eyes were taking notes. "You're... graceful under pressure."

Iya clicked her penlight off and slid it into her pocket. "Panic is costly," she said, a near-smile. "We can't afford it."

Something like amusement flickered across the doctor's perfectly held face. "I saw you in 214. You left as one person and came back as another. And suddenly the patient trusted you again."

"I feel like color matters," Iya replied, pouring water from the cooler. The stream sputtered, then steadied. "Blue makes me a stranger. Pink makes me the one who folds blankets right." She sipped, then added, "Sometimes moving two steps to the left changes the whole story."

The doctor tilted her head. "Isn't that deceptive?" Her voice carried no accusation—just curiosity, clinical and sharp.

"I pretend to be safe," Iya said, setting the cup down. "If I can give her that for twenty minutes, I will."

Dr. Johansson's gaze lingered—not the way families did when they wanted reassurance, not the way nurses did when they wanted direction. It was the watchfulness of someone who was studying more than behavior.

"You're not rattled by the dark," she said at last.

"I don't like the dark," Iya admitted, matter of fact. "People fall in the dark." She let the truth sit there, unadorned. "But the patients don't need my fear."

A pause. The doctor folded her arms, then unfolded them, a rare fidget. "I like machines that obey. Blackouts make me feel like I am practicing medicine in a dream where nothing responds."

"Dreams are cheaper," Iya said dryly. A small smile followed, soft enough to give the words permission.

"You don't tell people not to be scared," the doctor observed.

"Telling people not to feel is like telling them not to breathe." Iya leaned against the counter, arms loose, posture calm. "I ask them to do one thing they can do well. That nurse out there? Flashlights. It is a small win. Small wins stack."

The doctor nodded slowly, cataloguing the response. "You sound like someone who's signed more than her share of incident reports."

"I have." Another almost-smile, dry as salt. "Different kind of signature. Fewer pearls."

That earned the faintest tug at the corner of Dr. Johansson's mouth—a crack in the professional mask.

Lightning etched a vein across the window; thunder followed close, rattling the cupboard doors. The doctor flinched, almost imperceptibly. Iya pretended not to notice.

"Do you ever feel angry?" the doctor asked suddenly. "At the families who never come. At the promises that don't stick."

"Yes," Iya said. The word came fast, clean. "I try not to serve it to the patients."

"And to yourself?"

"I eat it in small bites," Iya said. "With water."

Dr. Johansson's brows lifted a fraction. "Does that work?"

"Most days." Iya straightened, smoothing the hem of her scrub top. "On the other days, I fold blankets until my hands remember what solving something feels like."

The generator's hum deepened; the overhead lights flickered, tested their strength, then held. A ragged cheer rippled from down the hall. The unit exhaled like a body unclenching.

"Well," the doctor said, as though tucking the conversation back into a folder. "Back to the modern age."

"Until the next storm," Iya replied.

They rose in unison. For a moment—no longer than a breath —they walked side by side into the brightened corridor. Then the doctor turned left toward her charts, and Iya turned right toward another crooked blanket.

The First Touch

The storm had passed, but its echo lingered in the halls. The machines hummed again, the nurses had caught up on charting, and the patients—or most of them—were settled.

Iya stood behind Mrs. Garcia's chair, her palms working lotion into the woman's fragile shoulders. Mrs. Garcia's head was tipped forward, her breathing soft and even.

"Pressure too much?" Iya asked.

Mrs. Garcia's eyelids fluttered. "No, honey. Feels like someone is remembering me."

The words struck a place inside Iya she tried not to name. She swallowed, steadying her breath. "Good. That is the point."

At the doorway, someone lingered. Dr. Johansson.

Her posture perfect as always, tablet in hand, but her eyes were fixed not on the patient, not on the chart—on Iya. Watching the way her hands moved, the way silence seemed to settle easier in the room when she was there.

When Iya finished, she tucked the blanket over Mrs. Garcia's lap, whispered a goodnight, and stepped into the hall. The doctor stayed still for a beat, then followed.

They didn't speak until later.

The corridors had thinned to night staff, the shift change quieting the unit. Iya was in the small rehabilitation room, tidying mats and stacking foam blocks. The kind of busywork she did when she didn't want to think.

The door opened with a hush.

Dr. Johansson stepped in, setting her tablet on the counter. For once she did not look perfectly untouchable. The pearls were there, the lipstick precise, but there was something else in her shoulders—a weight, unhidden.

"I watched you with Mrs. Garcia," she said, standing in the middle of the room as though she was not sure whether to sit or stay. "The way she went from restless to calm. That is not just skill. That's..." She trailed off. "It unnerves me."

"Unnerves?" Iya arched a brow, folding her arms lightly.

"I mean—it is more than care. You treat the body, yes, but you reach whatever lives underneath it."

"That's the job," Iya said simply, though her voice held no defensiveness.

"Some call it work. The rare ones call it purpose," the doctor murmured. She rubbed the side of her neck with two fingers, just at the base. "I get tension here. From work. From... holding everything together."

Her eyes flicked up, then down, as if surprised she'd admitted it.

Iya tilted her head. "You want me to help?"

The pause stretched, long enough that the hum of the lights filled it. Then—quietly— "Yes."

Iya crossed the space between them. She raised her hands, steady, precise, and set them at the edges of the doctor's shoulders. Her touch was not a lover's touch. Not yet. It was a healer's—firm, exact, but slow.

Her thumbs pressed into the muscle where stress had built a fortress. The doctor's breath left her in a sound that was almost a sob, almost a prayer.

"Breathe," Iya said softly. "You don't have to hold it here."

The doctor closed her eyes, posture softening. She tilted her head forward, baring the line of her neck, as if instinctively surrendering.

"I don't know how to let go," she whispered.

"You don't have to know." Iya's hands slowed, coaxing. "You just have to let someone else carry it for a minute."

The doctor's exhale shuddered, less controlled, more human.

"That," she murmured, eyes still closed, "is unnerving too."

"Good unnerving?"

"I don't know yet."

Iya's hands lingered a moment longer, then retreated. She folded them calmly in front of her, the space between them charged, alive.

The doctor straightened, smoothing her blouse, the pearls, the mask sliding back into place. But the air between them had shifted.

Neither spoke of it again. Not that night. Not the next. But when their eyes next met in the hall, something lingered.

And then—days later—the doctor sent a message:

No strings. No expectations. But… can we meet?

The Invitation

It started with a vibration against Iya's nightstand.

She lay on her back, staring at the slow whirl of the ceiling fan, her body heavy from the shift but her mind unwilling to rest. That was the thing about caregiving—your muscles tired but your chest still awake.

The screen lit. One name.

Dr. Johansson.

Iya let the phone glow in her hand. The ellipsis was louder than the words themselves—a hesitation, a plea wrapped in caution.

She did not answer. Not yet.

A minute passed. Another buzz.

I don't even know what I'm asking for. Relief? Quiet? To not hold everything together tonight.

Relief. Quiet. Not love, not sex. The language of someone circling need without naming it. Iya had seen it before—the same way patients clutched her hand and asked for pain relief when what they really wanted was company until the fear passed.

She typed a reply—deleted it. Tried another—deleted again.

This wasn't a moment to rush. Silence was part of the answer.

The phone vibrated again.

Forget it. This is unprofessional.

There it was. The retreat. The attempt to lace herself back into the corset of control. Iya let a small smile touch her mouth.

Finally, she typed:

You asked. I heard you.

Delivered. Read. Three blinking dots. Then nothing. Then dots again.

Are you saying yes?

Iya rested the phone on her thigh. She folded her hands, let the pause stretch. Most people scrambled to fill silence with apologies or reassurances. She let it breathe.

When she picked the phone back up, her response was measured, steady:

I do not work by the clock. I stay until it is enough.

Another pause. Then the doctor's final message:

Then come.

Iya set the phone face-down on the nightstand.

She did not rush to reply again. She did not need to. The Care had already begun.

The Home Appointment

The house was quieter than Iya expected.

Doctors' homes often carried the same precision as their offices: tidy, sterile, a curated order. This one did, too—bookshelves lined with medical texts and novels arranged by height, a rug perfectly centered beneath a pale couch, a bowl of apples in the kitchen that looked decorative rather than for eating. But beneath the polish there was something else: a stillness too sharp, like a hotel room someone had lived in too long without ever leaving a mark.

Dr. Johansson opened the door barefoot, robe loosely tied, pearls gone. Her hair was pulled back, but not with its usual severity. She looked... softer. And uncertain in a way Iya had never seen her before.

"You really came," she said, voice pitched between relief and disbelief.

"I always keep my appointments," Iya replied.

She stepped inside without waiting to be asked, her structured cream jumpsuit fitting her like second skin. Not showy, not reckless—professional, clean. But the way the zipper dipped into a quiet V was enough to suggest that this, too, was uniform.

The living room was dim. A single lamp on. The air hummed with an old love song, soft and unhurried. A bottle of wine waited on the coffee table, but neither reached for it.

Iya set her bag on a chair. "Tell me—where does it hurt tonight?"

The doctor's hand tightened on her robe's belt. Her voice wavered. "Everywhere."

Iya stepped closer, close enough for the doctor to catch the clean citrus trace of her perfume. Her mouth curved, slow and deliberate.

"Then maybe I'll have to touch you everywhere... until I find what hurts most."

The words landed like a shiver. Not a threat, not a joke—an inevitability.

The doctor's lips parted, but no reply came. She let Iya guide her to the couch. The robe loosened, slipping from one shoulder as if it had been waiting for an excuse.

Iya moved behind her, hands resting lightly on her shoulders at first—cool, steady. Then firmer, pressing into the muscle where tension lived.

"Breathe," Iya said softly. "You've been holding your body like armor."

The doctor obeyed, drawing in air as though it was her first full breath in weeks.

"I don't know how to stop," she whispered.

"Then stop trying to know" Iya murmured, her thumbs working slow circles. "You just let me carry it for a while."

Her hands moved with precision, coaxing the knots to soften. The doctor tilted her head forward, eyes closing, the posture of someone unused to vulnerability but starved for it.

Minutes blurred. The robe slipped further, silk against skin. Iya's hands traveled lower—across collarbones, down to the chest, where her fingertips lingered reverently.

The doctor's breath hitched. Her body leaned back into Iya's touch as though magnetized.

Iya bent low, lips brushing just beneath the ear. Once. Then lower, deliberate kisses along the neck, pausing at the hollow between collarbones.

The doctor exhaled a sound she had not meant to let escape —a mixture of relief and surrender.

"I shouldn't…" she began, voice frayed.

"You don't need to finish that sentence," Iya whispered against her skin. "Tonight is not about what you should not. It is about what you need."

The doctor's hands, trembling, let go of the robe's belt. The fabric opened, falling into a soft pool around her waist.

Iya's touch shifted—down the sternum, tracing the curve of breasts, firm but reverent. She did not rush. Each kiss, each stroke, was deliberate, as though committing the body to memory.

The doctor arched, control fracturing, a moan catching in her throat.

"Let go," Iya coaxed. "I will know when it's enough. You do not have to."

Guided, the doctor reclined back against the couch. Iya's hand supported her head, her other at the small of her back, lowering her gently like something fragile, something rare.

The robe parted completely.

Iya's lips trailed lower—over the chest, the abdomen, pausing at the edges of hipbones. Every kiss measured. Every stroke precise.

By the time Iya's hand slipped between her thighs, the doctor was trembling, gasping, caught between confession and release. The sound that left her throat was raw, startling even to herself.

And then—finally—she let go.

Her body arched, then broke open in shuddering waves, undone beneath Iya's hands.

The first surrender broke from her like a startled confession

—sharp, helpless, unpracticed. She arched, then fell back, blinking as if the room had tilted.

"Don't think," Iya murmured. "Breathe."

Silence pooled. The record turned. The doctor's hands—now open—slowly unclenched. A minute passed. The tremor in her legs dwindled, and with it the edge in her voice.

Then a smaller swell rose, unplanned, a gathering under the breath. Her eyes fluttered; her mouth found a sound that was softer this time, less shock, more want. Iya stayed with her, steady and patient, not rushing the climb, not counting it down. The crest came differently—rounded, warmer—and left her sighing instead of gasping.

"Good," Iya said, barely above a whisper. "Stay with me."

Another quiet. The kind that feels like the middle of the night—safe, heavy, honest. The doctor's face loosened where years had forced it to hold. She reached for Iya without grabbing, fingers brushing her wrist. The third wave rose slower, deeper, pulled from a place that had more to do with relief than urgency. When it broke, she shook—then laughed once, a wet, disbelieving sound. She pressed her palm to her own ribs as if surprised to find space there.

"There's more," Iya said, not asking.

A long inhale. A nod.

The last one was almost quiet—no theatrics, no fight left in it. It moved through her like weather finally passing: a long, low crest and then a soft collapse into stillness. Her eyes opened clear. The room felt larger.

The doctor's breathing slowed, her robe loose around her shoulders. She looked at Iya as though the room itself had shifted.

"That was... more than I expected."

Iya paused, zipping her jumpsuit with practiced ease. She let her eyes linger on the doctor's, a teasing smile playing at her lips.

"Then I'm glad I didn't disappoint."

The words hung in the air, heavier than the jazz still humming in the corner. heavier than the slow music humming in the corner. The doctor's pulse jumped under her own hand as if to confirm it.

Iya lifted her bag, calm and unhurried, leaving behind nothing but silence.

The Whisper

The facility looked the same—linoleum floors polished to a dull shine, oatmeal cooling on trays, the steady hiss of oxygen machines. Patients shuffled past, heads bowed, voices small. Nothing had changed.

Except Iya.

She moved with the same calm rhythm, but inside, a hum remained from the night before, an ember that had not gone out. It was not a plan, not a future, not even a desire. Just an awareness—that touch could mean more than routine. That a woman like Dr. Johansson could come undone beneath her hands.

By the third day, her phone buzzed. A number she did not know. Just one message:

"The doctor said you gave her... 'the Care.' I want that too."

Iya read it once, made sure her expression remained steady, then placed the phone face-down on the table. She poured herself tea, stirred honey into the cup, and drank as though the message had said nothing at all.

But when another message came that evening, she let it sit on the table, glowing in the dark of her apartment. She stayed on the couch in her scrubs, hair still damp from a shower, watching the phone as though it were another patient waiting for her attention.

"I do not want wine. I do not want talk. I just want to feel like she did."

The faintest smile touched her lips—not surprise, not pride, but recognition. A seed had been planted, and already it had grown a branch she had not expected.

Still, she did not reply. Not yet. Silence was part of the Care, even if she had not known to call it that until now.

Later, lying in bed, the room heavy with quiet, she whispered into the dark, half to herself, half to no one at all: "They think it's about pleasure… it never is."

She closed her eyes. Tomorrow, she would be back in the halls—steady, professional, invisible again. And somewhere, someone she had not met would already be whispering about her hands.

CHAPTER3:

THE SHAPE OF COURAGE

The Ritual

The backpack landed on the couch with a thud that rattled its zippers like a warning bell.

Maris groaned without looking up. She was already multitasking, hair elastic between her teeth, fingers pulling curls into a high bun, sneaker laces knotted tight. When she finally glanced at the pack, she let out a groan so theatrical it could have won an award.

"Ugh. Again? Didn't we just do this?"

"Once a month," Iya said calmly, checking the straps. Her voice was steady, like she was reciting a weather report. "That's the deal."

Maris spat the elastic into her palm, tied her bun with a tug, then pointed dramatically at Iya. "I never signed anything."

"You did," Iya replied, slipping her hoodie over her shoulders. "Every time you laced those shoes."

Maris narrowed her eyes, half glare, half smirk. "That's manipulation, not consent."

"Convenient memory loss," Iya countered.

"Fine," Maris huffed, grabbing her own backpack. It was smaller, packed like someone had just shoved things in until the zipper surrendered. A hoodie bulged out one side, a water bottle pressed against the fabric, and a granola bar wrapper crinkled in there somewhere. She zipped it with a grunt and slung it over one shoulder. "But if my legs mutiny halfway up, you are carrying me bridal-style. No excuses."

"Not happening," Iya said without hesitation.

"Ruthless," Maris shot back, putting a hand over her heart.

Iya rolled her eyes, but the corner of her mouth betrayed her with a smile. "Self-preservation, Maris."

"Wow. You sound like a motivational poster that got tired of being motivational."

"Then stop asking questions you already know the answer

to."

Maris muttered something under her breath about tragic friend behavior but still tightened her shoelaces once more for good measure.

The city had not fully woken up yet. Storefronts stayed shuttered, buses passed half-empty, and the sidewalks held only a scatter of people carrying thermoses instead of briefcases. The air had that weekend quiet, broken only by the occasional bark of a dog or the hum of a street cleaner.

Iya walked with her usual even pace, shoulders square under her backpack like it was molded to her frame. Maris trailed beside her, less graceful but keeping pace, complaints spilling out like fuel that kept her moving.

At the station, the platform buzzed with families herding sticky-fingered kids and couples gripping picnic baskets. Maris eyed her own sneakers, then glanced at Iya's bag again.

"See?" she muttered. "You pack like we are summiting Everest. It is a hill."

"Preparation isn't drama," Iya said, adjusting her straps. "It's respect."

"For the hill?"

"For yourself."

Maris groaned. "You say things like that, and I have to roll my eyes."

"You'd roll them anyway."

"Because you hand me material," Maris retorted, leaning into the train as it lurched forward.

The city began to slip away in layers—graffitied walls, rusted bridges, rows of brick apartments leaning on each other like tired old men. Then came wider skies, patches of water flashing light, and trees pressing closer to the tracks.

Maris drew a circle on the fogged glass with her finger. "It always feels like cheating. One second it is traffic and bus fumes, and twenty minutes later—bam. Trees. Bugs. Fresh air."

"Cheating," Iya said, "or balance?"

"Balance is yoga twice a week. This is..." Maris hesitated, then shrugged. "Fine. It is nice. But do not tell anyone I said that."

"Your secret's safe," Iya replied, lips twitching like she

wanted to laugh but would not give her the satisfaction.

They disembarked at a smaller station, where the air smelled sharper—wet leaves and stone rinsed clean. Maris inhaled dramatically, then coughed like she had bitten off more than she could chew.

"Okay, fine. Better. Do not smirk like you won."

"I didn't say anything."

"Your eyebrows did," Maris muttered, narrowing her eyes at Iya's perfectly neutral face.

The walk to the trailhead carried them past shuttered cafés, a playground squeaking under the weight of early-morning kids, and a dog stretched across a porch like it owned the block. The pavement gave way to gravel, then to dirt, marked by a wooden sign pointing into the trees like a dare.

Maris stopped, eyeing the incline like it had personally wronged her.

"Every month, I let you talk me into this. Every month, I regret it right here."

Iya smirked. "And every month, you survive."

"Barely," Maris muttered, but she followed anyway

The path curved upward, tree roots crisscrossing into little traps. Sunlight fractured through the branches, dappling their faces. Iya led with the steady rhythm of someone who never wasted motion. Maris trailed behind, half-grumbling, half-performing.

"You know what's funny?" Maris said, hopping over a root. "We call this 'fresh air' like the city oxygen is not the same. Same molecules, just more exhaust."

"Perspective," Iya said without turning her head.

"Science," Maris countered.

"Both," Iya replied.

Maris huffed but secretly liked her answer.

They reached a small rise where the trees parted enough to let the sky spill through. Maris dropped onto a boulder, pulled out her bottle, and guzzled like she had crossed a desert.

"See?" she gasped, wiping her mouth. "Wine never makes me this tired."

"That's because wine charges interest," Iya said calmly, sliding her bottle back into her bag.

"Interest?"

"You pay later. With headaches, regrets, things you cannot undo."

Maris squinted. "So, what's this, then?"

"Payment up front," Iya said.

Maris laughed despite herself. "One point to you. But only because you made it sound poetic."

The breeze shifted through the branches above. Iya tilted her head toward it. "Back home, they say if you want the wind to come, you whistle. Not because it makes sense, but because sometimes you need to give the world a sound to answer."

Maris blinked. "You're telling me to whistle at trees?"

"Whistle. Pray. Breathe. It does not matter. The point is not the sound. It is the pause you give yourself."

Maris angled her head, considering. "So... you're saying the universe is customer service, and I just have to make a noise to get connected?"

"Something like that," Iya said with the ghost of a smile.

"Fine. One point to you again. But if a squirrel shows up instead of the wind, I am suing."

They hiked again, sneakers crunching against gravel. Silence stretched, filled with birdsong and the faint rush of water somewhere downhill.

After a while, Maris said, quieter this time: "You really believe that? That life listens if you... whistle?"

Iya adjusted her pack, letting her breath catch the rhythm of her steps. "I don't think life owes you ease. But it pays attention to effort. Whistling is effort. Even if the only thing it gives you back is your own laugh."

Maris chewed on that. She wanted to roll her eyes again, but this time she did not. Instead, she smiled, almost against her will.

"Fine. But just so you know, if I whistle and the wind does not show up, you are buying me ice cream on the way home."

"Deal," Iya said.

And with that, they climbed higher, the trail folding into itself, the city forgotten behind them.

The Hilltop Encounter

The ridge emerged suddenly, like someone had pulled a curtain back on the sky. Trees thinned, the ground leveled, and for the first time since they left the city, they could see the world stretched out below—rolling hills layered in green, rooftops glinting in the far-off haze, a ribbon of water catching the sun like glass.

Maris immediately collapsed onto a sun-warmed boulder, limbs spread wide. Her backpack slid off with a thud.

"Tell my future grandchildren," she wheezed, "that their grandmother was brave but tragically betrayed by cardio."

Iya set her pack down with far more dignity, settling onto the edge of the rock. Her breathing was even, controlled, though a sheen of sweat touched her forehead.

"You're not even that tired," Maris accused, rolling onto her side.

"You're not either," Iya said, calm as stone.

"My soul is gasping," Maris muttered.

Iya almost smiled. Almost.

It was then that Maris noticed the couple close to them, resting on a handmade bench of old wood smoothed by use. They looked to be in their seventies, dressed in light layers and sturdy shoes. The man had silver hair and carried himself with an easy posture, his hand resting on a walking stick he clearly used more for balance than necessity. The woman sat close, hat pulled low, water bottle cradled in her hands.

They had the air of people who knew this place well—not tourists gasping for photos, but companions in a long, shared ritual.

The man chuckled at Maris' theatrics. "Ah, I remember those performances."

Maris propped herself up on her elbows, mock offended. "Excuse me, I'm fighting for my life."

"You're fighting for attention," Iya corrected, without looking at her.

The woman laughed, lifting her bottle in salute. "She is right, dear. We have raised two daughters. We know drama when we see it."

Maris put a hand to her chest, pretending to swoon. "Betrayed by strangers. In public. Tragic."

But she was already smiling.

"Mind if we share the view?" Iya asked.

"Of course not," the man said warmly. "Plenty of horizon to go around."

They moved closer, settling onto the other end of the bench with a polite nod.

For a few moments, the four of them sat in companionable silence, letting the wind wash over them. The breeze tugged at the woman's hat and carried the faint scent of pine and earth. Birds circled overhead, their cries sharp against the wide sky.

The man finally broke the quiet. "First time on this ridge?"

"Yes," Iya said with a nod. "We like to go walking once a month, but usually in different places. This is new for us."

"Ah," he said knowingly. "That is even better. New paths keep the mind awake."

Maris grinned. "So, like a gym membership—except we get a different branch every time?"

The man chuckled. "Something like that. Except the fees are sore legs."

His wife shook her head, smiling. "He always talks like that, even on trails."

Maris leaned back against the bench, smirking. "At least poets make sore legs sound romantic."

The man's eyes grew distant, the way people do when memory takes them by surprise. "You know, I once got lost here. Many years back. Before the signs were improved. Thought I was clever taking a shortcut."

"Lost?" Maris perked up instantly. "Like, properly lost? Search party and all?"

"Nearly," he said with a rueful chuckle. "I stumbled down a side path and ended up in a place I did not recognize. That's when I found it—a cave, tucked into the ridge. Not many know it is there."

"A cave?" Iya asked, her voice more curious than surprised.

"Yes. At first it terrified me. Pitch black, silent. My heart was pounding so loud I thought it would echo off the stone. But then, halfway in, I saw it—a dot of light, far off, faint but steady. That little speck gave me enough courage to keep moving. Without it, I might have turned back."

He let the memory hang there, eyes fixed on the horizon as though the cave might still be out there waiting.

The man's gaze lingered on the horizon. "The good thing about being lost is sometimes you stumble onto a path you would never have chosen for yourself. It looks too steep, or too dark, or too strange. But once you are on it, you realize you must make it worthwhile. You discover things you did not know existed—sometimes even things that make you happier than the road you thought you wanted."

He look at his wife ever so gently. "So don't be afraid to get lost once in a while. Just pay attention, and don't take foolish risks. Happiness is often closer than you think—but you still have to be responsible enough to keep yourself safe."

His wife reached for his hand, her touch gentle but firm. "That is what we tell our girls too. Try the things that scare you, while you can. Because one day your knees don't let you, your eyes blur, and you realize you have run out of chances."

She gave a small, bittersweet smile. "We are proud of them, of course. They are successful, busy, raising families of their own. We never wanted to hold them back. But the house feels quiet now. Too quiet sometimes."

The man squeezed her hand. "So, we keep walking. Together. As long as we can."

For once, Maris did not rush with a comeback. She stared at the ground, the laces of her sneakers suddenly fascinating. When she finally spoke, her voice was softer than usual. "So, like... the cave is basically a metaphor for courage?"

The man chuckled. "If that helps you remember it, sure."

"Okay, inspirational cave story—noted," Maris said, returning to her usual tone. "But if we go looking for it and bats fly at me, I'm suing both of you."

The couple laughed, the sound rich and unforced.

"Don't worry," the woman said. "You'll find more light than bats, if you're brave enough to step in."

"And don't take shortcuts," her husband added. "That's how I ended up there in the first place."

Maris grinned, her sparkle returning. "Noted. No shortcuts, no bats, no dying dramatically in a cave."

"You'd still make it dramatic," Iya murmured.

Maris elbowed her. "That's called branding."

The couple gave them rough directions to the cave—a smaller path beyond the next ridge, easy to miss unless you knew to look. "Most hikers want sunshine and views," the man explained. "Not many bother chasing shadows. But sometimes shadows teach you more."

When they rose to leave, he stood with surprising ease for his age, though his wife automatically steadied him with a practiced hand. They moved together in a rhythm that spoke of decades together—small gestures, unspoken cues, a kind of language only long love teaches.

"Enjoy your youth," he told them, smiling. "Don't waste it waiting for courage."

Iya and Maris watched them walk down the trail, their figures shrinking until they became two small silhouettes framed by the wide sky.

For a while, neither said anything.

Then Maris broke the silence. "So... cave of doom?"

Iya arched a brow. "That's what you got from all that?"

"No," Maris admitted quickly. She fiddled with her water bottle, then smirked to cover the crack in her voice. "I also got 'do not waste your knees' and 'light at the end of the tunnel.' But cave of doom is catchier."

Iya shook her head, but she could not help smiling. "You're impossible."

"Impossibly brave," Maris said, tugging her pack onto her shoulders again.

But even as she joked, the image lingered: a dark cave, terrifying at first, but halfway through—a dot of light, steady and waiting.

Neither of them said it out loud, but both carried that picture with them as they moved on, the lesson settling quietly in their chests like something they were not ready to admit yet.

Into the Cave

Iya unzipped her pack and pulled out two neat containers. The smell escaped first—garlic, soy, and vinegar mellowed into something rich and steady.

Maris sat up, incredulous. "Wait. Is that... adobo? Who brings adobo rice on a hike? Normal people bring trail mix. Maybe a sad granola bar."

"Someone who doesn't like sad food," Iya said, peeling back the lid. "Vinegar keeps it from spoiling. Garlic too. That is why people used to pack it for long trips, before refrigerators."

Maris stabbed a piece and let her eyes roll back dramatically. "Okay. Fine. This beats raisins any day. Five-star hike cuisine. Would survive the apocalypse again."

Maris blinked at the container in disbelief. "Wait... this is why the house smelled so good last night! I thought the neighbors were cooking. I was too sleepy to check, so I just drooled into my pillow."

Iya gave a small smile. "So now you benefit."

"Benefit? This is redemption," Maris said, already forking another piece. "Next time wake me up. I don't care if it's midnight. Garlic that strong is not something you sleep through—it is a public service."

"Okay," Maris said, snapping the lid shut and standing. "We have eaten like queens. Now we court danger."

"Or we walk back to the station like people with common

sense," Iya offered.

"Shh," Maris said, already smiling. "We met prophets. We were given a quest. It is rude to waste lore."

They took a photo of the bench to remember the spot, waved once toward the path where the couple had disappeared, and headed down the slope until the trail split. The main route continued wide and packed; to the right, a thin seam of dirt peeled away, shy as a secret. Maris pulled up the picture she had taken of the faded paint slash on the tree.

"This is it," she said, showing Iya the screen. "Same mark, same twist in the trunk. Look."

Iya glanced at the sky. Still blue, still generous. "We go a little way," she said. "We turn back if it feels wrong. No shortcuts."

"Scout's honor," Maris said, holding up two fingers.

"You were never a Scout," Iya said.

"I am now. Retroactively."

The side path led them under lower branches and through a pocket where the air got instantly cooler, the light chopped smaller by leaves. Ferns brushed their calves; the ground tilted, then settled. The noises of the main trail thinned to occasional bird calls and the small beating of their steps.

"Feels like we stepped off the map," Maris whispered.

"Maybe we stepped onto the real one," Iya said.

They found the mouth by accident, which made it feel like fate—an oval of shadow tucked into the ridge. No sign, no fence, just a dark breath in the middle of stone. Cool air drifted from it like the cave was exhaling. Up close the rock smelled like rain and old pennies.

Maris stopped two arm lengths away. "Okay. That is a serious hole."

"Not a sentence I thought I'd hear today," Iya said, but her voice was quiet too.

They stood a moment, listening to the small drip of water somewhere inside. The entrance was low; they would have to duck. Iya tested the ground with her foot and then her hand, finding the edges by feel.

"We set rules," she said. "Lights on. One hand on the right wall so we do not double back without knowing. Slow steps. If the ground changes, we say it out loud. If either of us wants to stop, we stop. We've got full batteries?"

Maris held up her phone. "Ninety-two percent and a reckless spirit."

"Keep the spirit within the rules," Iya said. She took out her own phone, turned on the flashlight, and the cave swallowed the small beam like it had been waiting.

They ducked inside together.

The light fell on rock the color of wet bark. Water had cut ripples in it over years; tiny glints of mineral woke as the beam crossed. The space narrowed, then opened, then narrowed again. Their footsteps made sounds that didn't belong to a trail—hollow, then dull, then the soft scrub of rubber on stone. A drop hit the back of Maris' neck, and she squeaked.

"It's just water," Iya said.

"From a prehistoric stalac-thing," Maris said, but she managed a breath that steadied.

Two meters in, the daylight behind them weakened to a smudge. Four meters, it was a memory. Their lights became the only sure thing, fragile little suns in a pocket universe. The temperature dropped enough to make their forearms pebble.

"I don't like not seeing the end," Maris said.

"That's the point," Iya said, and then added, softer, "We can turn back."

"No." Maris reached without announcing it and found Iya's hand. Iya's fingers were warm and sure. "I want to be brave on purpose. Just… hold on."

"I'm here," Iya said.

They walked like that: one hand each on the rock, the other threaded between them. After a minute, the darkness stopped feeling like a thing with teeth and simply became a fact—like gravity, or the price of rent. Their lights carved out small futures, step by step. The smell changed—less metallic, more earth. Somewhere deeper, water fell in a rhythm like a clock that had lost interest in minutes.

Maris kept up a quiet stream of nonsense to keep her nerves in check. "If a bat hits my face, I will pass out and you'll have to drag me like luggage. I am not light luggage. Also, remind me to write a Yelp review: 'Great ambiance, too dark, bring a buddy, five stars if you enjoy confronting your own mortality.'"

"Noted," Iya said.

Another few steps and the ceiling dipped; they bent at the waist to clear it. "Left foot up," Iya said, narrating as she tested. "There is a notch. Now down. Smooth surface. Right hand—stone gets slick here."

Maris copied her moves, the echo of Iya's voice becoming a rope of sound to hold.

Then they stopped. Not because of danger, exactly, but because darkness asked them to try something. Iya clicked her light off. The blackness was immediate and total, a cloth over the eyes. She heard Maris' breath hitch.

"Stay," Iya said. "Just thirty seconds. I want to know what it is."

"This is the part where a horror movie soundtrack starts," Maris whispered.

"Count with me," Iya said, calm, but not pretending she was not also listening for the cave's answer.

They counted. At nineteen, the dark did a trick: it felt less heavy. At twenty-one, Maris' shoulders dropped a fraction. At thirty, Iya clicked the light back on and the world returned in a spill of rock and shadow. They both exhaled, embarrassed and a little proud.

"Okay," Maris said, wiping her forehead like she had just done a math test. "Good to know I can stand inside a void and not die."

"Useful skill," Iya said.

They went on. The passage kinked left, then right. The floor rose in a shallow step. The air smelled older, somehow, like the inside of a forgotten library. And then—very small, almost not there—there was the faintest suggestion of brightness ahead. Not enough to see by, just enough for the eyes to fold around it.

"Look," Maris said, surprised by the softness in her own voice. "Do you see it?"

"I do," Iya said.

The dot was steady, hard to judge. The cave held it like a promise it was not in a hurry to deliver. They kept walking. The spot grew to the size of a bead, then a coin, then a thumbprint of daylight the color of diluted tea. The air shifted again, something green sneaking back into it. Their lights—so important a moment ago—looked cheap next to the sky distilled to a button.

Maris laughed once, short, and breathy. "He wasn't lying."

"They rarely are, the ones who've done the walking," Iya said.

They slowed without meaning to, the way people do when a ceremony nears the important part. It felt wrong to rush. They came to a spot where the path narrowed to a little choke of stone; they turned sideways, shoulders brushing rock.

"Hold on," Maris said, not because she was afraid she would fall, but because it felt like the right verb for both the place and the person.

"I've got you," Iya said.

They squeezed through and the opening widened, and the dot of light opened into a circle the size of a plate, then a window, then a door. Leaves made shapes beyond it. A sliver of sky. The cave let them go.

Outside, the world was indecently loud. A fly buzzed. Water chattered somewhere in shallow tiers. The air was warm again and tasted like sunlight. They stepped out onto a small apron of rock with trees shouldering close, and the ridge sloping down in green spills and patches of wild grass. They both blinked in the brightness like animals.

Maris put her hands on her knees and laughed for real. It sounded like relief had popped its cork.

"So that's what courage feels like," she said. "Sweaty and very unglamorous."

"And honest," Iya said.

They stood there, letting the light recalibrate the day. After a minute, Maris turned to Iya and held up their hands, still joined without either of them noticing they had not let go.

"Can I say something without you doing the monk face?" Maris asked.

"I'll try," Iya said.

Maris' eyes were clear now—no joke at the edges, no defense. "I know there are things you keep in the dark. I feel them, like... rooms you do not open when I am over. That is okay. Everyone gets to have doors. I just want you to know I am not trying to break them. I am just here, okay? If you ever want someone standing at the door with a flashlight, I am your person."

The breeze tugged a piece of hair across Iya's cheek. She did not look away. "There are parts I keep for me," she said, picking each word as if it were heavy. "Not because I do not trust you. Because I need some things that belong to me. I don't always know how to explain them without changing them. But—" She hesitated, then finished it. "But I want to be the kind of person who can share when she's ready. With you."

Maris' mouth quirked. "As long as you're not a serial killer, I'm your cheerleader."

Iya laughed, the kind that starts in the ribs. "I can confirm I'm not a serial killer."

"Great," Maris said. "My pom-poms are metaphorical, but they're very sparkly."

"I can imagine," Iya said.

They fell into a quiet that was not empty. The clearing felt made for a pause—two rocks like stools, a strip of shade on the left, a slant of light on the right where dust turned to glitter. Far below, a line of trail appeared and disappeared as people moved like punctuation in a sentence they could not hear.

Maris sat and tugged her water bottle free. "You know what the old man said about being lost?" she asked, unscrewing the cap. "I liked that. The good part of being lost is you stumble onto a path you never would've taken because it looked too scary or weird. But once you're on it, you kind of owe it something—you make it worthwhile. You find things you did not know were there. Maybe even things that actually make you happy."

Iya looked back at the hole they had come through. Seen from this side, it was a black coin set into green. "So don't be scared to get lost," she said, like she was testing the fit of the words. "But pay attention. Be responsible. Don't pretend danger is romantic."

"Exactly," Maris said, pointing with the bottle. "We looked around. We followed rules. We kept our hands on the wall. We did not do anything stupid. And we still got the light."

"Halfway in," Iya said.

"That's the annoying part," Maris said, rolling her eyes at the sky. "You have to go far enough to earn the dot."

They drank. A dragonfly stitched blue thread through the air and vanished. Somewhere a bird performed scales.

"How do we get back?" Maris asked after a while. "Same way? Or does this spit us onto that lower trail?"

"Let's check," Iya said, circling the clearing. On the far side, through a slice of brush, a narrow descent curved left and down. "This probably reconnects with the main path near the little bridge."

"Excellent," Maris said, standing. "I would like to get back by any route involving more sun."

They didn't mark the cave with anything more than a good look. No rock stacks, no initials, no breadcrumb they would hate themselves for later. Some places deserved to live as whispers.

On the way down, the trees made a canopy that turned the light green. The path held just enough roots to keep their feet honest. They traded roles without naming it— Maris leading when the ground was simple, Iya moving ahead when the slope steepened or the footing got slick. A small kindness passed between them each time the order swapped, a choreography made of glances and inches.

At a break in the trees, they could see another slice of ridge, familiar now: the bench where the couple had been, the tilt of a particular pine leaning into the sky. It made the world feel mapped by experiences, not just coordinates.

"I hope they're eating something good for dinner," Maris said. "They deserve stews and stories."

"They have both," Iya said, like she could see it.

"Do you miss your family like that?" Maris asked, gently.

"Yes," Iya said. "And also—no. I miss them in different ways. Sometimes it's loud, like on birthdays or when something big happens. Sometimes it's quieter—just wishing they were in the room. The good thing is, with calls and video, I still feel close. I know what's happening, even if I'm not there."

Maris grinned. "Yeah, thank God for Wi-Fi. Imagine doing all this back in the nineties—you would be spending a fortune on long-distance phone cards."

They reached the junction with the main trail, and the world got crowded again with weekend sounds—voices, clatter, a dog insisting on a stick three times too big for its mouth. The late afternoon had slid in sideways; shadows reached farther; the sky had softened to something the color of cooled tea.

At the water fountain near the trailhead, they rinsed their hands. The adobo had left a phantom—peppercorn and vinegar—stubborn and comforting. Maris sniffed her fingers and grinned. "Proof of life: lunch was real."

Iya dried her hands on her shirt and then, unable to help herself, smoothed the hem. "Next time: headlamps," she said.

"Next time: no bats, no dying dramatics, possible singing," Maris said.

"Please don't sing in a cave," Iya said.

"I can't make promises I don't intend to keep," Maris replied, and then bumped her shoulder against Iya's as they turned toward the station.

On the platform, the wind off the tracks lifted hair and paper leaves in the same careless way. Maris leaned into it and closed her eyes for a second like you do after a good swim. When she opened them, she caught Iya watching her—not suspicious, not evaluating. Just... there.

"What?" Maris said, because she felt seen and needed to disguise it.

"Nothing," Iya said. "I'm glad we went."

"Me too." Maris hesitated, then added, "If someday you want to tell me about the doors—any of them—I will be here. No crowbars."

"No crowbars," Iya agreed. "Just... a light, when I'm ready."

"Exactly," Maris said. "Your pace, your rules. I'll clap."

"As long as I'm not a serial killer," Iya said, eyes amused.

"Then I clap louder," Maris said. "And bring my pom poms."

The train slid in with its familiar brake-song. They found a window seat; the glass reflected two faces a little dirt-smudged, a little wind-wired, a little less guarded. As the trees gave way to bridges and brick, Maris rested her head briefly on Iya's shoulder, almost like checking a fact she already knew, the city drawing closer with every mile. Maris rested her chin on her hand, watching their reflections blur in the window.

"Hey," she said quietly.

"Hmm?"

"I know you don't tell me everything," Maris said. "And that's fine. Everyone gets to keep their own corners. Just... don't forget you don't have to carry all of it alone. Whatever it is, whenever you are ready—I will be here."

Iya held her gaze for a moment, steady. "That matters more than you know."

Maris nodded once, firm. "Good. Then it is settled."

She leaned back, a grin tugging at her lips. "But just so we are clear—you still owe me a wine night. That is non-negotiable."

Iya let out the smallest laugh, the kind she saved for Maris. "Non-negotiable," she agreed.

They rode the rest of the way in a comfortable hush. The cave was behind them, yes—but the dot of light had come along, settling somewhere easy to reach when the next dark room showed up.

The train in with it's familiar brake-song. They found a window seat, the glass reflected two faces a little dirt-smudged, a little wind-wired, a little less guarded. As the trees gave way to bridges and brick, Maris rested her briefly on Iya's shoulder, almost like checking a fact she already knew. The city drew closer with every mile.

For a while neither of them spoke. The quiet between them felt rather full rather than empty, the kind that happens after something honest has already been said.

Maris lifted her chin, watching they're blurred reflections in the window. "Hey", she said softly.

"Hmnnn?"

"I know you don't tell me everything," Maris said. "And that's fine. Everyone gets to keep their corners. Just don't forget you don't have to carry all of it alone. Whatever it is, whenever you're ready, I'll be there."

Iya held her gaze for a moment, steady. "That matters more than you know."

Maris nodded once, firm. "Good, then it's settled." She leaned back, a grin tugging at her lips. "But just so we clear, you owe me a wine night. That's non-negotiable."

Iya let out the smallest laugh, the kind she saved for Maris. "Non-negotiable," she agreed.

They rode the rest of the way in a comfortable hush. The cave was behind them, yes, but the dot of light had come along, settling somewhere easy to reach when the next dark room showed up.

"What?" Maris said, because she felt seen and needed to disguise it.

"Nothing," Iya said. "I'm glad we went."

"Me too." Maris hesitated, then added, "If someday you want to tell me about the doors, any of them... I'll be here. No crowbars."

"No crowbars," Iya agreed. "Just a light when I'm ready."

"Exactly," Maris said. "Your pace, your rules. I'll clap."

"As long as I'm not a serial killer," Iya said, eyes amused.

"Then I clap louder," Maris said. "And bring my pom-poms."

The train hummed steady beneath them, carrying the

rhythm of the day's climb. Outside, the city gathered itself again—steel, glass, noise—but inside the carriage, the light they'[A9]

CHAPTER 4:

THE FAMILY

The Dinner

It wasn't often Iya got nights like this—where she did not have to adjust her tone, smooth out her skirt, or weigh every word like it might be misunderstood.

Tonight, she wasn't a caregiver. Not a quiet professional slipping into silk and secrets. Tonight, she was just Iya: cousin, big sister, the dependable one who showed up.

They'd chosen a busy little restaurant tucked between a florist and a tattoo shop, the kind of place that smelled like garlic, warm bread, and ambition. Soft piano drifted above the noise of clinking cutlery and the low hum of conversation. The walls glowed under Edison bulbs that hung low like unspoken secrets.

Her cousins had already claimed a booth, their elbows knocking as they shoved menus at each other.

"Wow," said Bea, squinting dramatically at the menu. "No pictures. Suspicious."

"That just means it's expensive," Jonah muttered, flipping to the back for the drink list. "If a place won't show you the food, you're paying for vibes."

"And ambiance," added Carla, already leaning back like she was an expert. "Don't forget the ambiance. Five dollars per candle. Minimum."

They burst into laughter loud enough to earn a sharp glance from a couple in the next booth who were trying very hard to look romantic over their seared tuna.

Iya slid into her seat, rolling her eyes with a smile. "Can we try not to get banned from this place before the food even arrives?"

Bea ignored her. "Look at this, 'drizzled reduction.' What even is that? If they are charging me extra for drizzle, I want a refund."

Jonah grinned. "You do not drizzle reduction, Bea. You reduce a drizzle."

"That makes zero sense."

"It makes restaurant sense."

"Exactly," Carla said, raising her glass of water like it was champagne. "We're paying for words."

Iya shook her head but could not stop smiling. These nights weren't about the food, they were about this—the banter, the way her cousins could turn ordering appetizers into a comedy routine.

The food arrived in stages, each plate small and carefully arranged. Something with too much sauce in zigzags. Something else with toppings stacked like architectural models. But her cousins didn't waste time appreciating the artistry. They devoured everything.

"Okay," Bea gasped after a bite of spicy mayo. "Question: is food supposed to hurt, or is that just my repressed childhood memories reacting to flavor?"

"You're dramatic," said Carla, rolling her eyes. "That's literally just chili mayo, not a near-death experience."

"No. That's trauma with texture."

Iya laughed, shaking her head. "You're so dramatic."

"Me? Please. I am honest. Someone has to say it."

Jonah raised a fry like a pointer. "Honesty is free. This fry costs nine dollars."

Their laughter spilled over again, drawing another look from the couple next to them. But this time, Iya did not care. She was busy memorizing the sound of them—her family, alive and close, joking like the world was not heavy.

This, she thought, is why I work the way I do.

Not just for the paycheck. Not just for bills. But for this.

For the ability to say yes when her cousins asked her to join. For the ease of ordering without scanning the prices. For the freedom to soak in moments that did not come with a cost.

They did not know what it took. Didn't know about the other job, the hours past midnight, the silks hidden away in her drawer. And she didn't want them to. It wasn't their burden. It was hers. And worth it for this joy.

"Game time!" Jonah announced suddenly, wiping his hands on a napkin like a referee.

"No," Iya said automatically.

"Yes," Bea shot back, eyes gleaming. "We haven't played in

forever."

Carla grinned. "It's not a family dinner unless someone gets roasted."

Jonah leaned forward, conspiratorial. "Alright. Who is most likely to secretly date a celebrity?"

All fingers pointed at Mira, who almost dropped her sparkling water.

"What? I barely leave the house!"

"Exactly," Bea smirked. "Classic cover-up."

"Next!" Jonah snapped like a game host. "Who's most likely to get arrested for something stupid but justified?"

"Jonah," everyone said in unison.

He put a hand over his chest. "Wow. No hesitation. No hesitation at all."

"Justice is fast," Carla quipped.

"Okay, next one." Carla leaned in with a mischievous grin.

"Who's most likely to have a sugar daddy and never tell anyone?"

All heads turned toward Iya.

She groaned. "Why me?"

Bea raised her eyebrow, "Normal cousins do not book beach villas. They book Airbnb's with broken aircon and call it rustic charm. Someone must be funding that lifestyle, right?"

Jonah nodded. "Exactly. One minute we are broke cousins sharing fries, next thing you know we're sipping mocktails by the pool because someone decided to play rich benefactor."

"I budget," Iya said simply, sipping her water with exaggerated calm.

Bea added, "If you don't have a sugar daddy, then congratulations—you just became our sugar daddy."

Carla leaned closer, voice dropping like she was uncovering a conspiracy. "See? Classic sugar-daddy move. No branded bags, no flashy jewelry, no Rolex—just mysterious elegance and surprise vacations."

Iya set her glass down and raised her brows. "If I had a sugar daddy, do you think I'd waste his money feeding you clowns?"

That broke the table—laughter so loud the couple two booths over gave them another annoyed glance.

Jonah grinned. "I'm just saying—if anyone here has a rich person funding their midnight adventures, it's you."

Iya tried to hold a glare, but laughter bubbled out instead.

Loud. Messy. Exactly what family was supposed to be.

Iya sat back, soaking it in. For once, she did not feel split between versions of herself. Here, she was whole—just Iya.

The plates kept arriving, and so did the laughter. By the time dessert menus landed, the table was a battlefield of crumpled napkins, half-empty glasses, and stories that kept overlapping until no one knew who was supposed to be talking.

"Remember when Carla tried to cook rice in the microwave?" Bea said suddenly, pointing her spoon like an accusation.

Carla nearly spit out her drink. "It was an experiment!"

"You blew up the bowl," Jonah said, deadpan.

"Science requires sacrifice," Carla shot back, tossing her hair.

The whole table dissolved again, laughter spilling so loud it drowned out the clatter of cutlery from other tables. Even Iya leaned back, pressing her hand to her stomach, because her ribs hurt from how hard she was laughing.

Moments like this—messy, ridiculous—were the closest thing to peace she ever felt.

They teased, they exaggerated, they reenacted old failures like family lore. Nobody here was pretending to be polished, nobody was checking the clock, nobody was demanding anything of her except her presence.

For Iya, that was priceless.

"Okay, okay," Jonah said, trying to collect himself. "Final round. Who is most likely to become famous by accident?"

"Carla," Bea said instantly.

Carla blinked. "Excuse me?"

"Because you'd trip, fall, and somehow land in a viral video," Bea replied, smugly.

"Correction," Jonah added. "She'd sue the restaurant for unsafe floors and then become famous for the interview."

Carla pointed her fork at both of them. "Mock me now. But when BuzzFeed calls, I will remember this."

Even Iya laughed until her eyes watered. And for a split second, she forgot about both her jobs. She forgot about the polished apartments, the midnight shifts, the way her life split like a coin with two sides.

She was just here.

Just theirs.

The server came back to clear plates, slipping the check discreetly onto the edge of the table. Jonah reached for it automatically, but Iya was faster. She wasn't flashy about it— just a smooth gesture, sliding it toward her side of the booth.

"See?" Bea whispered dramatically. "Sugar mama strikes again."

Iya rolled her eyes and opened the little folder. Except—there wasn't a bill inside. Just a folded slip of paper.

She frowned, then looked up at the server.

"It's been covered," he said with a polite nod over his shoulder. "By a guest across the room."

There was a pause.

The cousins froze, forks mid-air.

"Wait—what?" Jonah asked, leaning forward like he'd misheard.

"All taken care of," the server confirmed. "Drinks, desserts, everything."

"By whom?" Bea asked, craning her neck like a detective at a crime scene.

The server only smiled, professional, and gestured subtly toward the back corner of the restaurant.

Iya followed his gaze.

And there she was.

Leah.

Alone at a table for two, posture perfect, a glass of white wine balanced effortlessly in her hand. She didn't wave. Didn't even smile. She just lifted the glass slightly, holding Iya's gaze for a breath too long—like a toast, but quieter.

Then she looked away, returning to her plate as if nothing had happened.

"Okay," Bea whispered. "Mysterious stranger alert. Who is that?"

"She looks rich," Carla added, eyes narrowing. "Like, scary rich."

Jonah whistled low. "You've got people buying you dinner in public now? You're definitely hiding something."

Iya closed the folder slowly, tucking the slip of paper back inside. Her voice was calm, steady.

"Daughter of a client," she said simply. "I used to look after her mother."

The cousins nodded, as if that explained everything.

Why wouldn't it? Caregivers had connections all over. Some families sent cards. Some sent flowers. Some, apparently, paid for surprise dinners.

Totally normal.

At least—that is what they believed.

Iya kept her expression even, but inside, she felt the faint touch of another world brushing against this one. Two lives, colliding under saxophone line and Edison lights.

And she wondered, just briefly, how long she could keep them from overlapping completely.

They poured onto the sidewalk in a wave of coats and leftover laughter. The florist next door was dark, glass vases catching the streetlight like quiet mirrors. A neon dragon buzzed above the tattoo shop, throwing a red crease across the pavement. Somewhere down the block, a guitar threaded a lazy rhythm through the night.

"Air," Jonah announced, stretching like a man reborn. "Finally—something they don't charge a service fee for."

"Give it a week," Carla said, "a start-up will monetize it."

They drifted toward the corner of the street, in their usual loose formation—near enough to bump elbows, far enough to walk without tripping. The street smelled like hot oil from a food cart and the clean bite of air that follows rain.

Bea bumped Iya's shoulder with a grin. "Okay, that was a flex. Client's daughter picking up the whole tab?"

"Coincidence," Iya said. "People remember good care."

Mira nodded. "And sometimes they say thank you twice."

"Great," Jonah said. "I welcome twice. Or thrice. Or whatever the word is for five."

"Greedy," Carla supplied.

"Iya, what if we all just lived together?" Bea declared suddenly. "You cook, I do skincare, Carla does nothing."

"Excuse me," Carla protested, "I offer moral support and dramatic readings of group chats."

They laughed at Bea's suggestion, like it was just another joke tossed into the noise of the night. But something in Iya tightened, soft and silent.

She wanted to say, "Because I'd never rest."

Because living with them would mean smiling even when she was empty, explaining where she went and why she came home late, answering questions she'd rather leave untouched.

Because she loved them too much to risk being seen too closely.

So instead, she laughed with them. Rolled her eyes. Said something like, "You'd turn my peace and quiet into a karaoke bar."

And they laughed harder, not knowing how much of her life was stitched together by answers like that.

Iya laughed until her ribs ached. Not because it was that funny—but because it felt like something she didn't have to pay for. Something she didn't have to protect.

They cut through a small plaza strung with fairy lights. A busker sat nearby with his case open; Carla dropped a coin with a tiny flourish. Notes lifted and softened the edges of their chatter.

Jonah clapped once, unable to resist stirring the pot. "If our lives were, a show, that bill moment was the mid-season twist."

"Only if there's a beach episode next," Bea said. "With snacks."

Mira tilted her head at Iya, not prying, just curious, the way family is. "You good?"

"Fine," Iya said, and it wasn't a performance. She felt... light. It helped that gratitude came with a receipt she didn't have to sign.

They paused at the fountain, water hissing in clean lines. Phones surfaced; someone snapped a crooked photo that caught too much forehead and not enough fountain.

"Print it," Jonah said. "Hang it in the Louvre."

"They only accept real art," Carla replied. "And pictures where I look less like a ghost."

"Alright," Jonah said, pivoting like a game host. "New theory about our elegant cousin."

"Dangerous sentence," Mira warned, smiling.

"By day," he intoned, "calm, competent, splits apart pill caddies like a magician. By night—"

"Sleep," Carla cut in. "Eight hours. SPF in the morning."

"Least cinematic answer," Bea sighed.

"No," Jonah said. "By night… secret agent."

"Pass," Iya said. "Too many meetings."

Bea leaned in, eyes bright. "Or—hear me out—escort."

Carla clutched her chest in mock scandal. "Ma'am!"

Jonah was already laughing. "Plot twist!"

Carla pointed at Iya, grinning. "Please. If she tried that, clients would demand refunds because she'd spend the hour correcting posture and forcing water breaks."

Mira snorted. "Five stars: learned to unclench jaw."

Jonah bent double, wheezing. "And if I tried it, they'd make me pay them just to have sex with me, the audacity!"

That finished them. Laughter arced under the lights, bright and ridiculous. Even Iya folded at the waist, palms on her knees, because the picture of Jonah tipping a disappointed client was too much.

"Congratulations," Carla finally said when she could breathe. "Pioneer of reverse prostitution."

"Trademark pending," Jonah replied proudly.

They drifted again, slower now, the night loosening each of them by a notch. A delivery bike slid past with a box that smelled like sugar; a couple crossed the plaza hand-in-hand; a taxi tapped its horn like a period at the end of a sentence.

Bea checked her phone and groaned. "My bus is either in three minutes or thirty. Schrodinger's transit."

"Text when you're home," Mira said, automatic.

"Hydrate," Iya added.

Jonah opened his arms too wide for a group hug and caught only elbows. "Come here, emotional disasters."

They let him gather them anyway—awkward, lopsided, perfect—then unraveled into goodbyes. The photo was declared terrible and kept; plans were made that no one wrote down.

As they peeled off—Mira toward the bus stop glow, Carla to her rideshare ping, Jonah back to tip the guitarist again—Iya lingered by the fountain. Across the street, a dark sedan signaled once and eased into traffic, taillights winking out. Maybe it had been there the whole time. Maybe it hadn't. She didn't go looking for meaning.

Hands in pockets, she felt the faint ridge of the folded slip tucked in her purse and let the night carry her toward her own route home. No speeches. No conclusions. Just the good noise of family still buzzing in her ears—and the quiet fact that, for now, gratitude could stay exactly what it looked like.

The city thinned out as the night deepened. Cafés pulled in their patio chairs, buses ran half as often, and neon signs buzzed louder than the voices left on the street. By the time Iya stepped off the plaza and onto the quieter stretch toward her apartment, the hum of her cousins' laughter still clung to her like perfume.

She walked alone now, heels clipping against uneven pavement, her breath visible in faint curls. It wasn't a long walk—fifteen minutes, maybe—but it was hers. Time to transition. Time to let the echo of family slowly fade into the silence of her other self.

At the corner, a group of teenagers huddled around a food truck, shouting orders over one another. One of them bumped into her, murmuring a distracted "sorry," already pulling at a paper cup dripping with cheese fries. She smiled faintly. No harm done.

Her phone buzzed. A message from Bea lit the screen:

Home safe? Or did the garlic bread kidnap you?

Iya snorted, typing back:

Alive. Garlic bread surrendered peacefully.

Bea sent back three laughing emojis.

Good. You are not allowed to Houdini out of family nights anymore.

Iya tucked the phone away. As if that was a simple thing.

At the next intersection, she hesitated. Left would take her home. Right would take her past the boutique hotel she sometimes used—a place that did not ask questions about late-night arrivals. She glanced right, just long enough for the thought to register, then pushed on left. Tonight wasn't for that. Tonight had been for family.

Still, the shadow of the other life hovered. That folded slip of paper in her bag. That lifted glass from Leah, wordless across the restaurant. Two worlds that brushed but did not collide. Not yet.

The streetlamp above flickered, humming. A car rolled by slow enough that she felt the shift in air, then sped up again when it caught the green light. She didn't look after it, though the weight in her stomach told her she could guess who might've been inside.

By the time she reached her building, the noise of her cousins had been replaced by something quieter: memory. The way Jonah nearly fell out of the booth laughing. Bea's exaggerated theories. Carla's mock indignation. Mira's patient side comments. All of it a reminder that her life wasn't just made of hours billed or secrets kept. It was this, too.

She let herself in, climbed the stairs, and unlocked her door to the small apartment. The space smelled faintly of detergent and the leftover stew Maris had probably made earlier. Shoes were by the door; a sweater draped over the back of the couch. Normal. Safe.

Maris wasn't asleep yet. She sat curled on the couch with a book, glasses slipping down her nose. She looked up when Iya walked in, smiling the kind of smile that belonged to someone who'd been waiting, but not worrying.

"Good night?" Maris asked.

"Loud. Worth it," Iya said, setting her bag down.

"Nice. I just spent three hours arguing with a journal

article about decision fatigue and grading discussion posts that were ninety percent vibes," Maris said, nudging the highlighter out of her hair. "My brain's oatmeal."

Iya laughed softly. "Academic cuisine."

"Exactly." Maris studied her for a second. "You look less clenched. Shoulders down for once."

"Family will do that," Iya said, pouring some water. She thought about mentioning the paid bill, the quiet toast, but didn't. "You eating?"

"Already did. There's stew if you're hungry." Maris stretched, gathering her notes. "I'm crashing before I start citing TikTok in APA."

"Please don't," Iya said.

Maris yawned. "Night, Iya."

"Night."

The apartment fell still, except for the hum of the fridge and a slice of traffic far off. Iya stood a moment longer in the kitchen, the echo of her cousins still buzzing in her chest, the folded slip of paper resting in her bag like a pebble she chose not to touch.

CHAPTER 5:

THE PERMISSION

The Husband

The café held its breath the way good cafés do—low voices, soft clinking of cups, steam curled from the counter like a thought escaping before it turned into words . Outside, late light slid across the glass and threw a pale band onto the floor by the window.

Mark sat in that band of light. Not dramatic—just a man who looked like he'd arrived early and then decided to stay very still so he didn't break anything invisible. The top of his coffee had formed a skin. He'd stirred it enough to look occupied and then given up.

When Iya walked in, he stood too fast and bumped the table with his knee. The cup wobbled but didn't spill. It felt like a metaphor, which she ignored.

"Mark?" she said.

"Yeah. Hi. Thanks for coming."

They shook hands. His palm was warm and a little damp —human, not slick. She took the chair across from him, angled toward the window. He sat like someone who'd been practicing looking calm and had worn out the muscles.

"Your message was… vague," she said, the way people say the weather is a little off—observation, not accusation.

He huffed a laugh through his nose. "I didn't know how to put this in writing. I still don't really know how to say it out loud."

"Try," she said.

He nodded, as if taking permission from the word itself. "I am married. Fourteen years. We get along. We run the house. We parent. We're… okay." He paused, searching the edges of his cup. "But the part that made us *us*—whatever that is—it's gone quiet. It's like living next to a radio that used to play your favorite song and now it's static. You can't prove anything's wrong, but you go to bed every night missing something you can't point at."

He didn't look up to see how that landed. People rarely do when they say something vulnerable.

Iya didn't fill the space. She let the machine hiss. A spoon clattered somewhere behind them. Silence is where truth grows or dies.

"We tried," he said finally. "Therapy. A couple retreats. Schedules. 'Intimacy calendars.'" He winced at the phrase. "We even did the thing where you're supposed to sit knee to knee and breathe together for five minutes a day." He glanced up, almost apologizing. "The best we could do was three minutes. Once. It felt like homework. She was polite about it. I was... determined. It didn't move anything."

"What did move?" Iya asked.

"Nothing," he said. "That's the problem."

He took another small breath, like a swimmer pacing himself. "It's not infidelity. There's no secret account, no hotel charges, no fight I can replay and say, 'That's when.' It's just... numb. We're good teammates. We can fix a leaky sink or tackle a school project at 11 p.m. But when I reach for her in the dark—" He stopped. "She doesn't pull away. She doesn't reach back. It's like touching someone who's looking out from far away."

Iya let that sit. She'd heard worse. She'd heard messier. But this was clean pain, which is sometimes harder.

"So why me?" she said, finally.

He shifted. This was the part that sounded like a rumor even in his own head. "Someone mentioned you," he said. "Not official. Not 'you should call her.' It came up in a conversation and then... wouldn't leave. She didn't recommend you. She just said she'd seen women walk away after spending time with you and they were... different. Not fixed. Just... back to themselves, a little."

"That's vague too," Iya said, a corner of her mouth softening.

"I know," he said. "But it was the first thing in months that didn't sound like a chore or a test we could fail together."

She lifted her cup and let the heat sit in her hands. "I'm not a coach, Mark. I don't give homework. I don't fix marriages. If you're hoping I can seduce your wife back to life, that's not my lane."

He shook his head too fast. "No. That's not what I want. I don't want her seduced. I want her to feel something and remember it's hers. Even once. Even if I'm not in the picture of that moment."

That sentence landed exactly where it needed to. It turned the air.

"Does she know you're here?" Iya asked.

"Not yet." He didn't justify it, which she appreciated. "I wanted to see if you were... real. If this was something I could offer without creating more pressure."

"And what do you want from me exactly?"

He stared at the cooling coffee long enough that she thought he might deflect. Then he looked at her and didn't blink. "I want her to have the choice," he said. "That's all. If she reaches for you, it won't be because I pushed her. It'll be because I finally stepped out of the way."

"That's not easy to say," Iya said quietly.

"It's not easy to live like this either," he said. "I used to think if I tried harder, I could drag us back. Turns out trying harder can feel like pushing."

She watched his jaw unclench and clamp again, the body's argument with its pride. Men came to her sometimes, but usually for the wrong reasons—curiosity, control, proof. He didn't smell like any of those.

"Tell me what you've done when you're alone," she said. "When you're not trying to be good at this."

He exhaled. "I stopped asking," he said. "Not out of punishment. Out of... mercy. For her, for me. I told myself it took the pressure off. It did on the surface. Underneath, I got lonelier and quieter." He rubbed his thumb along the cup's handle. "I tried to want less. That didn't work either. Desire is stubborn."

"Whose desire?" she asked.

He didn't expect the question and almost smiled because of it. "Mine, sure. But also, hers. I miss hers. She used to look at me with a kind of... mischief? That's the closest word. Not dramatic. Just alive. She hasn't looked at anything like that in a long time. Not me, not food, not a view, nothing."

"Would it scare you if this—me—works?" Iya asked. "What scares you if it doesn't?"

He considered both and picked the harder one first. "If it works," he said, "I'll have to live with the fact that I couldn't do it. That someone else could reach a part of her I can't." There wasn't bitterness in it, just the bruise of honesty. "If it doesn't work... then maybe this is just who she is now. And I have to decide if I can love her like this for the next forty years without turning into a ghost myself."

"Are you here because you love her," Iya said, "or because you're tired of not being loved back the way you want?"

He took the hit and sat with it. "Both," he said. "If I say only the noble part, I'm lying. If I say only the selfish part, I'm lying. I love her. I also want to be wanted. I don't think those cancel each other out."

"That helps," Iya said. It did.

He looked at her hands. "Do you have rules?" he asked. "For… whatever this is."

"I have boundaries," she said. "They're not complicated." She counted them out like stones on a table. "No secrets from the person who's supposed to know. No tests. No setups. No hidden cameras. No 'prove something to me' scenarios." She held his eyes. "I don't report back. I won't be your narrator."

He nodded. "I'm not looking for updates. I don't want a play-by-play. I just want her to have a door that isn't me."

"Good," she said. "Because I won't walk through it for her and drag her along."

He swallowed. "I don't want that either."

They let a server pass with plates. Somewhere behind them a couple laughed the kind of laugh that says, We're fine. It scraped a little, and neither of them looked.

"How did my name actually reach you?" she asked, circling back to the part that mattered to her. "Not the first sentence. The real way."

He pulled a folded napkin flat and smoothed it like a habit. "We were in a session," he said. "We weren't making any progress. Our therapist went quiet for a long time. She asked my wife what 'being touched' meant to her now. My wife said it meant 'being asked for something.' And the therapist said, very softly, 'There are forms of touch that ask for nothing.' She didn't say your name. Not then. It was after. I was leaving the building. We crossed in the hall. She said, 'This might not be for you. It might be for her. There's someone people see when they're ready to feel without performing. I won't write it down. If you remember it tomorrow, say it to your wife and make it hers to decide.'" He met Iya's gaze. "I remembered. I wish I could say I tried to forget. I didn't."

"That's less corny," Iya said, a dry acceptance. "And more believable."

"I wasn't trying to make it sound pretty," he said.

"I know."

He looked like a man waiting for a verdict he already suspected. She didn't offer one. She offered something else.

"Tell me one thing you miss," she said. "Small. Not sex. Not vacations. Not the big stuff."

He stared at the window again, at the band of light now inching off the floor. "She used to hum when she made tea," he said. "Not a song. Just... a sound. It filled the kitchen. I didn't know I loved it until it stopped."

"Does she know you miss that?" Iya asked.

"No," he said. "It's such a tiny thing it felt stupid to bring up. Like asking someone to fix a leak when the house is on fire."

"Sometimes you put out the fire by finding water," she said. "Even a cup of it."

He nodded, absorbing it without pretending it solved anything.

They let a longer quiet settle. It didn't feel like a stall. It felt like both of them rechecking their footing.

"I don't have a script for you," Iya said. "There's no right way to frame this that makes it painless. If you go home and turn this into a pitch, she'll feel sold and she'll shut down. If you turn it into a confession, she might feel cornered." She let a breath out. "Keep it simple."

"How simple?" he asked.

"Simple like this," she said. "Tell her you met me. Tell her why. Tell her she can reach out if she wants. Then stop talking."

He almost laughed. "Stopping talking is not my best skill."

"It's the most important one you have here," she said. "If this happens, it has to be hers from the first step. Otherwise, it's just another assignment."

He sat with that. "Okay."

"And one more thing," she added. "If she reaches out to me, I won't tell you. Not because it's a secret, but because it needs to live where it happens. If she wants you to know, she'll tell you. If she doesn't, that's also an answer."

He took that in, winced, and nodded anyway. "I can live with not knowing," he said. "I can't live with her never getting the chance."

"Good," she said.

He picked up his coffee and finally drank it, made a face, and put it down. Cold. He didn't apologize for the face. He looked relieved to have tasted something.

"Do you ever say no?" he asked, almost as an afterthought, but not really.

"Yes," she said.

"When?"

"When what I'm being asked for is control dressed up as care. When someone wants me to prove something for them. When the risk is someone else's dignity."

"Is this a no?" he asked.

"It's not a yes either," she said. "It's a door. That's what you asked for."

He nodded. "Right."

She slid her card across the table, not showy, just practical— her first name, a number. No title. No website. No brand.

"Don't present this like a solution," she said. "Hand it over like an option and then give her space. Don't hover in the hallway. Don't ask tomorrow if she's decided. Let it be quiet."

He took the card and didn't look at it. He tucked it into his wallet without ceremony, the way you put away something you don't want to scratch.

He turned the card over once before sliding it into his wallet. "If this ends up hurting me..." His voice trailed, then came back lower. "I guess that's mine to carry."

Iya didn't blink. "It might hurt. But hurt isn't the enemy

here." She leaned in just slightly. "Numbness is."

Mark sat with that. No comeback, no nod. Just sat there, as if the word numbness had finally been said out loud in front of him.

Iya held his eyes so he knew she'd actually heard him. "Then tell her my name," she said. "Don't dress it up. If she wants this, she'll call. If she doesn't, respect that."

He nodded once, like a promise he could keep.

They left the table as it was—cups, coffee rings, the small mess two people make when they've finally said the thing they came to say. Outside, the light had shifted. The band on the floor was gone. The room didn't feel different, but he did. That was enough for now.

The Wife

The café wasn't busy, but it carried the hush of a place where no one wanted to be overheard. Afternoon light filtered through the window, soft and pale, catching the steam that rose from cups.

Celine spotted Iya immediately. She had expected someone sharper, more obvious, someone who looked like they belonged in a different kind of room. Instead, the woman at the table was calm, ordinary even—ordinary in the way a locked door looks until you try the handle.

"You're Iya," Celine said when she reached the table.

"I am."

"You don't look the way I pictured."

"People rarely picture me right."

They shook hands—quick, clean. No spark, no theatrics. Just two women acknowledging each other in the middle of something neither could quite name yet.

Celine kept her coat on as she sat. "I don't even know why I came."

"Maybe because not coming felt worse," Iya said evenly.

That earned her a sharp glance. "Do you always answer like that?"

"Only when it's true."

Celine pressed her lips together but didn't argue. She ordered tea, and when it arrived, held the cup in both hands without drinking.

"I'm not sure what this is supposed to be," she said.

"It's not supposed to be anything," Iya replied. "It becomes what you bring to it."

"That sounds like a trick."

"No," Iya said, "a trick has an outcome already planned. This doesn't."

Celine gave a short, dry laugh. "You make it sound like I should want something."

"Not should," Iya said. "But if you didn't want anything, you wouldn't be here."

The words landed harder than Celine expected. She looked down into her tea. "That's the problem. I don't even know what I want anymore."

"Then that's where we begin," Iya said.

Celine looked up expectantly, but Iya didn't fill the silence with instructions or explanations. She just let the words sit, daring Celine to ask herself what "begin" could mean.

Finally, Celine took a sip of her tea. Her hand trembled slightly.

"I feel blank," she admitted. "I go through the motions. I tick off boxes. But it's like I'm playing a part I don't believe in anymore."

Iya's gaze stayed steady. "Do you want to believe again?"

Celine blinked. "I don't know if I can."

"That's not what I asked."

Her breath hitched. She tried again. "Yes. I want to. I just don't know how."

"Then that's enough," Iya said.

The silence between them shifted. Not comfortable, not easy, but alive.

"This still feels like cheating," Celine said at last, her voice low.

"Cheating is hiding," Iya said. "This isn't hidden. It's chosen. There's a difference."

Celine stared at her, unsettled. "Mark really said yes to this?"

"He didn't say yes to me," Iya replied. "He said yes to giving you a choice."

That landed like a stone in water. Celine gripped her cup tighter, her shoulders drawing in. "I hate that it feels like I need his permission just to sit here."

"You don't," Iya said. "But sometimes love looks like stepping out of the way."

The line lingered. For a moment, neither spoke.

Celine set the cup down. "And if I did say yes, what happens then?"

"Then we meet again," Iya said. "Not here. Somewhere else. And we begin."

Celine narrowed her eyes. "And what does 'begin' even mean?"

Iya leaned in, her voice dropping, deliberate and slow.

"It means we stop pretending you don't still feel. And then we see what happens when you let it out."

Celine's breath caught. She laughed, but it was thin, shaky. "You make it sound simple."

"It is," Iya said. "But simple doesn't mean easy."

The silence sharpened between them, charged with something neither wanted to admit aloud.

Celine stood, tugging her coat closed. "I'll think about it."

Iya stayed seated, calm, steady. She slid a plain card across the table—her name, her number, two times written neatly in pen.

"Do that. And when you decide, this is when I'm available. I don't move my schedule. If you want this, you'll come to me."

Celine hesitated. She picked up the card and slipped it into her bag like it might burn through the fabric.

Not a yes. Not yet. But when she walked out, she already knew she would keep turning the words over in her head: *see what happens when you let it out.*

The Awakening

The room didn't try to impress. No view to brag about, no chandelier pretending to be a moon. A low lamp honeyed the walls; the bed was turned down in a neat, forgettable way. Carpet softened the sound of their steps. It felt like a room that promised nothing and kept it.

Celine stood by the chair with her coat folded over one arm. She looked at the bed and then at Iya, the way people look at cold water before they step in.

"I almost turned back," she said.

"But you didn't," Iya answered.

"That doesn't mean I know what I'm doing."

"You don't have to," Iya said. "You only have to be here."

Celine set her coat on the chair with more care than

necessary. Underneath she wore a loose blouse and soft pants; nothing chosen for effect. A woman dressed for not being seen.

Iya didn't fill the space with reassurances. She moved close enough that Celine could feel her without being touched.

"If anything feels wrong, say stop," she said. "If you want to slow down, say slow." A small pause. "And if you want more, say more."

Celine tilted her head, testing the air between them. "And if I say nothing?" "Then I listen," Iya said. "Sometimes silence says the most."

Iya lifted a hand, palm up. No ceremony. Celine put her fingers there and felt the air change.

"Sit," Iya murmured.

Celine sat on the edge of the bed. Her shoulders were set high, as if they'd learned one shape and refused to forget.

"You carry it all here," Iya said quietly behind her, laying both hands along the crest of Celine's shoulders. Not a squeeze. A placement. A hello.

Celine started, then calmed. "Feels like... concrete."

"It's years of holding too much," Iya said. Her thumbs began a slow circuit along the ridge of tension, probing at what resisted, easing what yielded. "Let me lift what I can."

The first long breath came like an accident. The second was on purpose. Celine's shoulders lowered a fraction, surprised to find there was room to move at all.

"Tell me what happens," Iya said.

"I didn't realize how tight I've been," Celine murmured. "It's like I forgot... this part of me."

"Then remember," Iya said, and her hands traveled to the outer edges of Celine's shoulder blades, circling inward and down, following the groove beside her spine. Slow. Patient. Listening.

A small sound slipped out of Celine before she could swallow it. She lifted a hand toward her mouth and stopped midway, catching herself.

"Don't hide," Iya said, close enough that the words warmed the curve of Celine's ear. "Not here."

Celine's hand dropped to her thigh. Her breath unspooled in a long thread. Another sound followed, softer but cleaner, like a door no longer sticking.

"Lean back," Iya murmured.

Celine let herself tilt until her spine found Iya's chest. Iya adjusted without fuss, one arm slipping around Celine's middle—not trapping, just holding, a frame around a picture that was a perfect fit.

"You're safe," Iya said.

Celine nodded; she didn't try to swallow the tear that slid down. "I don't know why I'm—"

"Because you've been carrying more than anyone asked you to," Iya said, hands returning to their quiet work. "Let it out."

They let the minutes stretch until the room forgot to measure them. The first tremors of crying softened into breath. When Celine finally eased forward again, Iya was already moving, turning her with a light touch.

"Lie back," she said.

Celine lay on the bed, hair loosening against the pillow. She didn't undress. She didn't need to. Iya sat beside her hip, grounded with one foot on the floor, a lighthouse more than a wave.

"Okay?" Iya asked.

"Yes," Celine said, surprised by how solid the word sounded.

Iya's palm settled at the back of Celine's neck, a warm anchor, then skimmed along her collarbone, across the shallow rise of her chest, down to the warm edge of her stomach. She touched like someone following a map she refused to rush through; every pause was a question, every inch an answer.

Celine's body began to answer back. Nothing dramatic: breath catching, breath deepening, the tiny lift of her hips when a line of warmth met a forgotten path. She felt heat collect low and steady, like coals waking.

"Eyes on me," Iya said softly.

Celine opened them. Iya's gaze was steady—not hungry, not detached. Present. It felt indecent to be seen like that and kinder than anything.

"Good," Iya murmured, and the word itself sent a current through places Celine had written off as dead.

"Do you like being watched?" Iya asked, not teasing, not clinical—curious.

Celine startled at the honesty of the question. "Yes."

"Then watch me watch you," Iya said, her hand tracing a slow arc from the dip at Celine's waist back up the length of her ribs. "And keep breathing."

Heat rose in waves that didn't ask permission. Celine's thighs pressed together on instinct. The ache there felt almost impolite after years of silence. She didn't apologize. She let it bloom.

"More?" Iya asked.

"Yes," Celine said at once, and then, because the saying felt like crossing something important, again: "More."

"Tell me if I need to change," Iya said. Her fingers made a new circuit: along the outer line of Celine's hip, up the curve of her side, a slow, deliberate return to the place below her sternum where breath chooses speed. Celine's back lifted from the mattress as if her body had been waiting for that exact shape of pressure.

The first crest took her the way a sob does when you've been brave too long. It began low and spread everywhere, a pull rather than a push, gathering her into itself and breaking her open without breaking her apart. She made a sound she hadn't made in years—not loud, not polite, true. When she reached for her mouth, Iya's hand caught her wrist, bringing it down gently to the bed.

"Don't take yourself away from yourself," she said.

Celine let go. The wave moved through her in clean arcs. When it loosened its hold, she lay blinking at the ceiling, stunned. A laugh cracked out of her, bright and wet. "I thought that part of me was gone."

"It was waiting," Iya said, brushing hair from Celine's temple. "You asked it back."

Celine's answering breath turned into a shiver that wasn't fear. The coals were brighter now; the room felt as if the lamp had warmed.

"Again?" Iya asked, not as an offer, as a reading.

"Yes," Celine said, shocked by how easily yes now lived in her mouth.

"Slow," Iya said, and she kept her word. She didn't chase; she drew. The same paths, the same patience, a fraction more weight, a fraction more linger, like learning a song by playing the same notes until the space between them starts singing too.

Celine's body found the rhythm first and then forgot it,

which turned out to be the trick—no counting, no bracing, just letting the climb happen in its own strange path. She pressed her thighs together, then relaxed, then pressed again; her breath grew noisy and beautiful. When the second crest arrived, it was heavier and slower, like something that had been sleeping a long time and woke hungry. She rode it breath by breath, eyes on Iya, hands bunching the sheet not to hide, to hold.

It released her softly, and she broke into a grin so wide it embarrassed her. Then the embarrassment dissolved because there was nothing in the room asking her to be smaller.

"Okay?" Iya asked, not assuming.

Celine nodded, then shook her head, laughing. "I don't even know what that means anymore."

"It means you're here," Iya said. "That's enough."

The third wasn't planned. It came as a layered aftershock, a set of small undoing that added up to one more bright break. It surprised a gasp out of her and a sound that might have been her name said back to itself. When it eased, her whole body let go by degrees—jaw, throat, shoulders, belly—like turning off lights in a house, one room at a time.

When it was over, the room was quiet again. Celine lay back against the pillows, her chest rising and falling in steady rhythm, her body loose in a way she hadn't felt in years.

"Water?" Iya asked.

"Yes," Celine murmured, and it tasted like something better than water's usual promise. She drank half and then the other half, realizing how thirsty she'd been for everything.

Iya adjusted the pillow; the sheet came up over Celine's waist. No fuss. No sentimentality. Care that didn't need an audience.

"Still, yes?" Iya asked.

"Yes." Celine searched herself and found something else entirely. "I feel... honest."

Iya's mouth tilted a fraction. "Good."

She stood and slipped into her coat. Celine watched, a little dazed, as if the room might go back to being only a room the second the door opened.

"Will I see you again?" Celine asked. The question wasn't a plea; it was information gathering from a newly awake body.

"If you want to," Iya said. "You know how to reach me."

No promise, no choreography. Just the door left unlocked.

Iya stood, smoothing her coat over her arm. No words were needed. The silence spoke for them both.

As she reached for the door, she felt it—the faint weight tucked inside her pocket. Her hand brushed against the smooth edge of an envelope. Black, thick, elegant. Gold letters glinted faintly across its surface; initials curled like a signature of intent.

It wasn't handed over. It wasn't discussed. It was left.

Not as advance, not as demand. But as recognition. A way of saying: the Care was received, the moment is complete, and the silence will be kept.

Black for secrecy.

Gold for value.

It was the quiet ritual all her clients understood.

Celine sat up. She looked like herself but not the same self. It wasn't a makeover; it was a return.

"Thank you," she said.

"Take care of yourself," Iya replied.

The latch clicked. The hall was colder than it needed to be. Iya walked, the envelope a quiet presence against her ribs. She didn't open it under the hallway's indifferent lights. She didn't need to. Meaning weighed what it weighed.

In the room, Celine lay back on the bed, staring at the ceiling like it was the first sky she'd seen in a while. She felt the afterglow and the after-quiet, the way the nerves hum when they're newly convinced, you'll listen to them next time. She turned onto her side and laughed once, softly, into the pillow. No one heard it but her.

Down on the street, traffic dragged its tired brightness along the curb. Someone laughed too loud. A door thudded somewhere far away. Nothing in the city changed. Celine breathed in and felt all the way down. Everything did.

She sat up, gathered her things, and smoothed the bed with her palm, not to erase anything, just to mark the place where it had happened. At the chair, she lifted her own coat, slipped it on, and checked the pocket that was now empty. The lightness surprised her. Choice had weight; leaving it behind somehow made her lighter.

In the elevator she caught her reflection and didn't flinch. Her mouth was soft. Her eyes were bright with the kind of brightness you don't buy. She touched the place at her collarbone where warmth lingered and didn't apologize for smiling.

The doors parted onto the lobby. Night met her with its regular indifference. She stepped into it like a person stepping into a familiar street after finding the house keys she thought she'd lost forever.

She didn't look back.

The envelope said the Care had ended. But her body said something else had begun.

The Quiet Return

The city pressed against her as soon as she stepped outside. A lone bus sighed as it passed, neon signs buzzed faintly, and somewhere down the block, laughter spilled from a bar. Ordinary sounds. But tonight, they felt louder than they should.

She touched the pocket lightly, fingers grazing the seam. Not as reassurance—as acknowledgment. The ritual was complete.

She walked slowly, not because she was tired but because she wasn't ready to rush back into ordinary life. The sidewalk was damp from a late drizzle, and her boots left faint imprints on the concrete. The air carried that metallic city scent— wet pavement, faint gasoline, fried food from the corner shawarma place. All the little things that reminded her she was not in some sealed hotel room anymore, but back in the current of the world.

And yet, inside, she still carried Celine's tremors. The way her body had moved under her hands, the breaking open after years of silence. It wasn't lust that lingered with her now— it was something deeper, stranger. The sense of witnessing a flame that had almost gone out suddenly roar back, raw and insistent.

That always stayed with her longer than touch.

By the time she reached her building, her rhythm had steadied. The lobby light buzzed overhead, throwing a pale glow across the mailboxes. Someone had left a pizza flyer sticking out of hers; she ignored it, pushing through the stairwell door instead of waiting for the elevator.

The climb was grounding. Each step pulled her out of the hush she'd left behind and into the grit of ordinary life— the narrow stairwell, the faint smell of cooking from another unit, the chipped banister. She didn't resent it. This was her other world, the one that kept her balanced. Not luxury, not struggle. Just life, steady and unremarkable. A place no one asked her to be anything but herself.

She unlocked the door quietly, instinctively, as though not to disturb anyone. Inside, the living room was dim except for the faint blue glow of the Wi-Fi router. A mug sat abandoned on the coffee table, lipstick smudged at the rim.

Her roommate's sneakers were by the door, tossed in a way that spoke of rushing out earlier.

But the apartment was silent. Either she was asleep or out late. Good.

Iya slipped off her coat, hanging it carefully on the hook. She paused, hand brushing against the pocket where the envelope waited. Not yet.

Her room was her refuge—small, practical, but private. She closed the door behind her, flicked on the lamp, and sat at her desk. The envelope came out at last, placed neatly on the wooden surface. She didn't open it. She never did right away.

Instead, she reached for the leather-bound notebook she kept hidden beneath a stack of nondescript papers. A book no one had ever seen, and no one ever would.

She opened to a clean page. The scent of ink and paper met her like an old habit.

No names. Never names. That was her rule. She didn't need them anyway. One detail, one line, was enough to recall everything.

Her pen hovered before she wrote, slowly, deliberately:

C. / back / flame under ash

She stopped there, staring at the words. To anyone else, they would look like fragments. But for her, they were a map— a record of the evening, precise enough to spark memory, vague enough to protect.

She closed the book, slid it under the stack again, and leaned back in her chair.

The envelope still sat on the desk, gleaming faintly where the lamp caught the gold script. She ran a fingertip along the edge, not tearing it open. The ritual wasn't about what was inside. It was about what it meant: a silent contract between giver and receiver.

Her body exhaled slowly.

This was her rhythm, the way she carried each night back into herself. She didn't catalog details. She didn't replay every breath or sigh. She marked the essence—the truth of it—and then let it settle into silence.

She knew tomorrow Celine would wake different. Not transformed into someone new, but reminded of the woman she already was. That was enough.

Iya picked up the envelope, felt its weight, then tucked it into the drawer with others. A stack of secrets bound not by ink but by trust.

She sat for a moment longer in the stillness of her room, letting the hum of the city outside fade into the background.

Not climax. Not conquest.

The stillness after.

She reached for her pen one last time and wrote in the back of the notebook, where she kept her private fragments, her personal truths:

They'll say I cross lines.

But I don't.

I walk where I'm invited.

And tonight, a woman remembered her own body.

Not because of me.

Because she finally stopped hiding from it.

She set the pen down, exhaled, and let the room hold her in quiet.

For now, that was enough.

CHAPTER 5.5

THE PROVIDER

The common room smelled faintly of lemon polish and brewed coffee that had sat too long on the warmer. Evening light spilled across the floor, soft and golden, the kind of light that made the walls look kinder than they really were.

Iya set a tray of tea on the side table and glanced at the man by the window.

Mr. Edmund Veylan sat as though the chair were a throne he no longer wanted. His posture was upright out of habit, not pride. The suit jacket he wore was years old but still tailored—its seams holding the memory of boardrooms long left behind. His hands rested on the armrests; still large, still capable, though thinner now, veined and faintly trembling.

He was watching the courtyard. Not the garden itself, but the gate. As if expecting someone.

"Tea," Iya said gently, placing a cup within reach.

He didn't turn his head. Only his eyes flicked toward her, then back to the gate. "Thank you." His voice was low, like gravel smoothed by water.

For a while, silence stretched between them. Iya had learned not to break it too soon. Silence was part of care, too.

Finally, Edmund spoke. "You think love is built into the contract. You think providing buys you a seat at the table. But it doesn't work like that."

He turned toward her at last, his eyes pale but steady. "It's not that I never showed up. I did—sometimes. Birthdays, vacations, the odd weekend at the lake. But even then, I wasn't really there. I'd take the call in the middle of dinner, slip out saying 'five minutes,' and make it an hour. My kids would be splashing in the pool, and I'd be on the patio with a phone glued to my ear, nodding through a deal I thought couldn't wait."

He paused, his jaw tightening. "On our last family trip, I remember standing on the balcony at sunrise with a BlackBerry in my hand—the little brick of a phone with the tiny keyboard that executives treated like oxygen. Emails, calls, messages, all crammed into that thing. I tapped away while they built sandcastles below. I told myself it couldn't wait. I told myself they'd understand. I even took a picture of them from up there." His eyes narrowed. "I wasn't in it. I wasn't in any of it."

He let out a small breath, one that sounded like it had been sitting inside him for years. "I told myself it was for them. House, tuition, safety. But there's a kind of applause you only get at work. At home, no one claps when you close a deal. They just learn not to expect you fully." He looked down at his hands as though they belonged to someone else. "I didn't even notice. Not until the noise stopped."

The wall clock clicked, reminding the room it was still moving.

Iya nudged the cup closer. "Drink while it's warm."

He sipped once, then set it back in the saucer. The china gave a soft ring against itself.

"I made restaurant reservations I didn't keep. I bought tickets to a school concert and listened from the parking lot, phone pressed to my ear. I mouthed 'I'm sorry' through the windshield while my daughter searched for my face in the dark. She waved anyway. And I waved back like a man drowning."

Iya didn't offer balm. She kept her hands in her lap and let him walk the road of his sentences until he reached steadier ground.

"The worst thing," he said finally, "is that I congratulated myself for showing up at all. I treated presence like charity. Drop in. Be seen. Back to the airport."

"And now?" Iya asked.

"Now I have time," he said, smiling without pleasure. "Endless, shapeless time. It's funny how quiet gets louder when you know it's not going to end at five o'clock."

A cart rattled down the hall—plastic wheels, a stack of folded towels. Someone laughed, then hushed themselves.

Iya shifted in her chair. "You said earlier you worked for them. For your family."

"I did. And they believed me, because it sounded noble." He looked at the courtyard, where a maple held onto its last leaves. "But the truth is simpler, and I owe it to myself to say it plain: I worked for the part of me that needed to be applauded. The part that solved and signed and was told I mattered because I made numbers jump."

He rolled his shoulders, as though trying to sit more truthfully inside his suit. "My son used to ask if he could come to the office. 'Just to see where you go when you're gone, Dad.' I said, 'Maybe next month.' There are a lot of next months in this place." He glanced around the common room—the muted painting above the bookcase, the TV murmuring the news too softly for anyone to hear.

"You ask whose fault," he said, his voice low enough now that she leaned in to catch it. "I could say it's mine. I could say it's the story that raised me. I could say it's a market that never stops asking for blood. Any answer you want, I can make it sound good." His mouth tightened. "But none of those answers get me a do-over."

Iya followed his gaze to the gate. "You're waiting," she said gently.

"I am," he admitted. "Sometimes they come. Sometimes they don't. When they do, we sit. We're good at polite. My daughter gives me her life like a report. My son checks his phone. I try not to preach. I fail. We make plans we don't keep. Everyone pretends they're busy." He lifted his hands, then let them fall back to the chair. "Busy is a beautiful lie. It forgives everything until there's nothing left to forgive."

He looked at Iya, his gaze steady. "This is the part where I say I did my best. But I didn't. I did my habit. My habit was work."

Silence met him. Somewhere behind the nurses' station, a teaspoon clinked against porcelain.

Iya smoothed the napkin near the cup. "You want me to argue with you," she said. Not a question.

"I want someone to say I was right," he answered. "That the house and the tuition and the vacations bought me a pass. That I chose well." He shook his head. "But you don't lie for a living."

"No," Iya said.

A small smile cut across his face. "I knew that part the first week you started. You turned my chair to the window without asking if I wanted the TV. Everyone else assumed I needed noise."

"Sometimes the quiet is the work," she said.

He nodded gravely. "You asked what I wait for. I said forgiveness." His breath warmed the air between them. "It's true. But not all at once. Not a grand gesture. Just... small permissions. To be an old man in a chair who learned too late how to sit. To let a woman half my age hand me a cup of tea without me making it a transaction in my head."

His eyes returned to the maple. "I thought importance lasted longer. Turns out it's rented. They take it back at the door. And if you didn't build anything underneath—well," he tapped the armrest lightly, "you stay seated."

Iya adjusted the shade; a softer light spread across the carpet, less glare, more room for faces. "What would you have done differently?" she asked.

He thought, carefully, like a man reading a ledger for the first time with the right numbers in the columns.

"I would have learned how to be boring," he said finally. "Play the same card game on Thursday. Make pancakes badly. Sit on lawn chairs and watch the neighborhood do nothing. Call my wife in the middle of the day for no reason and not look at the clock." His jaw worked. "I would have let my children see me fail at something that wasn't work."

"Why that?" Iya asked.

"Because they only saw me winning," he said. "So, they learned to measure me in trophies. When the trophies stopped, what were we to each other?" He shook his head. "The men at the office—we were a club without a table. We had titles instead of friendship. I kept it neat, kept my distance. Later, there was no one to call who knew me without the card in my wallet."

The cart returned—fresh towels out, used ones in. A nurse paused in the doorway, took in the two of them, and nodded before moving on. The air carried faint sweetness of a floral diffuser someone had plugged in near the bookshelf.

"Do you hate them?" Iya asked. "Your family."

"No," he said, and the word was practiced enough to be true. "They did what people do. They used the language I taught them. I sent money when I should have sent myself. I made sure they had everything except me, and then I was surprised when they learned to live without me." He turned the cup a quarter inch. "They're not villains. They're graduates."

Iya nodded. "And you?"

"Remedial," he said dryly. Then softer: "But in the right school at last."

A low chuckle slipped from her. "This isn't much of a school."

"It is," he said. "No one passes, but everyone learns."

They sat with that for a while. TV voices lifted and sank. Someone down the hall called a name that wasn't answered, then called it again, louder. Rain began at the far window in a thin, careful pattern, like the sky deciding to try again.

Edmund looked back to the gate. "You know, it doesn't matter if you're a CEO or the president of a company. They forget you fast when you step down. I don't say it to be cruel; I say it because it's accurate. All those years of calls and meetings and hands reaching for you—then your name falls off the list. The room closes around the next person. That is how it works."

He let the truth land without force. "If you don't die young, you'll need one of you. A carer. Someone who stays when staying isn't glamorous. Not the ones who signed my bonus checks. Not the ones who wrote nice notes on company letterhead. The ones who know how I take my tea and which hip aches when the weather changes."

His eyes met hers. "You want to know what matters? It's the person who is still there when everyone else has somewhere important to be."

Iya's throat worked once. She swallowed the reflex to answer too quickly. "People don't put that on business cards," she said.

"They should," he replied. "If the world were measured right, your title would read—" He searched for it. "Keeper. That's the word."

She didn't look away. "And what are you now, Mr. Veylan?"

"A man who is learning to ask for water without apologizing," he said. "A man who is trying to say thank you like it's not a debt."

From the hall, the medication cart's brakes squeaked. A soft knock at the doorframe; a nurse smiled with two paper cups in her hand. "Mr. Veylan?"

He nodded. "Timing, as always." He took them without fuss, sipped from the small water, and handed it back. The nurse checked her chart and slipped away.

He watched the doorway a moment longer, then turned back. "I used to hold a room with one word. Now I wait for someone to push me to the dining hall. Life is efficient like that."

"You still hold a room," Iya said.

He arched a brow. "Do I?"

"You held this one," she said simply. "From the window to the cup and back again."

He smiled. This time it reached his eyes. "You're kind."

"I'm accurate," she said.

His shoulders eased. The room did, too. "Can I ask you something?" he said after a while. "Do you ever tire of it? Being the person who stays."

"Yes," she said. "I get tired. Then I come back."

"Why?"

"Because someone stayed for me once," she said, and left it there.

He didn't press. "That sounds like a debt you know how to handle."

"It isn't a debt," she said. "It's a lineage."

He studied his hands, the old strength still visible under the thinness. "I don't know how to join that."

"You already did," she said. "You told the truth in front of a witness."

He blinked slowly. "Is that all it takes?"

"It's a start," she said. "Starts are underrated."

The rain picked up, louder now. In the courtyard, a staff member in a bright raincoat jogged to the shed and came back with a bag of salt for the steps. The maple shivered, letting go of one more leaf.

Edmund cleared his throat. "Do you think I'm a bad man?"

"I think you were taught the wrong shape for love," she said. "And you wore it until it cracked."

He nodded, grateful and wounded at once. "That sounds right."

"Your shape can change," she added.

"At this age?"

"Especially at this age," she said. "The young don't know what they're changing from."

He chuckled softly. "You're good at this."

"It's my job," she said. "One of them."

He tilted his head. "You have another?"

"Everyone has another," she said. "Even if it's just who they are when they close their eyes."

He accepted that without pushing. The clock clicked again. Her shift would turn soon. She knew the angles of this light, the footsteps that would come with the evening round, the things that would need her elsewhere.

"Do you want the TV?" she asked.

"No," he said. "I want to sit with what I said for a while. If I turn something on, I'll drown it." He glanced at the gate one last time, less desperately than before. "Would you—when you come back—remind me of the pancake thing?"

"I will," she said.

"I might actually try it," he added, a boyish uncertainty slipping through the old authority. "They serve them on Saturdays."

"I know," she said. "You like the edges crisp."

He seemed surprised, then pleased. "Do I?"

"You do now," she said, standing up.

He lifted his hand, then let it fall, then lifted it again and left it halfway—between wave and reach. "Thank you," he said.

"For what?" she asked.

"For not rushing me," he said. "For letting me finish a thought."

She nodded once. "I'll be back after the round."

She turned the chair a degree so the glare wouldn't catch his eyes if the sun tried one last flare before giving up. She slid the cup closer again, just in case he forgot where he'd set it. At the door, she looked back.

He was no longer watching the gate. He was watching the maple hold on to its last leaves and the rain take its time.

Iya stepped into the hall. The cart's wheels squeaked, then rolled; a distant TV tried a joke and someone laughed on delay. She washed her hands in the small sink, watching the water silver her skin, then cut it off and dried them slow. Outside, the evening deepened. Inside, a man sat in a chair and practiced being present.

She carried the quiet with her down the corridor to the next room.

CHAPTER 6:

THE LINK

The Meeting

The restaurant breathed in low light and polished shadows, the kind of place where people whispered things they didn't want repeated. Rain streaked the wide windows, making the street outside look like it was melting.

Dr. Hannah Ceryn sat with her back to the room, as always. She liked seeing people arrive before they saw her. A habit born of both caution and curiosity.

Iya slipped in without a coat, hair damp, eyes sharp. She slid into the seat across from Hannah with an ease that suggested she belonged anywhere.

"You picked a quiet place," Iya said, brushing a strand of wet hair behind her ear.

Hannah's mouth curved faintly. "Not quiet. Private. There's a difference."

Iya tilted her head. "You don't like repeating yourself?"

"Precisely." Hannah lifted the menu without looking at it, then set it down like a prop.

The waiter appeared. Hannah ordered her usual glass of Syrah. Then she looked across the table.

"And for her—"

"Dark 'n' Stormy," Iya cut in smoothly. The waiter nodded and left.

A slow smile traced Hannah's lips. "Still your drink?"

"Still mine, yes. Though sometimes I let it choose me."

Hannah leaned her cheek into her hand, studying her. "I've never asked why."

"It looks like night at the bottom, daylight at the top," Iya said. "Sweet, until it isn't. And if you stir it wrong..." She lifted one brow. "It collapses."

"I should have guessed. You've always struck me as someone who prefers her metaphors drinkable."

"People think they know me because they've tasted rum

before. They forget it's the ginger beer that burns."

A low laugh escaped Hannah, velvet and restrained. "Sharp. Unexpected." She tilted her head. "Like you."

The drinks arrived. Iya wrapped her hand around the glass but didn't drink yet, as though waiting for the moment to deserve it.

"So," she said finally, voice calm but edged, "this is about Celine."

Hannah swirled her wine, watching the reflection of the chandelier fracture in the glass. Her tone, when it came, was deliberate. "She rang me this morning. Different tone entirely. Like a woman who finally remembered her spine."

"It was only one meeting," Iya replied.

"One is often enough with you." Hannah sipped, her gaze unflinching.

"That's not magic," Iya said evenly, "that's timing."

Hannah's lips curved in something between a smirk and a secret. "And timing, my dear, is the only magic most people ever get."

A pause hung between them, charged but not uncomfortable. Iya finally lifted her drink, the ginger sting catching the edge of her breath.

"You trust me with people you care about," she said quietly. "You're not careless with that."

"No," Hannah agreed. Her tone softened, but it was still laced with steel. "And let me be clear: I don't send anyone to you. I'm not arranging. I'm not... trading in secrets. That's not who I am." Her eyes flicked toward the rain, then back. "What I do is simpler—and harder. I listen. When I hear the ache beneath their words, when I know talk alone won't break it open, I remind them there are other kinds of care. And then I leave the choice with them."

Her gaze sharpened, almost cutting. "That's the difference. I don't lead them to your door. I just tell them the door exists."

Iya's mouth curved, not into a smile but recognition. "And so, you booked under a false name."

Hannah lifted her glass. "Naturally. I liked the idea that you wouldn't know who I was until I decided you should."

Iya let out the faintest laugh. "You thought you were mysterious?"

"I was careful," Hannah corrected, voice smooth as silk. "Mysterious is for show. Careful is how you stay alive."

For a moment, silence. Just the rain and the soft clink of glasses.

Then Hannah said, almost like a verdict:

"And that, I think, is why women like Celine end up with you. Not because I place them there. Because the idea of you doesn't feel foreign. It feels like something they've been waiting for, without knowing it.

The Question of Choice

The waiter drifted past with the confidence of someone trained to be invisible, topping off water, glancing at their glasses, vanishing again. Outside, the rain had eased into a shimmer—more air than weather—turning the street into a soft mirage.

Iya's fingers rested on the condensation band her glass had left on the table. "It still lands oddly," she said, tone even. "You —of all people—pointing anyone toward me."

Hannah gave her glass a quarter turn, as if aligning it with an invisible compass. "Odd," she allowed, "but intentional."

"Some would use less generous language." Iya's gaze didn't waver.

Hannah met it without blinking. "You mean the kind that makes me sound like I'm arranging assignations." The word was clean, almost clinical in her mouth, carried without apology. "I'm not."

"Convince me," Iya said. Not a dare. A test.

"I don't send," Hannah replied, voice warmer now, still measured. "I don't book, barter, or promise. When someone is circling the same problem for the hundredth time and language has stopped reaching them, I name a possibility. I say, 'There is another kind of care. If you want to hear about it, ask.' Some don't. It ends there. Some do. I give a first name or none at all and step back." She held Iya's eyes. "I'm not a broker."

Iya's mouth tilted with the smallest approval. "Better."

Hannah took a slow sip, as if tasting the word. "Good."

A couple at a neighboring table laughed; a spoon chimed against porcelain; the room settled again. Iya lifted her drink at last, the ginger heat catching enough to mark the moment.

"So what happens," Iya said, "when you 'name a possibility'?"

"They lean forward," Hannah answered. "Not toward you—toward themselves. They're not recognizing a person; they're recognizing permission. The idea is enough to shift the room inside them."

"Poetic."

"Accurate," Hannah countered, the corner of her mouth curving. "Poetry is what precision looks like when you say it out loud."

Iya let that sit. Then: "And ethics?"

"Intact," Hannah said, immediate. "Nobody is compelled. Nobody is coerced. I don't personally benefit if they go to you, and I lose nothing if they don't. I am not outsourcing my work; I am refusing to pretend my work covers every door."

"You realize you're unusual," Iya said. "Most would either deny the door exists or build a corridor to it and charge a fee."

Hannah's laugh was low, amused, unamused. "I'm aware."

The waiter reappeared with plates—grilled fish, winter greens, a bowl of roasted carrots shining with something citrus. He set everything down in a choreography that didn't require speech and left a small dish of salt as if he trusted them to finish their own balance.

"Do you ever regret it?" Iya asked when they were alone again. "Not the whisper. The step back."

"Regret?" Hannah tasted the word as if it were on the plate. "No." A beat. "I do, however, monitor."

"For what?"

"For projection masquerading as concern. Mine, not theirs." She set her fork down. "There's a thin line between offering a door and shoving someone through it because you've decided the room beyond is good for them. I don't cross it."

"Not even when they ask you to push?"

Hannah's smile was almost fond. "Especially not then. Consent is not enthusiasm. If they need me to propel them, they're not ready. Wanting is not the same as choosing."

Iya nodded once. "You sound like a therapist."

"I am one," Hannah said mildly, then added dryly, "however inconvenient that may be."

They ate for a moment in companionable quiet. Steam curled off the carrots. Outside, the mist thickened, blurring colors into suggestion.

"You enjoy the moment before," Iya said, breaking bread. It wasn't an accusation; it was an observation offered like a coin laid on the table.

Hannah's eyes warmed. "I enjoy honesty. And the moment before is where honesty declares itself." She glanced toward the window, watching her reflection ghost over the rain. "If I name a door and everything in them recoils, I'm grateful. Clarity is a gift. If I name a door and they sit taller—well. The body speaks first."

"The body lies too," Iya said.

"Only when the owner tells it to," Hannah replied, soft, exact.

Iya's laugh was a breath. "You do know how to place a sentence."

"So do you," Hannah said. "You just do it with your hands."

A beat. That landed.

"I assume you vet the stories that reach you," Iya said after a moment. "Not just who, but why."

"I do." Hannah folded her napkin once, twice. "No one arrives untouched by narrative. Some want a rescuer. That's not you.

Some want a secret to light their marriage on fire. That's not you either. Some want a reason to leave. I decline to be that reason."

"And the ones you don't warn away?"

"They're the ones who've been living like a room with all the windows painted shut." Hannah's gaze held steady. "When I hint there's another kind of air, they don't ask for proof. They inhale."

Iya took another sip, contemplating the line. "And if they ask for proof?"

"I tell them the same thing I tell myself," Hannah said. "Proof is what we name relief after the fact."

The corners of Iya's eyes creased. "You should embroider that on a pillow."

"God, no," Hannah said, scandalized in a whisper. "If I become quotable, I'll be unbearable." Then, with a sly tilt, "More unbearable."

The heat between them softened into ease. The waiter appeared to clear a dish; Hannah tilted her hand, a small gesture that said not yet, and he receded again, absorbed by the room.

"I had a woman once," Hannah said, voice lower, like a confidence set on velvet. "Brilliant, devastating mind. Talked herself into circles with flawless logic. She came every week, argued beautifully, cried politely, left the same. One day she said, 'I want to stop explaining my life and live it for a moment.' I told her there was someone she could speak to who did not require explanation. I said no more. She didn't ask for your number then. Six months later, she did." A small shrug. "That's the pace I trust."

"Patience looks good on you," Iya said.

"It's not patience," Hannah replied. "It's respect."

They finished the fish. The room's low soundtrack shifted —one track dissolving into another with the studied care of someone in the back who understood nights like this.

"You asked about ethics," Hannah said, returning to the earlier thread like a magician producing a card she'd palmed minutes ago. "Here's mine. I don't cross my own lines to help someone cross theirs. I don't hint out of loneliness or curiosity. And I never, ever mention you to anyone who would use you as a weapon against themselves."

Iya set her glass down. "They do that?"

"More often than you'd like," Hannah said. "Self-harm can wear very expensive clothing."

"And you, what—toss water on the wick?"

"I turn off the spotlight," Hannah said. "Starvation needs an audience."

They let that settle.

"Where do you put all of this?" Iya asked quietly. "The stories, the almost, the afters."

Hannah breathed in through her nose, out through a smile without teeth. "In a box in my head labeled Not Mine to Keep." Then, a beat later, more honest: "And sometimes in the long walk home."

Iya's gaze softened very slightly. "The walk is good."

"It is." Hannah tilted her glass in a small salute. "You take the long way too, I imagine."

"Always."

A table toward the back erupted briefly, then apologized to itself, volume slipping down again. The waiter hovered in the periphery, scanned their plates with his eyes, and approached. This time Hannah let him clear. He offered dessert; she declined with a smile and a glance at Iya that said we're not finished, but we don't need sugar.

"You haven't asked me the question," Hannah said when they were alone. "Most people do."

"Which one?"

"Why I ever came to you." Her tone was lazy, deliberately. "You act as if you worked it out before I did."

"I assumed you were careful," Iya said. "And that you prefer to know a door before you show it to anyone else."

Hannah's grin flashed quick, rare. "It was that. And curiosity. And a little envy."

"Envy?" Now Iya did lean in, intrigued but not naive.

"Mm." Hannah looked down at the wine lacing the bottom of her glass. "You get to be there for the hour after someone stops pretending. Therapy has to sit through every preamble. There's a kind of joy in the after that I only see through glass."

"You could break the glass," Iya said.

"I could," Hannah agreed, "but then I wouldn't be doing my work anymore." She set the glass down. "We each hold a piece.

That's what makes it clean."

Iya nodded, slow, the acknowledgment precise. "Clean matters."

"It does."

They let the quiet carry them for a full minute. The rain returned with delicate persistence, writing cursive no one could read down the windowpanes.

"Last thing," Iya said. "Say it plainly. For me, not for the room."

Hannah angled her body toward her, shoulder soft against the back of the chair, voice low enough to be private even here. "I am not sending anyone to you. I am not arranging or profiting or smoothing the way. When a woman sitting in my office is suffocating on language and I know I won't be enough, I tell her there is another door. I do not describe the room beyond it. I don't need to. If she's ready, she'll stand. If she's not, she won't. Either way, I am not the one who walks her there." Her gaze didn't waver. "I trust her. And I trust you to keep trusting yourself."

Iya held that a moment—the weight of it, the precision. "Thank you."

"For what?" Hannah asked, genuinely curious.

"For saying it clean."

Hannah inclined her head. "I thought you'd appreciate that."

The waiter returned with the check folded neatly like a secret. Hannah slid it toward herself without looking at the number. "Let me," she said. It wasn't a question.

Iya reached for her coat. "You always do."

"Privileges of being the one who chooses the restaurant," Hannah replied, dry as smoke.

"Also the privilege of not sounding like a pimp," Iya added.

Hannah's laugh was quiet and delighted. "I'll embroider that on a pillow."

"Please don't," Iya said. "You'd ruin your brand."

"My what?"

"Your aura of terrifying restraint."

Hannah lifted a hand, conceding the point. "Fair."

The plates had long been cleared, their glasses near empty. The restaurant had shifted into its after-hours rhythm—tables half-vacant, waiters quieter now, the hum of voices reduced to a low current under the music. Outside, the rain had slowed to a silver mist, turning the city into a blur, like a painting left too long in the weather.

Hannah rested her glass lightly against her palm, not drinking, just weighing it. Her voice, when it came, was velvet wrapped in steel.

"Care," she said slowly, "is a kind of currency. The rarer it is, the more people hoard it. Some will pay dearly for it, as you've seen. But others..." Her gaze lifted, sharp as a blade yet calm as water. "...others don't stop to ask if they deserve it. They take it because they're starving, and starving people forget their manners."

Iya didn't answer at once. She traced the rim of her glass with one finger, the ginger sting of her Dark 'n' Stormy still lingering on her tongue. The sound of her nail against the glass was almost inaudible, but Hannah caught it, as if even hesitation had a language.

Hannah leaned in, just enough that her words belonged to Iya alone. "You know what that means. Not everyone who whispers your name should ever reach your door."

The charged silence stretched between them, full of the things neither woman had said aloud.

Finally, Iya exhaled, slow. "I don't open the door for everyone."

"I know," Hannah replied smoothly. She set her glass down with a soft click, a punctuation mark to the thought. "That's how you survive."

The waiter returned quietly, clearing the last of the glasses. Neither of them moved until he was gone.

When they finally stood, the scrape of chairs felt louder than it should have. They walked to the door together without speaking, the distance between them measured, deliberate.

Outside, the mist softened the streetlamps into halos that wrapped the pavement in a gauze of reflected light. The air smelled faintly of wet stone and exhaust. They lingered under the awning, neither quite ready to step into the night.

At last, Hannah turned to her. "One last thing," she said, her tone deceptively light. "The problem with whispers is you never know whose ear they've already reached. What begins as reverence can sour into obsession. Be cautious."

Iya's gaze held hers, steady, unreadable. "Caution is the only reason I'm still breathing."

Hannah studied her for a beat, then inclined her head—an

acknowledgement, a verdict, a promise—and turned down the street. Her silhouette disappeared quickly, swallowed by fog and distance.

The rain clung to her hair, and with it came a memory she had long kept sealed—Johansson's voice, her touch, the farewell that had never truly left.

The Flashback

Johansson's hand lingered at Iya's cheek, trembling. Her forehead rested against Iya's, her voice breaking into something raw.

"You give me peace in a way no one else ever has. With you, I finally feel like I can breathe." Her eyes shone, but she didn't look away. "But if I stay... then I'm choosing that peace for myself and taking it away from the people who still need me. They need all of me—my time, my strength, my voice. If I keep you, I fail them."

Iya's grip tightened over Johansson's hand, desperate to hold it there. "So we punish ourselves instead?" she whispered.

Johansson shook her head, her lips brushing Iya's skin. "No. We give the best of ourselves away. That's the only way it's honest. And if we stay together, we'd start giving less to everyone else. That would eat at us. It would ruin what this is before it even begins."

Her mouth trembled, and then she kissed Iya—soft, brief, aching.

Not a beginning. Not even a promise. Just proof they could, and proof they wouldn't.

When she pulled back, her voice cracked. "Iya, you're my world. But we can't keep us for ourselves. Not when I can help more. Not when you can care for more."

Silence pressed between them, heavy as stone.

Iya's chest tightened until it hurt to breathe. She wanted to argue, to beg, but every word in her throat would only make the truth harder. She closed her eyes, and when she opened them again, her voice was steady. "Then this is goodbye."

Johansson's hand slipped away, lingering in the air for a moment like it didn't want to leave. She turned, pulling her coat tight around her shoulders. At the door she paused, back still to Iya, and her body shook once.

And then she left.

The click of the latch echoed in the quiet.

Iya sank into the chair, the fabric still warm. She pressed her palms together, holding them tight until the ache spread up her arms. Tears slid down her face before she could stop them, the kind that came from a place too deep to resist.

She had lost her only chance at something she wanted for herself. And all gone because both of them cared too much about everyone else.

The memory cut off as suddenly as it had arrived, leaving her chest tight. She had buried Johansson years ago, yet here she was—alive again, walking beside her in the rain.

Iya stood a moment longer, the mist catching in her hair, the quiet pressing in on her. Then she turned in the opposite direction, her footsteps slow, measured, each one carrying the weight of Hannah's warning:

Not everyone who whispers your name should ever reach your door.

The city took her in, but the whisper followed.

CHAPTER 7:

TETHERED

The Call That Should Not Happen

It was past midnight when the phone lit up.

Iya almost ignored it. Clients didn't call. They booked. They confirmed. They paid. Rules kept the worlds from bleeding into each other, and she had drawn those rules with precision.

But she froze at the name on the screen: Leah.

She let it ring three times before answering. "Leah." Calm. Professional. A boundary in one word.

A soft inhale, then her voice—low, velvet, pleased. "You answered."

Not hello. Not sorry for the hour. Just that. A victory.

"I don't usually take calls this late," Iya said, sitting up straight, the mattress dipping beneath her.

"I know." Leah's tone was deliberate, every word too slow to be casual. "That's why I risked it. If you answered, it means something."

"It means I was awake."

"No," Leah said, her smile audible. "It means you wanted to hear me."

Iya's jaw tightened. "Don't assume."

"Don't deflect," Leah countered instantly. "You don't pick up unless you want to. I bet you've ignored plenty of calls before mine."

Iya didn't respond. Silence was sometimes sharper than words.

Leah let the quiet breathe, savoring it like a cat watching a bird pause mid-flight. Then, softly: "Tell me what you're wearing."

Iya's breath caught—not in shock, but in recognition. Of course, Leah would push this far, this fast. "That's not how this works."

Leah gave a small laugh, throaty and amused. "Relax. I was

teasing. Sort of."

"Leah."

"I know your rules." Leah's voice dropped, huskier now. "I just like pulling on them. Seeing how tight they are. You should hear the sound they make when they strain. Like a bowstring."

"Boundaries don't need testing to matter."

"Of course they do. Everything worth having needs testing. Otherwise, how do you know it's strong enough to hold you?"

"You shouldn't call me like this," Iya said. "Not outside of what we agreed."

"And yet..." Leah's tone curled into a smile. "You're still here. Talking to me."

Iya's eyes narrowed. "Two minutes, then I hang up."

"Oh, make it one. Hurt me a little."

"Don't make this a game."

"Everything is a game," Leah said smoothly. "The only question is—are you the player, or are you the prize?"

"I'm neither."

Leah chuckled low. "That's exactly what the prize would say."

Iya pressed her palm against the cold windowpane, grounding herself. Outside, a car slipped past, headlights slicing through the dark. "You sound drunk."

"I'm not," Leah said. "I'm high on remembering you. That's worse, isn't it?"

"Leah—"

"You touched your glass before you left," Leah interrupted. "Set it half on the coaster, half off. Most people would never notice. But I did. It was deliberate. A little tilt. A little wobble. You wanted me to think about it later, and now I am. Still."

Iya froze.

Leah's voice softened, almost reverent. "I replay the way you listen. People think it's your ears. It's your body. Your spine straightens when you're holding the line. But when you soften..." Her breath caught. "God, I want to be the reason you soften."

"That's not noticing," Iya said tightly. "That's staring."

"Don't flatter yourself," Leah teased, a dark smile in her voice. "I don't stare at everyone. Just you. Because you make it impossible not to."

"You're in dangerous territory."

"Mmm," Leah purred. "Dangerous is the only territory worth owning."

Iya exhaled sharply. "Fifty seconds."

"Fine," Leah said. "Then I'll use them well. I can still smell your shampoo on my scarf. Still see the way you leaned back when you decided the night was over. Not cold, not cruel. Just… untouchable. Do you know what that does to a woman like me?"

"You're romanticizing obsession."

"No." Leah's voice was clear, sudden, cutting through the line like glass. "I'm telling you the truth. I collect you. Every glance. Every movement. And you hate it because you know I'm not wrong."

"That's unhealthy."

"That's inevitable."

Iya closed her eyes. She hated how steady Leah sounded, how there was no apology in her tone—only certainty.

Control had always been Iya's native language; she spoke it fluently, without effort. But Leah's voice rewrote the syntax— every word landing where Iya's calm should've been. For the first time in months, Iya felt the balance tilt—not violently, but precisely, the way a scale betrays what it's been carrying.

She wasn't used to being seen without permission. Leah's certainty left her exposed, not because it was cruel, but because it was sure. And what unnerved her most wasn't the danger—it was the recognition.

Her breath came slow, deliberate, an imitation of calm. The air felt heavier now, pressing against her skin, as if the room itself waited to see if she'd recover her footing.

She wanted to hang up, to end it cleanly. But control isn't the same as escape.

And what unsettled her the most wasn't Leah's confidence— it was the truth tucked inside it. She had answered.

"Ten seconds," Iya said.

"Then give me something I can keep."

"No."

"You already have." Leah's laugh was low, almost tender. "You answered."

The timer on Iya's chest clicked down. She ended the call. The silence afterward felt thick, like air after a storm.

Her phone buzzed once more. A message.

Thank you for not making me feel small when you said no.

Another followed almost immediately.

I moved the glass fully onto the coaster in my head. It's steady now. Goodnight.

Iya stared at the screen, pulse heavy in her throat. She set the phone face-down and slid it under a paperback, as if paper and ink could weigh down whatever thread had just been tied between them.

But when she lay back down, damp hair against the pillow, the voice still lingered. Not poetic. Not vague. Direct. Sharp. Intimate. The kind of voice that didn't ask—it tethered.

And the worst part: Iya had let it.

The Weight of Normal

Morning at the facility didn't ask how you slept. It simply arrived—clean light, humming vents, the quiet choreography of a place that kept people moving when their bodies wanted to stop.

Iya clocked in at 6:58. Two minutes early didn't give her space to breathe, but just enough to prove she still believed in being ahead of the day. She tucked a stray flyaway into her braid, clipped her badge, and let the familiar smells wrap around her—detergent, oatmeal, the trace of antiseptic that lived in the walls.

"Mm-hm," Lorna said from behind the med cart, not looking up yet, pen scraping a checklist. "You come in here with those eyes like carry-on bags and expect me not to charge baggage fees?"

Iya's mouth twitched. "Good morning to you, too."

Lorna lifted her head. The headscarf today was deep maroon with tiny gold dots; it made her look like she'd been born under good lighting. "Girl, don't 'morning' me with that half-smile. You want coffee or a life coach?"

"Coffee," Iya said. "Life coach later."

Lorna made a satisfied noise and reached for a Styrofoam cup. She poured, handed it over, then watched Iya the way a nurse watches a monitor: reading for patterns, deciding what was noise and what was a real signal.

"You good?" she asked finally.

"I'm here," Iya said.

"Mm." Lorna's mouth shaped a knowing line. "A lot of people show up. Not everybody is here."

She didn't press.That was part of her power—she could tease like an aunt at a cookout, then set the joke down and give you quiet long enough to tell the truth, if you had one to give. Iya didn't. Not one she could say out loud. She sipped the coffee, grateful for the heat, and checked the board.

Room 204: Santos. Room 210: McKenzie. Lift assist at 7:15. Vitals pre-breakfast.

Work gave you a list. Lists were mercy.

They moved. Lorna pushed the cart. Iya peeled gloves from a box, the powderless pair snapping at her wrists. The hallway was still, that odd hush of morning before televisions started talking and family members arrived with tote bags and questions.

"Mrs. Santos?" Iya knocked softly, then entered. The older woman blinked awake, eyes bright, then clouded, then bright again—as if the day were testing how much light she could hold.

"Good morning," Iya said. "You want the blue blouse or the one with the little flowers?"

"Your voice," Mrs. Santos said, studying her. "You sound like someone I used to know."

Iya adjusted without thinking, warmth in her tone, a gentle lilt. "Maybe I am. Maybe she sent me to help, hmm?"

The lines at the corners of Mrs. Santos's eyes softened. "Yes. That makes sense."

Iya washed hands, measured blood pressure, took a pulse—steady, then steadier. She made small talk while the numbers rose on the screen, understanding how big small talk can be when you've forgotten the shape of your own day.

"You slept okay?"

"I dreamed I was at the beach," Mrs. Santos said. "Waves kept coming, but they didn't reach me. They just… tried."

"Persistent waves," Iya said. "We like their effort."

A shadow of a smile. "We do."

Shirt, buttons, collar smoothed. Iya worked quickly without rushing. Care was a tempo: move too slow and you lose dignity; move too fast and you lose the person. She wheeled Mrs. Santos toward the common room, brakes gentle, blanket tucked, feet positioned on the pedals so ankles wouldn't drag.

Outside in the hall, Lorna waited with a wipe in one hand and a story in the other.

"Now listen," she said as they moved, her low voice carrying like a secret everyone was meant to hear. "Last night my nephew calls me, says, 'Aunty, I think my girlfriend's mad at me.' I said, 'What you do?' He said, 'Breathed.' I said, 'Okay, baby, then stop doing it in her direction for a minute, your breath kind of stank.'" She rolled her eyes. "These children. No conflict resolution, just vibes."

Mrs. Santos laughed, surprised at herself, the sound like a door being opened just enough to feel air.

"You hear that?" Lorna said, pleased. "Made her laugh before eight. I'm a miracle worker."

They parked Mrs. Santos near the window where the sun slid in like a guest who knew the code. The television in the corner muttered about traffic and weather; the oatmeal smell got stronger. A volunteer arranged puzzles on a table no one would finish.

"McKenzie next," Lorna said, scanning the list. "Me or you?"

"I'll take him," Iya said.

Room 210 had the heavy quiet of a person planning not to cooperate. Mr. McKenzie stared at the ceiling as if he'd made a pact with it. Iya greeted him, offered choices—blue sweater or gray, wash now or after tea. Choices were dignity disguised as options.

"Don't matter," he said. "It's all the same in here."

"It's not all the same," Iya said evenly. "You wearing blue today. Looks good on camera."

"What camera?" Suspicion sharpened at the edges.

"The one in your granddaughter's phone," Iya said. "She visits at ten. You going to let her post a photo of you in that wrinkled T-shirt?"

He hesitated. "Get the sweater."

She nodded, no victory in it, only forward motion. She set up the sling for the lift, checked the straps, explained each step. Lorna came in to take the other side of the transfer. The machine hummed and the old man rose like a reluctant balloon.

"I ain't heavy," he muttered.

"You're precious," Lorna corrected, voice even, eyes on the straps. "And precious things get handled right."

The line wasn't flashy; it just landed with a small, true weight. Mr. McKenzie grunted like he didn't care, then held still the exact way people do when they've decided to trust you.

They got him settled. They checked the skin at his hip where pressure liked to make trouble. Ointment, barrier, reposition —the unglamorous heroics of routine.

As they wheeled him out, Lorna slowed, looked at Iya. The teasing from earlier had slipped; what remained was attention.

"You with me?" she asked.

"I'm with you," Iya said.

"Good." Lorna's voice stayed soft. "Cause sometimes you move so clean I can't tell if you're present or you just a well-trained ghost."

Iya nearly smiled and nearly winced. Both felt true. "I'm here."

"Stay that way," Lorna said. "These folks can tell the difference."

They split for the medication pass. Iya crushed a pill in applesauce, labeled and logged, then brought it to Room 206.

"Morning, Ms. Patel," she said. "Oatmeal or toast?"

"Oatmeal," Ms. Patel said, then whispered, "Both," like she was robbing a bank.

"Criminal," Iya said, deadpan.

By 8:30 the building had woken fully. TVs shouted, shoes squeaked, laughter leaked and disappeared. A son argued gently with his mother about her sweater. A husband sat so close to his wife it looked like he was keeping her intact by touch alone. A nurse called for a chart, got three by accident and said thank you anyway.

Iya moved inside all of it, efficient, polite. Her body worked the way a seasoned dancer hits marks without thinking. And yet, the thread from last night still tugged when she wasn't looking. Not strong. Just present. 'You answered'.

She hated how the sentence fit in the spaces between tasks.

At the hydration table, Lorna handed out water like a woman daring people to say no to their own throats. She glanced over and saw the set of Iya's shoulders, the small brace she used when her mind was somewhere else.

"Walk," Lorna said, nodding toward the side hall.

"I have vitals due in—"

"Twenty minutes," Lorna said. "You'll do them better after sixty seconds with me."

That was the thing about her: in this mood, you didn't argue because arguing felt like disrespecting the weather. They walked to the window at the end of the hall where a parking lot made its best attempt at being a view.

"Talk," Lorna said.

"There's nothing to talk about."

"Mm." Lorna's mouth did that thoughtful purse again. "You're not obligated to give me your business. But I like you. I want to keep liking you with all the information." She tilted her head. "You in trouble?"

"No," Iya said, a little too quick. She adjusted. "Not the kind of trouble you're thinking."

"Okay," Lorna said. The word covered a lot of ground. "You still sleeping?"

"Some.

"You know 'some' is how liars say 'no,' right?"

That got a real smile out of Iya. "You're very kind."

"I'm very observant," Lorna said. Then, quieter: "I've seen your type burn out. The ones who want to do it clean. The ones who believe the job eats only what you offer it. It eats more. So, you make your own plates."

Iya looked out at the cars. A woman in a red coat unfolded a walker like a secret ritual. "I'm making plates."

"Good," Lorna said. "Make them big. And eat from them yourself. You don't got to tell me who's calling you at midnight. Just don't answer like you owe them something."

The words hit with that specific Lorna-weight—not sermon, not warning, just fact delivered the way you deliver medication: measured, necessary, in the correct dose.

"I don't owe anyone," Iya said.

Lorna considered that, eyes kind. "You owe you."

They stood in a pocket of quiet where the building couldn't reach, where even Leah's echo couldn't quite intrude. Lorna didn't touch Iya—she wasn't the touching type unless it did work—but the space between them felt held.

The pager on Iya's hip buzzed. She checked: lift assist in 212. "I need to—"

"Go," Lorna said. "Handle your list."

Room 212 was a puzzle: a woman who liked to joke with nurses and fight with gravity. Iya and an orderly did the transfer, laughter threaded through the mechanics. They settled the woman into her chair with a soft thud and an "oof" like somebody finishing a good stretch.

On the way back to the station, they passed the family board—dry erase names and visit times. Someone had drawn a little heart next to "10:00—Nina." Underneath, in shaky handwriting, someone had added, "Bring the red scarf."

The word scarf tugged the wrong memory—Leah's low murmur: *I can still smell your shampoo on my scarf.* The thread tightened, small and mean. Iya kept walking.

At 9:15, Lorna met her at the sink. They washed hands in a practiced duet, water arcing, paper towels crumpling like pacts.

"You ever notice," Lorna said casually, "how the long days feel shorter if you let one person be easy?"

"One person?"

"Girl, pick somebody, you can't save everybody. Just pick one person and make their day easier. That's enough."

Iya thought of Mr. McKenzie and his blue sweater. "Okay," she said. "I'll start with him."

"That's right," Lorna said. "We don't run the universe, but we do run this hallway." She paused, then added, softer: "Just don't run yourself."

They moved again. Work swallowed time the way the sea swallows footprints. At ten, Nina arrived for Mr. McKenzie, phone ready, smile rehearsed. He scowled for show, then sat up straighter and told her blue was a strong color. Nina laughed. The photo caught something it probably wasn't trying to: a man who felt seen.

Lorna slid up next to Iya, voice all Auntie again. "Look at him. Instagram model. I'm going to start charging appearance fees."

"You'll retire next week," Iya said.

"And miss all this glam?" Lorna scoffed. Then, after a beat, her tone dropped a register—not heavy, just intentional. "You did that. Remember. People will see your work and call it luck."

They rode the day to midmorning. Breakfast trays vanished, lunch marched in—soup, sandwiches, the endless conspiracy of hydration. A new admission was due at noon; the family had questions; the bed needed a second set of rails.

In the tiny staff room that pretended to be a break space, Iya sat for the first time. The chair complained; the vending machine blinked one working light. Lorna tossed two creamers toward Iya's cup without asking; both landed. She pretended not to be proud.

"Okay," Lorna said, settling into the chair like a queen accepting an inferior throne. "This where you tell me the rest of that story you're not telling."

"There isn't a story," Iya said. She realized she sounded tired of her own sentence.

Lorna rested her elbows on the table, fingers laced, eyes steady. When she spoke, her voice had that Viola cadence—measured, almost quiet, the kind that makes a room hush because it wants to catch every word.

"Listen. You are good at this. Not just the charts and the lifts. You are good with people. That is expensive work—in here," she tapped her chest, "and in here." She tapped her temple. "If somebody is calling you at hours that steal from this"—she gestured toward the hall, toward the residents, toward everything they protected—"you need to look them in the eye, even if it's through a phone, and tell them you do not pay with the part of you that keeps other people upright. That's non-negotiable."

Iya said nothing for a moment. The machine hummed. The air vent breathed. She could feel the sentence inside her, settling. Not a sermon. A boundary she could borrow until hers felt solid again.

"Okay," she said.

Lorna nodded once, satisfied. The weight lifted; she let the smile back in.

"Good. Now eat that spring roll before it files a complaint with HR for neglect."

Iya laughed, the sound looser than it had been all morning. She took a bite. Crispy, savory, a little greasy—exactly the kind of comfort that reminded her she was still human.

The pager on the wall beeped. Break over. They dumped cups, stood, rolled shoulders in a shared, unspoken stretch.

Back in the corridor, the day resumed its rhythm. A nurse asked for a second set of hands; a daughter needed a moment in the hall to cry about something that wasn't the sweater. They gave what they could, held what they couldn't fix, kept moving.

At as Iya leaned to fix a blanket corner under Mrs. Santos's ankle, her phone buzzed—one short pulse in her scrub pocket. Work messages. She didn't check. Another buzz, a longer one. She glanced, reflex only.

Unknown Number: *Apologies for the hour last night. I'll book properly this afternoon.*

A second later, the contact label updated as if the phone wanted to make it worse. Leah.

Iya locked the screen without opening the thread. She tucked the blanket, smoothed the sheet, adjusted the pillow. Mrs. Santos sighed, the contented kind that says somebody did their job right.

Lorna appeared at the doorway, reading the room the way she read everything. She didn't ask. She didn't need to. She just tipped her chin once, a small, precise question: You good?

Iya returned the same chin tip, same precision: I'm here.

Lorna's mouth curved. "Lunch in fifteen," she said. "Try something with vitamins? Your face is out here doing public service announcements."

"About what?"

"About taking a nap," Lorna said. "You are a billboard for pillows."

She left. The air in the room felt normal again—blankets,

light, a television trying to sell a product no one here needed. Iya checked the clock. She calculated what she could finish before meal trays landed: two vitals, one quick transfer, a chart note. Lists were mercy.

She stepped into the hall, the sound of her sneakers steady on the floor. Outside the window at the end of the corridor, a gust lifted a row of small maples planted in a neat line. The leaves shook, then settled, as if the wind had only wanted to remind them who was boss.

Iya tightened the tie at the end of her braid. She had work. The tether from last night tugged once, faint and insistent, then faded under the weight of the day.

She moved. The building moved with her.

Lunch Break, Uninvited Thoughts

By middaythe facility had found its rhythm. Lunch trays clattered back into the kitchen, televisions gossiped from every corner, and the shuffle of wheelchairs filled the halls like a slow parade. The energy of the place always dipped just before lunch, a strange hush before the second half of the day stretched out.

In the staff lunchroom, the smell of reheated leftovers mixed with burnt coffee. The table wobbled despite the layers of napkins wedged under one leg, and someone from the night shift had abandoned a half-empty box of mini donuts. Only the plain ones were left; the chocolate had been stolen first, as always.

Iya set down a foil container, still warm. When she peeled back the lid, the sweet, garlicky scent of tocino drifted into the room, sticky and rich. The fried eggs and garlic rice nestled beside it glistened like a quiet promise.

One of the younger nurses dropped her sandwich instantly. "What is that?"

"Tocilog" Iya said. "Tocino, fried eggs and rice. I marinated the pork on my day off, cooked it this morning. My grandmother always said food tastes better if it's shared."

"Sharing is caring!" the nurse sing-songed.

"Yes," Iya said, a sly smile tugging at her lips. "I'm sharing the belly consequences with you guys."

The table cracked up.

Lorna was already leaning forward with her fork like a weapon. "Baby, please. I'll take all the belly consequences. Y'all can fight over what's left."

The laughter grew louder. Someone grabbed a plate; another pulled napkins. Even the shy CNA reached for a spoonful.

The lunchroom, which usually felt tired and gray, filled with chatter that smelled like garlic and sweetness.

"Girl, this is brunch," one nurse said. "Who cooks like this before a shift?"

"She does," Lorna announced, pointing her fork at Iya.

"My grandmother always made too much. I guess I inherited that part. You actually remind me of her sometimes," Iya said.

"Hold on—did you just call me your grandmother?!", Lorna said, feigning offence.

"I did not! I said you remind me of her," Iya laughed, hands up in defense.

"Mhm," Lorna sighed dramatically, eyes narrowing in mock suspicion. "Nope. Too late. You aged me twenty years in front of witnesses." She stabbed another piece of tocino. "Fairy godmother. That's my title. Sequins, magic wand, good lighting. You can keep your grandmother talk."

"Fairy godmother," Iya repeated, chuckling. "Fine."

"Better," Lorna said, chewing happily. "At least fairy godmothers get sparkle."

The laughter rolled again, filling the room with an easy warmth. For a moment, it was just coworkers being coworkers—banter, food, teasing that kept the day from feeling too heavy.

"Okay," Lorna said, licking her fork clean. "Tell me something. What do you young people even do for fun these days? Don't say TikTok, or I'm retiring on the spot."

"Bars," one nurse said.

"Concerts," another chimed in.

"Netflix," the shy CNA offered.

"Lord have mercy," Lorna said, groaning. "So... basically, you drink, you shout, and then you stare at screens? Y'all are boring."

"And what did you do for fun?" Iya asked, eyebrow raised.

Lorna smirked. "Honey, in my day, fun cost two dollars and came with ketchup. That's all I'm gonna say."

The table roared again.

Iya laughed with them, really laughed, her shoulders loosening in a way they hadn't since last night. Food, teasing, coworkers who didn't pry too hard—it was the closest thing to ordinary she had.

Then her phone buzzed once in her pocket.

She ignored it, spooning garlic rice onto her plate.

Another buzz. This time she slipped the phone out under the table, glancing at the screen.

Leah: *I want to see you again. Official. No games this time.*

Her breath caught. Official meant safe, contained, professional. But nothing about Leah felt safe.

Her thumb hovered over the screen. One answer would secure the boundary. Another would invite the storm.

She locked the phone without replying, sliding it back into her pocket.

Lorna was still holding court, laughing about how "young folks" paid twelve dollars for avocado toast. The others teased back, calling her old-fashioned.

The laughter was contagious but Iya's smile faded as quickly as it came.

Even here, in the middle of laughter and rice and garlic, the tether pulled. Thin, invisible, but insistent.

Official. No games this time.

She stared at the half-empty container of tocilog. Food was supposed to be grounding. Sharing was supposed to make it lighter.

But no amount of sharing could untie the thread that Leah had already knotted around her.

The Thread That Does Not Break

By the time her shift ended, the world outside had shifted to gray. The sky hung low, heavy with the kind of clouds that threatened rain but didn't commit. Iya walked home in the muted chill, her bag slung over one shoulder, her braid damp against the collar of her scrubs.

The streets of the city hummed with their usual indifference —buses sighing at curbs, strangers speaking too quickly into phones, the clatter of lives that didn't know hers. It was a relief to be swallowed by anonymity.

At home, the apartment greeted her with its silence. Her housemate wasn't in yet. No television, no radio—just the soft thud of her shoes on the floor and the click of the lock behind her. She set her bag down, peeled off her jacket, and stood in the middle of the room as though deciding what version of herself to wear.

She moved through the motions: kettle on, hair tie loosened, blinds half-drawn. Each task was meant to anchor her in the present, to prove the day had ended. But even here, even in the quiet, the thread tugged.

Her phone lay face-down on the counter. She hadn't checked it since lunch. She didn't want to.

And yet.

She flipped it over. No new notifications. Just the last message, sitting there like an open door.

I want to see you again. Official. No games this time.

Iya's thumb hovered above the screen, then lowered. Not

to reply—just to hold the phone a second longer, as though touch alone could steady her.

She set it down again, face-down, like hiding it would make it less real.

She made tea. The water hissed against the bag, steam curling. She wrapped her hands around the cup, savoring the heat. She told herself she was drinking calm. Drinking distance.

But when she finally sat on the couch, the cup resting between her palms, her gaze slid to the counter again. To the phone lying silent, waiting.

She hated the way silence could feel like an invitation.

The tether didn't pull hard, not tonight. It didn't need to. It only had to exist.

CHAPTER 8:

IN OTHER HANDS

The Quiet That Means Something

Morning came in thin, uncommitted light. The blinds held it at the edges the way a hand holds water—enough to see by, not enough to drink.

Iya lay still and listened to the room breathe. The fridge hummed. A neighbor's door closed and reopened with the soft panic of someone who forgot their keys. Somewhere below, a bus rumbled and moved on. The city did not care that she hadn't slept. That, at least, was reliable.

Her phone was on the counter where she'd left it the night before, face down. She told herself she liked the sight of it like that: domesticated, harmless, just another rectangle in a room of rectangles. She told herself a lot of things in the morning.

She made tea. Steam rose quietly from the kettle. She did not reach for the phone until the mug had warmed both palms. Then, finally, she crossed the small space, flipped the device over, and looked—not because she expected anything, but because not looking was worse.

No new messages.

The last message in the thread stared up at her the way a photograph does when you've left it out on the table: unavoidable without actually moving. She didn't open it. She didn't need the exact words to remember the shape they made. She locked the screen and set the phone down again with the same care you use on a sleeping child—gently, as if any noise would spell trouble.

Silence was supposed to be neutral. Iya wasn't sure. It had a temperature. It had an angle. It slid under the door like cool air and waited.

She braided her hair at the sink, fingers moving out of habit, and caught herself glancing at the counter between loops. Nothing. Good. Or not good—just... useful. She dressed. She collected the day: badge, wallet, keys, the small tin of mints, because routine could be a religion if you repeated it with enough devotion.

On the street, the air smelled faintly of rain—a clean that hadn't happened yet. She walked instead of catching the bus. The longer route let her pass the old convenience store with the uneven awning and the bodega cat that refused to be hired. A man in a delivery van sang to the radio in a voice that had never asked for permission. A woman in a cobalt coat argued with a parking meter.

Iya liked mornings for this: the soft parade of strangers who expected nothing from her. You could belong to the world without the world belonging to you.

Her pocket buzzed. A phantom, she thought, before she checked. Nothing. Just her body offering a memory of what it thought should be there. She exhaled, half laugh, half surrender, and kept walking.

At the corner, she stopped for the light and allowed herself, for the space of one red-to-green, to wonder what Leah's silence was doing. Punishing? Composing? Waiting for a better entrance? The thought arrived already dressed in Leah's voice—low, velvet, certain—and Iya cut it off like a thread caught on a nail. Not today.

She typed a reply she did not send: *No bookings for a while. Please respect that.* She read it twice, then pressed and held until the letters trembled and disappeared. This was a relief and a regret at the same time.

At the next block she chose a different street than usual, not because she needed to but because choosing felt like owning something. A café leaked the small, mean smell of burnt espresso into the air. A teenager skateboarded past as a pigeon strutted like it had discovered the concept of sidewalks and intended to take credit.

Her phone stayed quiet. The quiet didn't.

She stepped into a pharmacy for lip balm and came out with

the wrong flavor because she hadn't actually looked at what her hand had picked up. The cashier had called her "hon." The receipt was long enough to use as a scarf. She smiled at herself and put it all in her pocket like evidence.

The facility's building climbed up ahead, all glass and insistence. She let herself stop half a block away, hand around the strap of her bag, and closed her eyes for three breaths. In for the list. Out for the noise. In for the work. Out for the rest. She opened her eyes on the third and felt assembled enough to move.

Inside, the lobby said good morning the way it always did: automatic doors sighing, a plant trying to look tropical under fluorescent lights, a poster reminding everyone to wash hands the way you remind children to use their inside voice. She nodded to the security guard. He nodded back with the exact amount of interest reserved for people who come every day.

Her phone was a small, polite weight in her pocket. She pretended not to notice it noticing her. At the elevator, she caught her reflection in the brushed metal—uniform neat, braid smooth, face giving nothing away she didn't sign for. It would do.

The elevator opened on the smell of oatmeal and bleach. Routine rose to meet her like a familiar tide, and she let it take her ankles, her knees, her waist. She checked the board. She washed her hands. She took gloves. She made herself a patient chart with one small, private instruction at the bottom: Do not touch the thread today.

Her finger hovered over her pocket anyway.

She took it away.

The morning unfolded on schedule—this was its talent. A resident wanted orange juice with exactly two ice cubes. Another needed the blue sweater because blue was strong for photographs. A daughter cried in the hallway about a thing that wasn't really the sweater, and Iya stood with her long enough for the tremor to turn into a story and the story to turn into a breath.

In each room, the same quiet skill: make the space feel like it can hold the person who's in it. She could do that. She could be that.

Between rooms, the silence followed, light on its feet. Leah had always known what to do with space: fill it, starve it, make it sing. This was a different trick. This was restraint performed like a ribbon—looped, placed, waiting for someone else to pull.

Midmorning, she put her phone on do not disturb and turned the screen brightness down until it looked like a tired moon. She placed it face down on the counter in the staff room while she refilled a pitcher. The itch in her palm quieted. She poured water, listened to it hit plastic, and thought about nothing except not spilling.

When she picked the phone up again, there was still nothing to see. The absence had learned to smile.

She almost preferred the pressing—Leah's voice shaped into sentences that wanted things. At least that was a storm you could put a window between. This was weatherless. This was a room you couldn't prove you were in until you tried to leave it.

On her way back to the hall, she tucked the phone deep into her pocket and imagined it was just a wallet. Just a key. Just a thing. The thought felt like a lie that was trying to be kind. She let it.

Work would do the rest, she told herself—the lists, the steps, the small victories that stack up into a day. The tether was slack. She could walk without tripping on it. She could. She would.

Her hand closed over the door handle to the unit.

Outside, somewhere beyond the walls, the city shifted gears. Inside, a call bell chimed. The world was asking for what it always asked for.

Iya answered the right thing first. The other would have to wait.

The Package at Work

The lobby smelled faintly of rain when Iya came back from rounds. A courier stood at the desk, slim parcel in one hand, clipboard in the other. The elegant package was small enough to look harmless. Dark ribbon, no return address.

"Delivery for... Iya Maldiano?" he asked, squinting at the label.

Her chest tightened. She signed before her face could betray her.

The box was light, almost nothing inside, but it sat in her palm like a stone.

"Somebody's got admirers," the receptionist teased.

Iya smiled in the way you smile at strangers you'll never see again—polite, disposable. She slid the package into her bag with the same efficiency she used to tuck a blanket corner. Out of sight, but not out of mind.

When she turned, Lorna was leaning on the nurses' station, one eyebrow raised.

"Mhm," Lorna said, voice smooth as the maroon scarf tied

around her head. "Whatever's in that box got you standing like it's made of bricks. You good?"

"Just something I ordered," Iya said quickly.

"Alright," Lorna replied, shrugging. "Long as it doesn't explode in my med cart." She went back to her chart, humming low under her breath.

Protective, not prying.

Iya exhaled, grateful and unsettled at the same time.

She carried the parcel down the hall like contraband. Each step felt watched, though no one was looking. At her locker she shoved it under her folded sweater, shut the door, and twisted the lock until it clicked sharp.

Out of sight. Out of reach.

Except it wasn't. Not really.

By lunch, the breakroom was alive with chatter—plastic containers clicking open, microwaves humming, the smell of reheated noodles competing with hand sanitizer.

One of the younger CNAs leaned across with a grin. "So,

who's spoiling you? Saw the courier this morning. That box looked fancy."

The others laughed and chimed in, the kind of teasing that makes workdays feel like family dinners with too many cousins.

Iya stabbed some leftover rice with her fork, expression steady. "I'm only generous with regrets I don't want to keep."

"Rule of life, darling: chew carefully. Some things taste sweet but choke you later," Lorna said, pointing her fork.

She gave the line a dramatic pause, then shoveled some more noodles. "And don't look at me like that—I'm talking about food. But if it also applies to people, well…" She shrugged, lips twitching. "That's just bonus wisdom."

The table cracked up, loud and easy, but Iya's smile was slower. Because for her, it wasn't just food. The words sat heavier, almost too on target, like Lorna had slipped truth into the laughter the way you hide medicine in jam.

Sunday

Room 214 smelled faintly of yesterday's tea, and lavender lotion that had soaked too long into the sheets. Mrs. Harding sat on the edge of her bed, cardigan buttoned wrong, hair in stubborn wisps that refused a comb.

"She's been refusing everything," Lorna murmured at the door, her voice steady but frayed at the edges. "Shower, change, even just brushing her hair."

Mrs. Harding looked up, chin lifting. "I don't need any fussing. Harold likes me just the way I am."

The words landed sharp. Harold had been gone nearly ten years. Iya didn't glance at the calendar on the wall that read Wednesday. She stepped into the room as though the answer had just arrived to her.

"You're right," she said warmly. "He does. But isn't it Sunday today?"

Mrs. Harding blinked. "Sunday?"

"Yes," Iya said, tone playful, coaxing. "Sunday morning. And when Harold comes home from church, won't he want to see you looking your loveliest?"

A flicker lit Mrs. Harding's eyes. Not recognition, not facts— just the feeling of being in the right place in the right time. Sometimes that was enough.

She let Iya guide her to the bathroom. Warm water loosened her hair, soap softened the day's edges. They talked about hymns she might hear, about Harold stopping to chat with the pastor before walking home.

By the time they returned to the bedroom, Mrs. Harding was humming softly. A blue blouse slid over her shoulders without protest. Iya smoothed her hair, corrected the buttons, dabbed a little powder on her cheeks.

"There now," Iya said. "Harold won't know what hit him."

Mrs. Harding smiled at her reflection for the first time that day.

In the hall, Lorna leaned against the doorframe, arms folded. She tilted her head, watching Iya close the drawer. "See? That wasn't so bad."

"No miracle," Iya murmured. "Just Sunday."

But the words lingered longer than they should have. Sometimes truth was too heavy for certain hands to hold. Sometimes the kindest thing wasn't Wednesday,

The Booking

After the rain, the city gleamed like glass—streets darkened to ink, lights stretched across puddles in fractured reflections. Iya took the quieter side of the block, the one with the deep awnings and the bakery that turned off its sign and left the ovens to cool like sleeping animals. Her bag rode light against her hip. Tomorrow was her day off. Tonight, she had chosen this.

The building didn't boast. It didn't have to. Stone and glass met with the kind of precision you get when architects are allowed to be fussy in peace. The lobby was designed to be forgettable: neutral art, furniture that discouraged lingering, scent faint and citrus-clean. The concierge looked up, gave a nod of acknowledgment and returned to a screen full of nothing. That was the comfort here: you entered, you disappeared.

The elevator slid upward without complaint. In the brushed steel, Iya's reflection answered her back—plain scrub jacket traded for a simple black blouse, braid tied low, face composed into the unobtrusive calm she wore when rooms expected things. The part of her that was good at stillness showed up first. The rest followed.

The hallway carpeted silence. At the right door, she knocked twice—measured, soft—and the latch clicked almost immediately.

The woman stood there like a press photo. The blouse was sharp; the sleeves were rolled with precision; her hair obeyed the comb without question. The look said control without effort. Only her shoulders gave her away: a little too square, as if they'd been holding themselves on purpose for hours. Only her eyes told the truth: tired and unwilling to admit it.

"Please don't ask me about my day," she said. Not brusque. Just finished with words that made statements. Her voice carried the low certainty of someone who signs other people's paychecks. "I just want to be someone's person tonight. Not their boss."

"I won't ask," Iya said. "I'll just be here."

Inside was curated restraint. Pale wood floors and furniture with angles that claimed seriousness. A rug attempted warmth and achieved money. On the marble island, three lilies lifted at precise, staggered heights, perfection pretending to be casual. Beyond the tall glass, the city glittered like it had never met fatigue.

Iya did what she always did with new rooms. She moved the lampshade a fraction to soften the light. She drew the curtain just enough so the window stopped acting like a stage and became a view. She took in the line of the couch, the distance to the table, the way the air carried the faintest trace of lemon from the counters. She didn't put on music, preferring the silence.

She gestured toward the couch. "Sit. Nothing to perform here."

The woman produced a tiny, surprised laugh and sat—heels aligned under the table with an unconscious precision that would have frightened dust. Her spine was long, a line disciplined into existence. Hands tented lightly in her lap, fingertips meeting like the roof of a small cathedral.

Iya chose the cushion near the armrest. Close, but not crowding. She warmed a trace of oil between her palms until her hands carried heat and nothing else. "Your hands first," she said. "They've been working overtime."

The woman hesitated. It was the hesitation of someone who didn't give things up lightly—information, hours, control. Then she offered her right hand as though submitting evidence. Iya received it with both of hers, not seizing, not testing. Holding. Her thumbs found the center of the palm and pressed slowly, evenly, a breath longer than would have been polite if this were anything else.

The woman inhaled too fast, surprised at herself, then let it out slower, like memory returning to a muscle. "I'd forgotten this," she murmured. "How much a hand can tell on its own."

"You don't have to explain," Iya said. "Your body already knows."

She traced the tendons under the thumb, read the small signatures that stress leaves behind. Tightness at the web between index and thumb—phones and pens. Tenderness along the outer edge—keyboard. She smoothed those spots with patience, taught them how to release without making a speech about it.

When she let go, the woman's fingers didn't retreat into fists;

they settled open, undecided, unarmed.

The left hand was the same map in a different weather system. Iya learned it quickly—callus softened under expensive lotion, a whisper of ache along the wrist where bracelets had been removed and weight had been measured all day. She worked the base of the palm in small circles that meant I see where you hold yourself.

"What do you need tonight?" Iya asked after the rhythm had steadied. "Not your schedule. You."

The woman's eyes closed. The answer slid out like a confession that had been waiting in the hallway. "Permission. To not lead. To not decide. To stop."

"Then stop," Iya said. "I'll do the rest."

That landed. It hit somewhere behind the eyes, a place posture can't fix. The woman tipped her head back against the sofa and exhaled—a sound that seemed to surprise her with its own weight. The long muscles along her neck let go by a degree. The kind of degree that changes weather.

Iya didn't fill the space. She let the room do some work.

The woman's knees drew in slightly, an unthinking curl, the way a body admits it would rather be small. She didn't speak. She didn't need to. Bodies ask long before mouths do.

Without announcing, Iya shifted a few inches closer, shoulder brushing shoulder, then set her arm along the back of the sofa. Not claiming. Present.

Habit is a loyal guard. The body held for a heartbeat as if waiting for the other shoe to drop, and when it didn't, gravity made its case. The woman leaned—first an accident, then on purpose—until her temple found Iya's collarbone and stayed. Her hair grazed fabric. A breath shivered out of her, then returned softer.

Iya matched her exhale, not theatrical, simply available. Minutes stretched. Silence grew thicker, but not empty—shaped, held. The room warmed by a degree. The woman's shoulders forgot to audition, descending one notch at a time. The little muscle at the angle of her jaw let go.

"Those shoulders," Iya murmured eventually, dry and kind. "They've been clocking overtime."

A short laugh answered—half protest, half gratitude. "They don't know how to stop."

"They're allowed," Iya said. "You're not on duty here."

The laugh dissolved into quiet. The woman's hands, which had been posed—useful, competent—became simply hands. Fingers lengthened on the cushion, palms down, unoccupied. She breathed. Iya let her.

The climb is always made of quiet inches. One more inch: the woman shifted nearer, almost imperceptible. Another inch: her knees tucked a little, as though her body had remembered for itself that curling is not the same as failing. Iya answered inch for inch. She adjusted until angles made sense. No choreography, only geometry.

She eased her down the couch, a slow fold. The woman curled on her side; Iya behind her, an arm a light arc across the waist. Not heavy. Not pinning. A weight that said nothing except you're allowed.

The change was immediate, like a room that had been waiting to exhale. The woman's back softened to meet Iya's front. Her breath found a different clock. Her hands, the ones that operated phones and pens and the levers of other people's days, lay open and empty on the cushion, relieved of purpose.

Iya didn't fill the quiet. She attended to it. She let her palm rest against the woman's ribs, not counting, but modeling a slower answer if the body wanted it. In: a tide. Out: a departure that didn't require apology. In. Out. Something old and animal claimed its space.

After a while the tiniest tremor moved under Iya's hand— a stutter before the exhale, the almost-sob of a person who doesn't do that. It passed. Two tears warmed the pillow and vanished. No one wrote them down.

Minutes formed a shape. The city outside blinked and rearranged itself. The room hummed lightly in the way electricity hums when it has not been asked to perform miracles. Here, there were only lungs remembering their original job. It felt indecent, how much that could change in a body used to being useful.

The woman's mouth softened; her brow forgot it had a task. The line of her spine let something go that posture had been handling like a contract. Her body asked a question without words. Iya answered by not moving.

And then, in the half-light of almost sleep, the whisper came —the truest things always do when there's no audience left to impress.

"This is better than sex."

Not a performance. Not a provocation. A field report from the place beyond roles.

Iya didn't reply. She wasn't the echo. Her palm rose and fell with the woman's breathing and said the only thing that mattered: I'm still here.

Sleep took the woman with a gentleness that felt like permission. It arrived not as a victory but as a return. Her body settled the way bodies do when no one is measuring them. In this room, she looked ordinary. Human. That was the gift—once the role slid off, there was someone beneath it. It should not have felt miraculous. It did.

Stillness is an act if you do it right. Iya stayed. She matched the weight of her arm to the pace of the other woman's breath. She waited long enough for the depth of sleep to prove itself—three long inhales that didn't ask for company, three more that rode out steady—before she eased away. She drew a throw from the back of the couch and laid it lightly over shoulder and hip. Not fussing. Respect.

The apartment had reset to a softer version of itself. The lilies were still too perfect. The city still glittered in the slice of glass left open between curtain and frame. The clock on the oven glowed a number with no urgency.

Shoes in hand, bag on shoulder, Iya moved to the door. Her fingers brushed something that didn't belong to the threshold—the weight of it announced itself even before the texture did. A black envelope lay flush to the floor, matte and dense, edges crisp as if they had opinions. Letters sank into the surface in gold, not flashy, commanding by quiet: The Care.

Already waiting. Already prepared. Someone had known this ending would arrive and left the proof for it. It was not a surprise. It still landed like a verdict.

She didn't open it. She slipped it into her bag and turned the handle carefully so the latch would not declare her departure to a sleeping room. The hallway held its hush. The elevator arrived when it was ready. She liked it better for taking its time.

Outside, the rain had turned to a memory. The street smelled faintly of metal and something sweet left over from a café that had locked its door an hour ago. She walked the lit side because nights are to be met face-first. A bus hissed at a corner and resumed its route. Somewhere, a laugh lifted that did not belong to anyone in particular.

She didn't check her phone. That belonged to a different room. She let the quiet from this one ride home with her instead, tucked into the space above her sternum where good silences settle.

The stairwell in her building had that familiar cleaner smell that loses its conviction after eleven. The apartment received her with the uncomplicated mercy of objects that expect nothing. Bag on the counter. Lights to low. Water in a glass. Breath that returned to the speed of a place that knows your name.

She set the black envelope down and didn't reach for it. Gold letters held their small glow like a secret. No lilies, much smaller windows. The quiet was hers alone.

She washed her hands longer than necessary—not in the way of someone scrubbing off a job, but like a person telling her skin it had finished its shift. The water ran. Stopped. The room reasserted its ordinary.

No aftermath here. Not tonight. The next page could do that work. Tonight's work had been done: a slow climb, a surrender, a body given the rare permission to be small and safe and unremarkable.

Iya turned off the kitchen light and let the apartment fold itself around her. Outside, the city kept its counsel. Inside, air moved in and out without report. The rest could wait.

Ms. M

Iya set her bag down on the counter. The black envelope lay exactly where she'd left it, matte against the laminate, gold lettering catching the light. She didn't open it. Gratitude wrapped in ceremony didn't need to be read. She already knew what it said: Thank you for holding me when I couldn't hold myself.

She poured water, drank slowly, set the glass down with quiet precision. Small anchors. A way to make the silence behave.

Her phone lit on the counter.

Leah: *You're learning I don't like silence.*

A second message followed before she could even think.

Leah: *The scarf doesn't smell like you anymore. I might need a new one.*

Iya closed the screen and left it face down. She would not hand Leah the satisfaction of an immediate reply.

Instead, she pulled her notebook from the drawer and flipped to a clean page. Her pen hovered, then moved:

Some truths belong in one room only.

Some need disguises before they're allowed out.

She closed the book, tucked it under a stack of receipts, and reached for her phone again. This time, the name was different.

Hannah.

The link. The conduit. The friend of a friend who understood discretion wasn't optional. Hannah didn't chatter, didn't pry —she opened doors and kept them shut to the wrong eyes.

Status? the message read. Short. Efficient. The kind of word that doubled as care.

Iya opened a draft, fingers moving quickly.

Hannah,

Moving forward, clients should use Ms. M. No exceptions.

She stared at the sentence, then added nothing else. No soft edges, no smile in the words. This wasn't about warmth. This was about a mask, one she needed now more than ever.

She signed it simply: —M.

The message sent, leaving a faint aftertaste of finality.

Ms. M. A door. A wall. A choice.

For a moment, she let herself believe it might be enough. That the new name would hold the line between who she was and what she did. That it could keep people like Leah in their place.

Her phone lit again.

Leah: *Funny how some women pay you to take their armor off...*
and some of us just want to keep you in ours. Guess which one I
am?

The words chilled her more than they should have. The
executive tonight had handed her weight over willingly, had
fallen asleep in her arms like surrender was a gift. Leah's
words carried the opposite: not surrender, but capture. Not
rest, but possession.

One client had trusted her enough to sleep. Another wanted
her awake, tethered, caught.

Iya set the phone down, face to the counter, but the words
clung louder than silence. The envelope glimmered in the
corner of her vision. Gratitude, prepared and polite.

The phone buzzed again. Obsession, raw and uninvited.

She tied her braid tighter before bed. Some knots had to hold.

Leah

Iya doesn't know what she does to people.

She moves through a room the way sunlight does—soft,
steady, not asking permission. She thinks she's ordinary. She

thinks she's careful. She doesn't see the way the air changes when she's near.

I do. I always do.

The first time her hand brushed mine, it wasn't anything. A steadying touch, a half-second. She'd never remember it. But I remember. My whole skin remembers. That moment has lived in me longer than most relationships I've had.

She offers things in teaspoons—one glance, one word, one act of kindness measured so exactly you almost think it was accidental. But it's not. She chooses where she pours herself. She chose me once.

Other women rent her. I've heard the whispers. They pay for hours. I got seconds. And yet my seconds feel purer than their hours. They don't know her the way I do. They want to own her. I only want her to see me. To really see me.

Sometimes, when she speaks, it sounds like she's talking to the room. But I know it's meant for me. A warning, a test, an invitation—doesn't matter. I hear her. I hear what she won't say.

I tell myself I'm patient. That she's just cautious, that she needs time. That she doesn't trust easily. Fine. I can wait. I've waited through worse. I've lived through empty years where no one even remembered I existed. Waiting for her isn't hard. It's the opposite—it's my purpose.

Nights are the worst. That's when her voice returns. Not in dreams—dreams are sloppy, inconsistent. I hear her in the real silence, in the hum of the fridge, in the tick of the wall clock. I remember her exact tone, the way she clipped a word or softened a sentence. I replay it until the memory feels fresher than the day itself.

People think obsession is loud. Screaming, breaking things, losing control. They're wrong. Real obsession is quiet. It's folding the same thought so many times it becomes a blade. It's cleaning your apartment at 2 a.m. because you need the space ready if she ever decides to walk through the door. It's buying a bottle of her favorite soda even though she may never drink it, just so it waits in the fridge like a promise.

They'd call me crazy if I said it out loud. They don't understand how care works. She cares differently. I've seen it. She pretends it's business, but she gives more than business. She can't help it. That's why people cling. That's why I cling.

I told myself once, if she ever really looked at me—really looked—I'd never need another thing again. And sometimes she does. She doesn't notice it, but her gaze stops on me a second longer than it should. That's all the proof I need.

That's how I know she feels it too.

Everyone else wants love. That word is cheap, overused. What I want is rarer: recognition. I want her to know she can't hide from me, because I see her already. I see the doors she keeps locked. I know what's behind them must be beautiful, dangerous, worth protecting. And someday, she'll open one. For me.

Until then, I wait. I watch. I collect the seconds she drops, and I turn them into whole seasons.

One day she'll understand.

And when she does, she'll realize it was always supposed to be me.

CHAPTER 9:

SMOKE SIGNALS

The Message

The phone buzzed against the nightstand at 5:17 a.m.

Not a loud sound, not even intrusive—just the soft, steady vibration of glass against wood. But in the stillness of the room, it might as well have been a siren.

Iya's eyes cracked open. The air was dark, the ceiling only a suggestion above her. Fifteen minutes until her alarm. Fifteen minutes that were supposed to belong to her. The last stretch of silence before the world asked her to pour herself out again.

She could've ignored it. Should've. But the way the light spread across the wall pulled her in. She reached, almost without thinking, and tilted the phone toward her.

One preview. One line.

Leah: *I didn't sleep again. Thought about you. Sorry. Hope that's not weird.*

Iya's stomach folded inward. She hadn't even fully woken up and already her body was bracing itself.

Not the first message. Not the first odd hour. Leah had a way of finding the cracks between days—sending little fragments of herself at times when no one should be awake enough to respond. Midnight. Two a.m. Now, 5:17. That fragile space between the end of night and the beginning of duty.

The words stared back at her. Too soft to dismiss. Too sharp to hold.

I didn't sleep again.

Not information. Not confession. A quiet indictment: you weren't here, so I couldn't rest.

Thought about you.

Sweet, tender, dangerous. It should have felt flattering. Instead, it curled around her like a ribbon tied too tight. A line that made her feel less chosen than claimed.

Sorry. Hope that is not weird.

The bow tied neatly around the package of obsession. Polite enough to seem harmless. Clever enough to trap her if she stepped closer.

Iya let the phone hover in her hand. Thumb poised to unlock. She didn't.

Don't answer. Not this hour. Not this tone. Don't feed it.

Her chest rose and fell. She placed the phone face-down on the nightstand, as if weight alone could hold it there. It buzzed again. Twice more.

Each vibration was small, but it carried through her. Like a pulse she couldn't unhear. Like a presence in the room.

Iya rolled onto her side, away from the glow. The wall in front of her was bare, but the message had already burned itself into it, letters etched in fire.

She shut her eyes. Opened them again. Shut them once more. Nothing changed.

Not scared. Not yet.

But she could feel Leah close, as if the words had a body. As if the text had curled up on the pillow beside her and whispered straight into her ear.

I didn't sleep again. Thought about you.

Iya pressed her lips together. Silence. Always silence. That was her answer. That was the only power she had left to keep.

Her alarm went off at 5:30. A bright, ordinary sound that should have woken her. But by then she was already upright, blanket folded back with the precision of habit, shoulders squared against the day.

The phone lay untouched on the nightstand, its screen dark now. Waiting. Always waiting.

She didn't pick it up. Didn't need to. The words were already stitched into her skin, the way smoke clings to fabric—subtle, persistent, impossible to wash out quickly.

The message would wait.

It always did.

Hairline Cracks at Work

By seven, the unit had found its morning voice—fluorescents humming, carts whispering over tile, doors sighing open and shut. On most days, Iya slipped into that rhythm without thinking. Today, it felt a half-step too fast, as if the hallway were moving and she was standing still inside it.

Her first slip arrived with the laundry.

A small stack of freshly folded clothes waited on the counter; she balanced Mrs. Alvarez's things on her forearms, the fabric warm with the clean, faint smell of detergent and steam. In the room, she opened the top dresser drawer and slid in a soft green cardigan, smoothing the fold with her palm.

"That's not mine," Mrs. Alvarez said from her chair—mild, not scolding. "Mine's the blue one. Buttons down the front."

Iya checked the collar. The laundry tag read A.L.—Alvarez and Lee, too similar when your head was half a beat behind your hands.

"You're right," she said quickly, drawing it back out. "Wrong room. I'll fix it."

Harmless. Easy to correct. Still, her pulse tapped once against her throat as she stepped into the hall. Small cracks weaken walls.

A call light blinked near the end of the corridor. She angled her cart toward it; three steps in, a coworker lifted a palm from another doorway—two-person turn. She pivoted without thinking, counted with him, adjusted, checked for skin pulls, thanked him. When she finally reached the blinking room, the light had gone steady.

Mr. Ng looked at her with the kind of tiredness that pretends to be anger. "I've been pressing forever."

"I'm sorry for the wait," she said, placing a cup of water where his hand could find it. "I was helping next door."

He took a sip and said nothing. She took the silence as a complaint. She left the room with the apology clinging to her like static.

Back at the cart, she opened a chart too fast. Names blurred —two Al— entries stacked on the same page. Her pen hovered over the wrong line before she caught herself and nudged the note to the correct file. The correction was a victory but still felt like tripping over nothing in front of people you knew.

Focus.

The hallway smelled like lemon cleaner giving way to breakfast toast from the kitchen. Toast always found the corridors, the warmth creeping into sterile air. On most days she liked it, but today it only reminded her she hadn't eaten.

Her pocket buzzed.

She didn't need to look. She did anyway.

Leah: *You seemed far away yesterday. I don't like it when you disappear.*

Her throat tightened. She shoved the phone back fast, but the words had already sunk their claws in. Far away. Disappear. As if Leah owned her personal space. As if silence itself were a betrayal.

A bed alarm chirped in Room 9. She was already moving.

"Hang on, I've got you," she said as she reached the rail, voice steady by design. Mrs. Kline was pushing herself upright, slippers untied.

"Church," Mrs. Kline said. "I'm late—my mother—"

"Later," Iya answered softly, setting the slippers where a foot could find them. "You're early. Early is devotion."

Mrs. Kline paused, the fog in her eyes thinning a degree. They sat for a beat. The alarm went quiet under Iya's hand.

Back in the hall, a towel slid off the side of her cart and kissed the floor. She stooped, retrieved, replaced it on the bottom shelf where floor things go and clean things survive. A glove snapped when she tugged it—thin latex ribbon. She found another. The mask strap tickled her cheek where the elastic had started to fray. None of it mattered alone. Together, the morning felt like it had teeth.

Lorna came down the corridor with a clipboard tucked to her chest, her steps the exact speed that kept others from speeding up. She didn't ask questions. She tilted her chin: I see you.

"Stay by the windows for a while," Lorna said in passing. "Feels better there."

"I was thinking the same," Iya said, meaning thank you and I'm trying in one line.

She took the long loop past the courtyard window. The light there was honest. She stood in it for one breath and watched leaves not care what time it was.

The phone buzzed again. One line on the lock screen before it slipped to dark:

Leah: *I could come by. Two minutes. Just to see you.*

Her thumb hovered. The idea of Leah in this air, in this hallway, near these people—no. The word formed cleanly in her chest even if it never reached her fingers. No.

She slid the phone deeper into her scrub pocket until its weight settled against her hip and stopped trying to float.

A call light blinked. She moved too quickly this time; the cart's front wheel clipped the doorframe and jolted. "Everything okay?" a resident asked gently from a chair just inside.

"Yes," Iya said, too fast, a thin edge on the word she didn't mean to leave there. The resident blinked, startled, and looked down at her hands. Guilt punched once, clean and center. She pushed the cart forward, jaw tight.

A wheelchair footrest resisted its hinge, sticking on nothing. She pressed, it released with a loud click that sounded like it had a temper. The hallway TV coughed out a commercial jingle three notches too loud; Lorna drifted into the common room and turned it down without ceremony, like smoothing a wrinkle with her palm.

Iya reached Mr. Ng again with a fresh straw she didn't strictly need to bring. "Here," she said softly, placing it on the tray. He nodded once, not unkind.

Her pocket felt heavier. The words from earlier layered over each other like film negatives. Far away. Disappear. *I could come by.* The shape of them pressed against her ribs as if language could bruise.

In the next doorway, a resident leaned forward. "Could you —" she began.

"In a minute," Iya answered. The words snapped before she could sand them smooth.

The resident recoiled a fraction; the kind of flinch people pretend they didn't do. Iya felt the heat rise up her neck. That's not who you are, she thought.

From the corner of her eye, she caught Lorna returning to the hall. Not rushing—never rushing. Just arriving at exactly the pace that didn't make a scene.

Lorna stepped close enough that only Iya could hear. No lecture. No diagnosis. Just a lifeline.

"Girl... don't," she murmured, voice low and steady. "Exorcise. Supply closet. Two minutes."

Iya closed her eyes and let out a breath that wasn't relief so much as surrender. "Two minutes," she said, already turning.

Exorcise was what they called it—half joke, half survival trick. Not the gym kind. The demon kind. Two minutes in a closet to scream into your hands, shake it out, breathe, and come back human.

The supply closet held its small universe: lemon cleaner, metal shelves, labeled bins, a mop that always leaned as if listening. She shut the door, pressed both palms over her mouth, and let the sound out—a rough, breathless, not-quite-scream that stayed inside her hands. Two short jabs into the air, then a wide, ridiculous hook that made her half-smile at herself. Shoulders up. Shoulders down.

In. Two. Three. Four.

Hold. Two.

Out. Two. Three. Four.

Again.

Again.

She wasn't reset. Not really. But the coil unspooled a notch. Enough space opened in her chest for air to move without scraping. On the top shelf she kept a spare scrub top, folded tight—sunny yellow. She swapped it for the one clinging to her skin, rolled the used top into a neat bundle, and tucked it into a laundry bag. A small trick she'd learned with certain residents and, sometimes, with herself: a new color can be a new temperature in the room.

She checked her watch. One minute, fifty-three.

Back in the hall, the unit sounded exactly as it always did. Lorna emerged from the call-light room with an empty cup, glanced once at the yellow sleeve, and tipped her chin good; breath found.

Iya touched Lorna's shoulder in passing. A thank you without taking up more space than the day could spare.

She wasn't fine. The edge still lived under the skin. The words in her pocket still pressed their shapes against her. But the two minutes had carved a handhold into the morning. One breath steadier than the last. Enough to keep moving without splintering.

At the nurse's station, the printer spat another sheet in the same tired font. Down the hall, someone laughed at a joke the TV had already told twice. In her cart's top bin, the soft green cardigan waited to be walked to Mrs. Lee's dresser, tag facing up so it wouldn't go wandering again.

Nothing was fixed.

But for now—she could breathe.

The Glance

The yellow scrub top did its job: brighter, lighter, something new to carry on her skin. The coil in her chest had loosened but not disappeared. She knew it wouldn't.

The unit hummed with its usual patterns—wheels over tile, muted televisions, the occasional cough breaking through the hall. Routine should have steadied her. Instead, every sound seemed outlined in ink, too sharp against her ears.

At the nurse's station, a coworker glanced up as she passed. Just a glance, quick and neutral, but long enough to sting.

"You okay?" he asked, not unkind.

"Fine," Iya said, the answer immediate, too smooth. She tucked the green cardigan under her arm—Mrs. Lee's, finally going to the right dresser—and walked on before he could hold her with his eyes any longer.

Fine. Always fine.

She slipped into Mrs. Lee's room, placed the cardigan in the top drawer, and smoothed it flat. Mrs. Lee thanked her absently, already folding tissues into precise squares at her table. Iya envied the calm of the repetition.

In the hallway again, she felt it: another pair of eyes. Not accusing. Not even curious. Just watching. Lorna was at the far end, leaning against the counter, clipboard balanced on her hip.

Lorna didn't speak. She didn't have to. She gave a small tilt of her head, the kind that said, I see the storm, but I won't name it. Not unless you want me to.

The gesture cut deeper than any question could.

Iya forced her shoulders back, pushed her cart toward the common room.

She wasn't falling apart. She wouldn't let herself. The slips, the sharp edge of her voice earlier—those were cracks, not collapses. She could still hold.

But she felt it, the way smoke lingers after you've tried to clear a room. You can open every window, change every shirt, spray every scent—and still, the trace clings. People smell it even when you think you've scrubbed it away.

Leah at the Edges

By the time she sat down, the trays were cleared, the linens changed, and the clock leaned past two.

The staff lounge was barely more than a box. No windows. A fridge that hummed too loud. A microwave that smelled permanently of burnt popcorn. Two chairs, one always wobbly. Still, to anyone who worked the floor, it was a kind of sanctuary—four walls where no one called your name.

Iya lowered herself into the steadier chair. The cushion squeaked as if reminding her she hadn't sat in hours. Her whole body seemed to sink at once, not into comfort but a pause. She didn't realize how much she'd been holding until she stopped moving.

Her phone pressed heavy in her pocket. She took it out.

Three messages stacked neatly on the screen.

Leah: *Did I do something wrong?*

Leah: *I just want to know you're there.*

Leah: *You make me feel sane. Don't take that away.*

Iya stared. Her pulse didn't spike, not like it had in the morning. Instead it slowed, heavy as a stone sinking in water.

The phrasing was Leah's gift—soft on the surface, edged beneath. Polite enough to pass as vulnerable. Sharp enough to catch if you tried to hold it.

She set the phone down on the table, screen up this time, as if looking away might make it worse.

The silence didn't last long. The phone buzzed again.

Leah: *You don't know what it does to me when you vanish. I can't breathe right until you come back.*

The words curled into her like a claim, turning silence into suffocation, as if her presence alone controlled Leah's lungs.

She pressed her palms together, elbows on the table, eyes closed for a second. The lounge was quiet except for the fridge hum and the faint shuffle of footsteps outside. But inside her head, Leah's voice filled the room.

Did I do something wrong?

Soft, almost girlish. Innocent on the surface, but barbed.

I just want to know you're there.

Sweetened with need.

You make me feel sane. Don't take that away.

The kind of sentence that carried both praise and a threat: you hold my balance, so if I fall, it's on you.

Iya opened her eyes. The table in front of her looked suddenly foreign, too clean, too sharp around the edges. She pressed her thumb against the wood grain until the pressure steadied her.

The phone buzzed again.

Leah: *When you don't reply, I wonder if you're punishing me.*

That one cut deeper than the rest. Testing. The word hung heavy, dressed in a kind of intimacy that wasn't earned. It was psycho-sexy, the way Leah always seemed to write: soft, vulnerable, but with that undertow of control, like a voice curling around you until you couldn't tell if you were being seduced or trapped.

Iya sat back, spine pressing against the chair. The instinct to respond pulsed under her skin, a reflex born from caregiving itself: when someone cries out, you answer. When someone says they need you, you show up. It was in her bones to soothe.

But this wasn't care. It was something else. Something that blurred the line between need and possession.

Her thumb hovered over the screen. She could type a dozen things: I'm at work. Please stop. Later. Don't do this. Each possibility carried its own weight, its own consequence. None of them would be enough.

She locked the phone, shoved it into her pocket. Silence was her only reply.

But silence didn't feel neutral anymore. It felt like a choice she had to hold, like balancing glass in both hands. One slip and it would shatter, cutting her on the way down.

The clock above the microwave ticked toward 2:20. She had maybe three minutes left before she needed to be back in the hall. Her body wanted to stay in the chair until it molded to her. Her mind wanted to pace.

Instead she just sat, staring at the fridge, breathing evenly until the tightness in her throat loosened.

When she finally stood, her legs protested. The weight in her pocket followed.

Out in the hallway, the rhythm of the unit greeted her again: call lights, footsteps, voices pitched in the middle register of routine. Lorna passed her without stopping, clipboard in hand. She didn't speak, didn't ask. Just glanced once at Iya's face, then tipped her chin—the same small gesture as before: I see it. I won't name it. But I'm here.

Iya straightened her shoulders, pushing her cart back into motion. She wasn't undone. Not yet. But she could feel the smoke clinging, thin and stubborn. No matter how many doors she closed, it seeped under.

...Her pocket felt heavier. The words from 5:17 and 7:00 —whatever—layered over each other like film negatives. *Far away. Disappear. I could come by.* The shape of them pressed against her ribs as if language could bruise.

She wasn't undone. Not yet. But she could feel the smoke clinging, thin and stubborn. No matter how many doors she closed, it seeped under.

And then, unbidden, another voice rose—softer, steadier, just as unforgettable.

Johansson's hand had lingered at her cheek once, trembling. Her forehead rested against Iya's, her voice breaking into something raw.

"You give me peace in a way no one else ever has. But if I keep you, I take that peace from the people who still need me. Iya, you could be my world. But we can't keep us for ourselves. Not when I can help more. Not when you can care for more."

The memory cut off as suddenly as it had arrived, leaving her chest tight. Johansson had walked away because she loved in the widest sense—because care, to her, was too large to keep.

Leah clung because she couldn't see beyond her own need.

Both hurt. But one had been love made honest by sacrifice. The other was hunger sharpened into demand.

Iya drew a breath, steadying herself, and pushed her cart forward.

Fractures

The afternoon dragged like wet cloth. Not the rush of the morning, when everyone needed to be washed, dressed, fed. Not the soft winding down of evening. Just the long middle stretch, where the work never stopped but never had urgency either.

This was when the restlessness came.

Residents wandered, shuffling toward doorways that didn't lead home. Others called out, half in frustration, half in fear. A few just sat and waited, the silence around them demanding to be broken by anyone passing.

Patience was currency in these hours, and it was the one thing Iya felt short on.

"Miss? Miss!"

Room 11 again. Mrs. Carter was on the bed's edge, eyes sharp, fingers working at the blanket like it had wronged her.

"You forgot my medicine."

Iya stepped in quickly, hands gentle but voice even gentler. "The nurse will be here soon, Mrs. Carter. I'll check in with her."

"I don't want the nurse. I want you."

The words tightened something behind Iya's ribs. Not my role. Not my lane. But she smiled anyway, smoothing the blanket over Mrs. Carter's knees. "I hear you. I'll remind her again."

Mrs. Carter muttered, unconvinced, but let herself fall back against the pillow.

Out in the hall, Iya's pocket buzzed.

Leah: *You didn't answer. Did I scare you?*

Her thumb hovered. She didn't open it. She shoved the phone deeper into her scrub pocket until it pressed against her thigh like an unwanted hand.

Another call light blinked. Room 14.

Mr. Ng was half out of bed, only one slipper on.

"You'll fall," Iya said, steadier than she felt, guiding him back against the mattress.

"I rang ages ago," he muttered. "No one listens."

"I'm here now," she said. She crouched, found the slipper under the chair and slid it onto his foot. Blanket tucked. Alarm reset. Her hands moved with practiced calm. Her chest did not.

The television in the lounge erupted with a laugh track, too loud, the kind that drilled through walls. "Turn that racket off!" someone yelled. Another voice countered, "Leave it on!" The two complaints tangled in the air.

Her pocket buzzed again.

Leah: *I dreamed about you during my nap. Woke up smiling. Do you ever dream about me?*

Iya froze in the doorway, one hand pressed to the frame.

The words wrapped around her ribs, velvet over barbed wire. *Do you ever dream about me?* Written like seduction, pressed like demand.

She forced herself down the hall. Mr. Daniels sat in his wheelchair at the corner, arms crossed, scowling.

"You left me here. I've been waiting forever."

She took the handles and forced a calm voice. "Let's get you comfortable."

She wheeled him toward the lounge, adjusted the footrests, checked the brakes. Every movement precise, professional. Inside, her jaw was clenched so hard her teeth ached.

By the time she parked him by the window, her pocket buzzed again.

Leah: *Your silence feels louder than any words. It's like you want me to suffer with it.*

Her stomach dropped.

Suffer. The word burned. As if silence itself were cruelty. Almost tender on the surface, but with teeth underneath. Psycho-seductive. The kind of phrasing that blurred into obsession.

Her hand closed over the phone through the fabric, squeezing until the hard rectangle dug into her palm. She should've left it in her locker. She thought that every shift. But she never did.

Because what if it was her sister back home, needing her? What if it was a client, a woman who'd chosen her because no one else could meet that need? It wasn't about bills. She could pay those. It was about being the person who answered. Being the one who knew how to fill a silence.

Still, in this moment, the phone didn't feel like purpose. It felt like a trap, buzzing with demands she hadn't agreed to.

Her chest tightened, her breath shallow. For a moment it rose —the scream, raw and unshaped, pushing against her throat.

But it never came out.

It stayed locked inside her mouth, burning behind her teeth until her jaw ached with restraint.

She pressed her nails into her palm until crescents bloomed. Shoulders up. Shoulders down. A breath in, sharp. A breath out, longer.

From somewhere down the hall, Lorna's laughter carried. Not directed at her, not even close by. Just a story spun for a resident, light and easy. It cut through the air like fresh wind through smoke.

Iya leaned on the sound for half a second, just enough to remind herself the floor was still under her.

Then she straightened.

The hallway looked exactly the same—TVs humming, slippers scuffing, call lights blinking. Nothing had changed. Except the smoke in her lungs, thicker now, impossible to ignore.

She wasn't fine. She wasn't undone. She was both at once.

And anyone who looked close enough could smell it.

The Walk Home

Shift change always felt like a door closing behind her. Not a slam but the soft click of a latch, the kind that said enough for today. Iya peeled off her gloves, rubbed sanitizer into the lines of her hands until they squeaked, clipped her badge loose.

"Go home," Lorna said at the station without looking up. "Eat something. Leave the ghosts here."

"I'll try," Iya said.

Outside, the air was a different size. Cooler, wide. She left the building's hum behind her and the evening folded itself open —traffic breathing, a dog barking somewhere up the block, the thin metallic rattle of a cyclist's chain. She could have waited for the bus, but the stop was crowded, a little too much body heat. She walked.

It took a block for her shoulders to remember they were allowed to fall. Another block for her jaw to unclench. The day held on anyway, the way a scent clings even after you step out of the room that made it. She could still feel the weight of Mr. Ng's slipper in her hand. She could still hear Mrs. Carter's "I want you". She could still sense Leah's words where they'd pressed against her skin from inside her pocket.

Her phone sat heavy against her thigh. She slid it into her bag instead and tugged the zipper shut, the way you might treat a live wire.

Leave it. Just for the walk.

She tried to pay attention to the ordinary things. A kid dragging a branch along the fence, testing which bars sang. A woman on her stoop, clipping mint from a pot with kitchen scissors. The sky doing that late-hour trick where it can't decide whether to fade or deepen.

She took the long way, past the little bakery that had already closed but still smelled like sugar in the grout, past the laundromat windows where shirts turned in the drum like slow fish. She let the movement pull the day through her, sieve out the bigger pieces. She breathed in, out, counted to four, even though no one could see.

At the second light, she almost reached for the phone again. Not to answer—just to look. To make sure the world hadn't tilted in her pocket without her.

She didn't.

Hold the quiet. Hold it like glass.

Silence, she knew, was not nothing. It was a thing you carried. At work, silence could be comfort if you set it down softly. Sit beside someone, breathe with them, let the noise in their head thin itself out without forcing it. With Leah, silence was something else entirely. It was a boundary that got read as insult. A door she closed that Leah insisted was slammed shut.

Your silence feels louder than any words.

She heard the line again and kept walking. She thought about the residents who needed her because their bodies had forgotten how to do certain things, and the ones who needed her because their minds had let go of a few ropes. Need, she knew, wasn't always grasping. It could be simple. Honest. A hand opened out because the ground had shifted.

Leah's need was different. It came wrapped in velvet but was sharp underneath. It asked her to be oxygen and then accused her of theft when she took a breath for herself.

At the busier crosswalk, a little boy in a red jacket burst from his mother's grip and ran two steps toward the curb before she caught him by the hood. He laughed like falling wasn't real. The mother didn't laugh; she held him until he softened. Iya felt something in her chest answer that gesture. The clean, uncomplicated nature of it. The safety. The way hands could be a wall and a blanket at once.

She didn't have that kind of claim anywhere. She had an apartment, a job, and a second life that didn't live on paper. She had people who needed her in very different ways. None of it was hers in the way a mother could mean it. Maybe that was why Leah's words snagged where they did—because they hinted at a kind of belonging she didn't trust and might not even want.

Two more blocks and the day loosened another stitch. The sky finally committed to deeper. Streetlights blinked awake, one by one, as if deciding not to leave the evening unsupervised.

Her bag vibrated.

She stopped walking without meaning to. The sound wasn't loud. It didn't need to be. It existed in the same part of her that turned toward a name said softly from a bed.

She didn't take the phone out. Not yet. She put her palm over the place where it hummed and let it finish. When it stilled, she kept her hand there a second longer, as if the quiet could be pressed into the device like a stamp.

When she finally unzipped the bag, she didn't open the message. She just glanced at the preview.

Leah: *Tell me you miss me back.*

Five words. Not a question. An instruction.

She slipped the phone away again, slower this time. On the bench at the corner there was an old flyer half-torn from the wood—lost cat, tabby, answers to Ginger. Someone had written FOUND across it in thick marker. The letters were crooked. They looked like relief had made the hand shake.

Iya thought of writing FOUND across her own day. Not because anything miraculous had happened, but because she had not disappeared. Not into anger, not into apology, not into that place where answering felt like the only option. She had held the line. It was a thin line, but it was hers.

Her building came into view—four stories, brick scabbed with old paint, three steps up to the front door that always stuck in damp weather. She pushed her shoulder into it until it relented with a low groan.

Inside, the hallway smelled like someone else's dinner and the cleaning fluid they never diluted enough. The light over the mailboxes flickered. She climbed the stairs slow, hand sliding along the rail where the varnish had gone to satin from a thousand other palms.

At her door she paused again, listening for nothing in particular. Quiet wasn't empty; it had a shape. In her apartment it meant her breath and the tick of the kitchen clock. It meant no one else's need for a few hours.

She set her bag on the counter and left the phone inside it, zipper closed. She opened the window above the sink two inches and let the cooler air come in. The evening smelled faintly like rain that hadn't decided to fall yet.

She washed her hands a second time, long after the sanitizer had done its job, because water had a way of convincing the skin it was clean. While she dried them, the urge to check her phone rose again, then passed like a wave that chooses not to break.

She stood by the window and let the traffic's distant breath be the only sound.

She could answer later. Or not. Silence was not a punishment; it was a room she could sit in without explaining herself. If someone insisted on turning it into a weapon, that wasn't on her. She could hold that thought, even if it shook.

Across the street, apartment windows flicked on one by one —small squares of other lives making their own weather. Somewhere, someone laughed. Somewhere else, a kettle began to sing. She let the picture steady her.

Her phone vibrated once more in the bag. She didn't move. Not yet.

Two minutes, she thought. Not the closet kind. The home kind. Two minutes to breathe, no witness, no performance. Then she'd decide whether to open the door the message was knocking on.

She watched the sky slip from blue to almost-black and counted her breaths until they felt like hers again.

She gone the whole day without replying — a small, invisible victory that belonged only to her.

CHAPTER 10:

BETWEEN SHIFTS

Morning Reset

The kettle hissed softly before the sun came up, the sound filling the stillness of the apartment like a held breath. Iya switched it off before it could whistle, the faint click of the switch sounding far too loud in the early quiet. She glanced toward Maris' closed bedroom door—no movement, no light spilling from the crack beneath it.

The living room was caught in that half-light between night and morning, when shadows seemed softer and edges blurred. Outside, the city was just beginning to stir: a low, distant rumble of a car, the faint slap of wet tires on pavement, a dog barking twice before its owner's voice hushed it.

She scooped coffee grounds into the press, the smell already working its way into her bloodstream. Steam rose as she poured the water, curling in slow, lazy threads toward the ceiling. The ritual steadied her—the way it had for years—but today it felt heavier, as if her mind was already ahead of her, moving into places she didn't want to go yet.

Most people assumed she'd have moved into a bigger place by

now. She could afford it—a kitchen with more counter space, a view that wasn't just the building across the alley, maybe even a balcony for summer nights. But a solo apartment would be too exposed. Too easy for people to start asking questions.

With a roommate, she looked like anyone else balancing work and life—splitting rent, swapping laundry days, arguing over who left the dish towel damp. It was a camouflage that fit too well to give up. And if she was being honest, there was something about the presence of another person in the space—footsteps in the hallway, the low hum of a television from the next room—that kept the quiet from turning sharp.

Mug in hand, she walked to her bedroom and set it on the desk. The narrow bookshelf against the wall was crowded, spines worn from years of shifting and packing. She ran her fingertips along them until she reached the spot she always stopped: between a dog-eared copy of *The God of Small Things* and an old poetry collection whose pages had gone yellow at the edges.

The plain, faded-navy notebook slid out with a soft rasp. Its cover was unmarked; corners slightly bent from being pulled free again and again. She'd kept it hidden for years — close enough to reach for without thought, invisible to anyone not looking for it.

She sat on the edge of the bed and opened it to the last page, the paper faintly scented with ink and time. Without pausing, she began to write:

Light finds its way in, even through the smallest cracks. But sometimes you have to hold still long enough to notice it.

She read the line twice, the curve of her handwriting almost unfamiliar in the dim light. Her pen hovered above the paper for another sentence, but nothing came. She closed the notebook and slid it back between the books, nudging the spines until they aligned perfectly.

Her phone buzzed. Leah's name lit the screen. 6:02 AM.

Good morning. Hope I didn't wake you. The words were warm, almost friendly—the kind you might send to someone you were close to. Too close.

She turned the phone face-down on the desk, letting the silence swallow the vibration still humming in her palm.

Time to get ready for work.

Facility Shift

The automatic doors sighed open, letting out a wave of warm, processed air mixed with the usual faint scent of oatmeal, disinfectant, and something softer—a smell she'd long ago stopped trying to name. It was the scent of lives in progress, lives in waiting.

The morning hum of the care home was already in motion: a wheelchair rolling somewhere down the corridor, a soft voice coaxing someone to eat just a little more breakfast, the occasional trill of a call bell breaking the rhythm.

Iya's first stop was Mrs. Gillespie's room. The older woman sat on the edge of her bed, slippers dangling from her feet, her cardigan bunched around her shoulders as though she'd just decided she was cold. Her eyes were fixed on the wall—not vacant, but waiting, like someone expecting the curtain to rise.

"Morning," Iya said, her voice low, almost musical.

Mrs. Gillespie's head turned slowly, and then her face lit up. "Oh, you're here. Did you bring the lemon pie?"

It took Iya only a second to adjust. "Of course," she said, stepping closer, her tone dropping into a conspiratorial whisper. "It's in the kitchen. But you know the deal—breakfast first, or the pie might disappear."

A flicker of amusement passed over Mrs. Gillespie's features. "That would be a tragedy."

As Iya helped her into a fresh cardigan, their fingers brushed briefly. It was a fleeting touch, but it carried weight. Moments like this were small, almost invisible to anyone else—but they were the glue holding the day together.

Down the hall, the squeak of a laundry cart broke the stillness. Mr. Klein appeared around the corner, his slippers making a faint shuffling sound against the floor. He stopped when he saw her, eyes narrowing in that sharp, assessing way of his.

"You're careful," he said without preamble.

Iya paused, adjusting the cart in her hands. "Careful?"

"Not the clumsy kind," he said, leaning slightly on his walker. "The kind where you keep yourself hidden. People like you... you disappear before you're even gone."

She studied him for a moment, trying to decide whether it was a compliment, a warning, or simply one of his blunt observations. With Mr. Klein, it could be all three. Before she could answer, he resumed his slow, deliberate journey down the hall.

The break room was quiet when she stepped inside, except for the sound of the kettle working its way toward a boil. Lorna leaned against the counter, spoon in hand, waiting— the metal handle tapped softly against her mug in a steady rhythm.

"Girl, you've been quiet all morning," Lorna said without looking up. "Who's camping in your head rent-free?"

Iya shook her head, managing a small smile. "No one."

"Mhm." Lorna's gaze lifted, sharp with amusement. "Pick your battles. Some folks will pitch a tent in your head and stay there until you evict them."

The kettle clicked off, steam curling upward. Iya didn't answer. But she knew exactly whose tent was in her head, and she wasn't sure eviction was going to be simple.

The lounge emptied after the mid-morning break, leaving only the low hum of the vending machine and the faint scent of tea lingering in the air. Iya sank into one of the mismatched chairs, letting herself exhale in a way she couldn't on the ward floor.

Her phone buzzed on the table. She glanced down, expecting the worst: another message from Leah. Instead, the screen lit up with a familiar notification—the volleyball group chat.

Anyone in for tomorrow? Court is booked at 7. Need 2 more players.

Her thumb hovered above the screen. She hadn't played in weeks. The last time she'd gone, the game had been chaotic in the best way—mismatched teams, strangers becoming partners within minutes, the sound of sneakers squeaking against polished wood, and the hollow thud of the ball echoing off high walls.

She loved the rush of diving for a save, the sting of the floor on her forearms, and the way the group cheered like it was a championship point even though it was just another Thursday night. For two hours, she'd forgotten about schedules, client requests, and the careful compartmentalizing of her life. It was just her, a ball, a court, and the next point.

She typed: *Count me in.*

A flurry of thumbs-up emojis followed almost instantly, along with a joking reminder from one of the regulars: *No mercy this time, Iya.*

She smiled despite herself, locked the phone, and stood. Tomorrow would be loud, sweaty, and unimportant in the grand scheme of her life. Which was exactly why she needed it.

The Cryptic Inquiry

By midday, the air outside had thickened into the kind of heat that clung to skin and slowed the streets. The glass doors of the care home sighed open behind her, releasing a puff of cooler, conditioned air that dissolved instantly into the evening warmth.

Iya crossed to the narrow bench tucked along the side entrance—her usual spot for breaks when she wanted to be away from both patients and staff chatter. From here, the noise of the city was muted: the steady rumble of a bus, the muffled clang of construction two streets over, a snatch of conversation from a pair of smokers leaning against the building's far wall.

Her phone felt warm in her hand, the metal case holding a trace of her own body heat. She scrolled through notifications —a reminder about tomorrow's volleyball game, an ad for discounted takeout, and then the one that pulled her atention in like a magnet.

The encrypted app's icon glowed with a single unread ping. She hadn't opened it since last night, when the message had arrived.

It was still there, exactly as she'd left it:

Absolute discretion required. Details to follow in person.

No greeting. No name. Just two initials she didn't recognize, a date, and the assumption she would be available.

Beneath it sat her own reply from the night before:

Understood. Awaiting details.

The little indicator beneath her words was still the same

—delivered, but unread. Whoever had sent it hadn't even looked at her response.

That unsettled her more than if they'd replied instantly. Silence could mean a lot of things. It could be disinterest. Or it could be the kind of confidence that didn't need chasing.

She slipped the phone into her pocket, but the weight of it seemed heavier now, pressing against her leg as if it wanted her to keep thinking about it.

She leaned back against the bench, tilting her head up toward the sliver of sky framed between the building and the alley wall. A cloud moved across the fading light, dimming it for just a moment before it returned, brighter than before.

It was just another job, she told herself. But even as the words settled in her mind, she knew they didn't quite fit. Jobs like this didn't just happen. They found you. And when they did, they almost always wanted something more than what they were asking for.

Game Night

The gym smelled faintly of polished wood and sweat, the kind of mix that felt both stale and electric. Bright lights buzzed overhead, making the court glow against the shadows of the bleachers. Sneakers squeaked with every pivot, the hollow thunk of the ball echoing off high ceilings before giving way to shouts, laughter, the smack of hands meeting in triumph or apology.

Iya hadn't been here in weeks. She felt it in her shoulders at first, in the stiffness of her calves as she warmed up. But once she stepped onto the court, the old rhythm returned like a muscle memory that lived deeper than fatigue.

"Rotate!" someone shouted, clapping twice.

She jogged into place, tied her hair higher into a ponytail, and let herself lock in. The ball arced over the net, spinning slightly. She dropped low, arms out, absorbing the sting of the pass before flicking it upward to the setter. One clean move, one clean line.

The next rally was longer—volleys snapping back and forth, sneakers skidding, the ball flying just past fingertips before being dragged back into play with a desperate save. By the time it came her way, Iya was ready. She leapt, wrist snapping forward, and the ball shot down with a sharp smack against the wood. Point.

The cheer that went up wasn't stadium-level, just a mismatched chorus of friends and strangers, voices raised more out of shared adrenaline than obligation. Still, it filled her chest with something warm and unguarded.

For two hours, she wasn't a caregiver, wasn't a confidante, wasn't anyone's secret. She was just motion—sweat, focus, breath, laughter.

Between games she crouched at the sideline, gulping water from a dented bottle. Her grey zip-up clung damp at the collar. Around her, people joked, called dibs on positions, stretched against the wall. The ordinary chaos of pickup ball.

That was when she felt it—a gaze that lingered a second too long. She glanced toward the bleachers, where a few scattered spectators sat. One woman wasn't on her phone, wasn't chatting, wasn't restless. She was just watching. Steady. Eyes fixed not on the ball, but on Iya.

The look was calm, unreadable. But it held, long enough that Iya felt it under her skin. She turned away, tied her shoelace tighter, and went back in for the next round. By the time she glanced back, the woman was gone.

She shook it off. Just a stranger, she told herself. People watched games all the time. But the weight of that gaze followed her longer than the ache in her knees.

Evening Detour

After the last game ended she stepped back into the night, her body buzzing with exertion. Sweat cooled on her temples, her chest still rising with the rhythm of movement. For two hours, she'd remembered what it was like to belong entirely to herself.

The air outside was cooler now, touched with the faint

sharpness that came after a gym's heat and sweat. Streetlamps washed the sidewalks in pale circles, and the sky above was a deep, settled navy, the kind that swallowed edges and left only light to define the streets.

The street outside the gym was alive but not chaotic. A streetcar rattled past, its windows flashing tired faces framed by neon ads. The smell of something fried drifted from the corner takeout, mixing with the faint sweetness of the bakery sweeping its last crumbs into the street.

She took the long way home. Past the pharmacy with its tired buzzing sign. Past the florist brushing petals into a dustpan, pausing every few strokes as if even sweeping required patience. The details of the city felt sharper after a shift— every gesture, every smell standing out against the blankness of hospital corridors.

Outside the coffee shop, she slowed. Same chipped sign. Same wobbly table by the window. But the barista was new, pouring steamed milk like it was a science experiment. In the back corner, a couple sat too close, their voices low. She couldn't hear the words, but she recognized the rhythm—the body language of people trying to decide if they still belonged in the same story.

Everyone thinks they'll recognize endings, she thought. But most of the time they arrive quietly, like a door that stops opening without anyone deciding to lock it.

Half a block later, the faint chords of a guitar rose through the air. A busker stood outside the convenience store, case open at his feet. The tune was uneven, a little frayed, but honest. Iya dropped a coin without breaking stride, the clink swallowed by the next chord.

Streetlamps blinked awake overhead, casting soft halos on the sidewalk. Light pooled in uneven circles, catching the faces of strangers who were each carrying their own stories home.

Her phone buzzed. Leah.

We should talk. Dinner.

The words looked harmless enough on the screen—polished, almost generous—but something in them felt practiced. They read like lines rehearsed in a mirror.

She slowed. She could ignore it. Delay. Pretend she hadn't seen it until morning. But she knew, even before the thought fully formed, that the invitation wasn't about "talking" or "clearing the air." It was a test.

Her phone buzzed again.

Just dinner. Promise.

She stopped walking for a moment, thumb hovering above

the screen. The word "promise" tugged at her. Polite. Disarming. A word meant to soothe suspicion while refusing to give detail.

A phrase came to her, unbidden, like a line written on the inside of her ribs:

"A promise without detail is just bait."

She slipped the phone back into her pocket and walked on, letting the glow from shopfronts guide her the rest of the way home.

Late Night Weigh-In

By the time Iya reached her building, the street had thinned. A delivery driver leaned against his car, scrolling through his phone between orders. A couple shared a cigarette in silence. A lone cyclist locked their bike with the weariness of someone who'd done the same routine a hundred nights before.

Inside, the hallway lights cast everything in tired yellow. The air smelled of detergent from someone's laundry and the peppery tang of whatever was cooking two doors down. She closed her door quietly, letting the quiet wrap around her.

Maris stood at the stove, the kettle just beginning to rumble. A jar of honey sat open beside a chipped mug.

"Long day?" her roommate asked, not turning.

"Same as always," Iya said, setting her bag on a chair. The steam curled upward, soft and slow.

She opened the fridge without looking, eyes on the dim light inside. "How would you handle someone who keeps crossing your line?"

The spoon paused mid-air. "Depends," Maris said, tone casual but steady. "Are they worth keeping?"

"I'm not sure yet."

"Well don't decide on an empty stomach." A faint smile. "Eat first. Decide later. Hunger is a bad editor."

Iya let out a soft laugh despite herself. "You always make it sound easy."

"Most problems are easier when they're not yours to figure out."

The kettle clicked off, filling the small space with silence before the hiss of water into the mug. The room smelled of tea leaves and honey, faint and grounding.

She lingered a moment longer, leaning against the counter. Maris' words sat with her. Were they worth keeping?

In her room, she slid the faded-navy notebook from between two books on the shelf. Sitting on the bed, she let the pen hover before writing:

Some bridges you burn to keep the fire warm. Others, because the other side isn't worth visiting.

She stared at the words, the ink still wet. They felt true. Heavy, but true.

A line floated through her mind, something her mother once told her when she was younger and trying to make sense of people who left without warning:

"Not every goodbye deserves grief. Some are just clean air finally reaching you."

She closed the notebook, slid it back between the spines, and reached for her phone. Two words.

Alright. Dinner.

The reply came instantly.

Perfect. 7 PM.

The glow of the screen lingered in her eyes even after it dimmed. She lay back against the pillow, the room quiet around her.

The time between now and tomorrow felt both impossibly wide and painfully small.

CHAPTER 11:

DINNER WITH TEETH

The Arrival

The host smiled the way people in restaurants like this were trained to smile—polite, efficient, as though nothing bad could ever happen under the shelter of low lamps and expensive glassware.

"Reservation for two," Iya said.

"Right this way."

The dining room moved like it had been choreographed: servers gliding soundlessly between tables, napkins unfolding at just the right second, glassware catching stray light like tiny mirrors. Tables were close enough to overhear, but spaced far enough to allow the illusion of privacy. Candles blurred faces, softening strangers into something like company.

"Here?" the host asked, gesturing to a neat two-top in the center.

"Corner," Iya said, her voice calm but firm. She tipped her chin toward the table at the edge. From there, she could see the entrance, the server alleys, and—most importantly—the mirrored column that gave her a slant view of the bar. Back to the wall. Habit.

The host didn't falter. "Of course."

She sat with her shoulder against the wall, the table already arranged like a little stage play—folded linen crisp as pressed uniforms, two knives aligned with ruler precision, water glasses waiting to capture candlelight. She placed her phone face-down beside the bread plate, inhaled steady and counted: four beats in, six beats out. Reset.

The room pulsed with its own quiet rhythm—forks tapping, glasses chiming, laughter swallowed mid-breath. To her left, a couple leaned too close together, their conversation urgent but hushed. To her right, a solitary man turned the pages of his book with the reverence of prayer. Iya catalogued these details the way she always did. Observing was easier than feeling.

Then the door opened, carrying with it a gust of cooler air.

Leah.

Perfume came first—floral, deliberate, the kind that announces itself before the person does. Her coat was draped casually over one arm, but her stride was precision itself. She crossed the room as if she'd been expected, a smile already sharpened into place.

"There you are," Leah said, as though Iya had been the one keeping her waiting. Her eyes swept the room once—exits, corners, mirrors—and then returned to Iya. Noted.

Iya rose briefly, chin tilting in acknowledgment. "Right on time."

Leah slid into the opposite chair, smile precise. "For you? I'd never be late. Not once." She let the line sit before adding, softly, "Maybe I like the idea of you waiting—just not for me."

The server materialized with magician's timing. "Good evening. Would you like to see—"

"The Barolo's beautiful," Leah cut in, voice smooth as glass.

"Dark 'n' Stormy," Iya said, not looking at her.

Leah's smile deepened, her gaze fixed on the untouched glass as though it already belonged to her. "The way you choose things... it feels final. Like there's no version of the world where you don't get what you want."

Iya set her glass down lightly, her tone calm but edged with steel. "It's not that I always get what I want. It's that I know what I don't want."

Leah studied her for a beat too long. Then she smiled, as though she'd just been handed something worth tucking away for later. "Duly noted."

Iya let the silence stretch past comfort, deliberately. Then, casually: "You don't look tired."

Leah leaned in, her voice dropping to a whisper soft enough for only Iya. "Maybe I am tired. But not of you. Never of you."

The words lingered in the air like smoke. Seduction twisted together with warning.

Playful Surface

Their first plate arrived: crostini lined in tidy rows, Gruyère melted golden at the edges, each slice crowned with a dark sheen of garlic–onion jam. The scent rose between them—rich, savory, sweet enough to cut through the smoke of the candles.

Leah gestured lightly with her wrist. "After you."

Iya picked up one slice, movements precise, unhurried. Leah broke hers in half, but her fingers lingered, deliberate, like even the act of handling bread was staged.

"You know," Leah said, her voice low and coiled like ribbon, "you're hard to pin down."

Iya took a slow sip of her Dark 'n' Stormy, the ginger sting sparking across her tongue before she set the glass back down. "That's not an accident."

Leah's mouth curved. "So you admit it. You keep people guessing."

"I keep people where they need to be," Iya replied evenly. "Guessing is optional."

Leah tilted her head, narrowing her gaze as if adjusting a lens. "And where do you think I need to be?"

Iya's patience frayed. She cut into her crostini, crust shattering under her knife. "Right now? In that chair. Before you overthink a piece of bread."

Leah's laugh was low, amused. "Clever. But still a dodge."

"Not a dodge," Iya said, finally meeting her eyes. "A correction. I'm sharper when I'm hungry."

Leah leaned back, tracing the rim of her wineglass with one fingertip, as if sketching a circle to trap Iya inside. "There it is. Even appetite becomes an edge with you."

For a moment, the silence stretched—taut, expectant, like the pause before a blade's drop.

They let conversation skim the surface for a few minutes. The city's fickle weather. A new café Leah claimed she'd "stumbled into," though her precise description suggested she'd mapped the street first. Overpriced rentals that made them scoff together, their laughter sharper than the wine.

But Leah never floated long.

"Do you live alone?" she asked lightly.

"No."

"Roommate?"

"Yes."

"Close friend?"

"Close enough."

The clipped answers stacked like bricks. Leah didn't push. Not yet. She just catalogued each word, eyes sharp as if she were piecing together a puzzle she believed she could finish.

The Match

The mains arrived: Leah's lamb, seared to dark edges and perfumed with rosemary; Iya's sea bass laid across wilted greens, citrus beurre blanch glinting in candlelight. The plates landed in silence, the server almost reverent.

Iya cut a neat piece of fish and lifted it to her mouth. Normally she'd savor lemon against butter, texture against texture. Tonight, the flavor dulled under the pressure of Leah's gaze.

"You don't eat like someone enjoying herself," Leah murmured, her tone bending between compliment and trap.

"I'm eating," Iya said, lifting another forkful.

"Yes," Leah drawled, watching the way her knife rested between bites. "But measured. As though each mouthful tells me something you'd rather hide."

Iya's eyes lifted, steady. "Or maybe it's just dinner."

Leah smiled, as though the pushback was the prize. "You make restraint look like theatre. Most people crack when they're holding back. You? You make it look designed."

Iya set her fork down, the click against porcelain deliberate. Her voice didn't rise. It didn't need to.

"It's not theatre. I can go hungry, but I can't stand nonsense."

The line landed sharp, a blade placed carefully on the table.

Leah froze for a heartbeat, then smiled wider, as if peeling back a new layer. "Then I'll be careful never to bore you."

Iya leaned back slightly, glass in hand. "That would be wise."

Leah's gaze followed, lips grazing the rim of her glass before she lowered it. "You know, you play these moments like a game."

"It's not a game," Iya said evenly. "It's boundaries."

"Boundaries can shift," Leah whispered. "That's what makes them fun."

"Or they hold," Iya countered. "That's what makes them

worth having."

Leah tilted her head, candlelight slicing her expression in half. "You talk like someone who's already chosen the ending."

"I haven't chosen anything," Iya said. "That's the difference. You plan ten moves ahead. I stay present. And right now, dinner's getting cold."

Leah laughed softly, pleased. "So,dinner's just dinner."

"It's only ever dinner," Iya replied, cutting another bite. "Anything else is someone trying to write the ending before the story's halfway through."

Leah leaned in, her voice silk pulled over steel. "And you don't like anyone writing your ending."

"No," Iya said simply. "I don't."

The silence between them stretched thin, like a wire. Neither blinked.

The Slip

The plates cleared. Only the candle remained, flickering with each draft. The table looked too neat, too white, like a stage waiting for its next act.

Iya wrapped her fingers around her fresh Dark 'n' Stormy, ice chiming softly. She'd barely touched it when Leah tilted her head, voice languid.

"So… volleyball."

The word cracked the rhythm. Iya froze. "What about it?"

Leah swirled her wine. "You're good. Quick. Sharp. That spike of yours—clean. The kind that makes the air hold its breath."

It was too exact.

"You've never seen me play," Iya said flatly.

Leah's smile curved slow. "Couple of weeks ago. Wednesday. Community gym near the river. Grey zip-up. Hair pulled back. You nearly took a man's head off with a kill shot. He never saw it coming."

The details sliced. Not rumor. Not accident.

"You were there," Iya said.

Leah gave a small laugh. "You make it sound like a crime." Then, softer: "Would it bother you if I was?"

Velvet words. Sharp teeth.

"That's not coincidence," Iya said. "That's surveillance."

Leah's laugh came soft, smoothing edges. "Surveillance sounds... harsh. I call it curiosity. Don't you think people are truest when they don't know they're being watched?"

"The truth should belong only to them," Iya replied, voice flat.

The candle leaned in a draft, one half of Leah's face lit, the other slipping into dark.

Leah rested her chin on her hand, smiling still. "You looked alive, Iya. More than you do here. Unguarded."

The word pressed hard.

"Everyone has a place they don't perform," Iya said.

"Not you," Leah whispered. "Even in play, you're performing —for that feeling. For yourself."

"Then maybe you saw wrong."

Leah didn't argue. She didn't need to. Her silence claimed victory.

The server appeared with dessert menus, shattering the air. Iya scanned hers without reading. Leah didn't bother.

"Tiramisu?" Leah asked.

Iya slid the menu shut. "Not tonight. I've had enough."

Leah's smile lingered. "Pity. I was hoping you still had room."

She wasn't talking about dessert.

The Exit

The check came, neat in its black folder. Leah reached without pause.

"I'll take this."

"I can pay my own way."

"I know." Leah signed swiftly, eyes flicking up. "But I enjoy paying for what I enjoy."

The line sat between them like a claim.

The server whisked the folder away. Silence reclaimed the table.

Leah leaned back, posture relaxed but sharpened by intent. "Do you want a ride?"

"No. I'll walk."

"It's late."

"I like late."

Leah's smile curved slow. "People say that... until they see who else is still around."

The line lingered—half threat, half seduction.

They stepped out together.

The street was damp from earlier drizzle, pavement slick

with shattered reflections. The city's hum felt distant, hushed, amplifying every sound: a bicycle chain creaking, a poster flapping, the click of Leah's heels.

They walked a block in silence, too close for strangers, too far for friends. Leah's gaze didn't land directly, yet Iya felt it press against her skin.

At the corner, Iya stopped. "This is me."

Leah glanced down the side street. Quiet. Too quiet. "You sure?"

"Yes."

Leah studied her, enough to edge on discomfort. Then her smile slid back into place, precise as a blade into its sheath. "Goodnight, Iya."

"Goodnight."

Leah's figure slipped in and out of pale streetlight until the dark swallowed her.

Iya turned toward her building, keys sharp in her palm. Halfway up the stairs, her phone buzzed.

One new message.

I had a good time tonight.

She turned. The street hadn't changed—wet pavement, flickering lamp, quiet windows.

But the stillness didn't feel neutral anymore.

It felt claimed.

Back in the apartment, she was clear in her mind. "*There's a line between being wanted and being kept. The danger is how easily one disguises itself as the other. A hand reaching for you can feel the same, whether it means comfort or control. Desire isn't the enemy—it's the cage it pretends to build out of care. Tonight, I felt the difference in my bones. Wanting can be kind. Keeping can be prison. And I refuse to live behind someone else's lock.*"

CHAPTER 12:

THE QUIET ROOM

Morning Rounds

The unit woke the way an old house does—one light at a time, one sound finding another. A kettle hissed somewhere down the hall. A cart wheel clicked each time it met the same nick in the floor. In 6B, the television was turned on low for company, not content.

At the board, Iya saw the small star penciled beside Veylan, Arthur. Added after midnight. The quiet code: watch closely. She read the night note once, then again, the way you reread a map before a drive you know by heart. Comfort measures in place. Daughter updated. Breathing irregular.

She paused at Arthur's door and stood just inside the threshold. "Morning, Mr. Veylan," she said softly. Announce, wait, enter. Consent in small things.

The blinds were open an inch. The light pushed past the maple outside and through the narrow seam, a soft stripe on the far wall. Arthur lay propped on pillows, head turned slightly toward that stripe. His eyes were open but heavy, lids sinking between blinks. Each breath made a small hollow sound in his throat.

"You brought the weather voice," he rasped after a moment. The sentence was thinner than last week, broken at the edges.

Iya drew the chair close until her knees touched the bed frame. "Forecast says mild sky," she said. "And oatmeal later—with a side of scandal."

The corner of his mouth lifted, then settled. That was as far as his smile could travel today.

She warmed a washcloth in the basin, rang it out just until it was a weight of heat in her hand, then passed it over his forehead, temples, along the line of his jaw. His eyelids lowered under her touch. The muscles around his mouth loosened.

"Still want the cedar?" she asked, keeping her voice even, small.

He nodded once, a slow hinge.

She rubbed a drop between her palms, close enough for him to catch it without effort. He inhaled—shallow, then shallower—and something in his shoulders let go.

"Workshop," he whispered. A pause. "...cedar... screws..." Another pause to gather breath. "...stubborn."

Iya smoothed the sheet along his ribs, a gesture of reassurance. "That cedar smell—it was always yours."

A faint flicker crossed his lips.

She took his vitals the way you take a pulse you already know: not to be surprised by the numbers, but to make sure you heard them right. The oximeter glowed cool on his finger. The numbers dipped, climbed, hovered. His hand was cool to the touch. She covered it and held it for one full breath and then another, lending warmth.

"Want me to open the blinds another finger?" she asked.

He shaped a tiny no. "Not... all at once," he breathed. "Let the day... earn it."

"I'll let it try," she said, and left the blind where it was.

The nurse stepped in with the night chart, the two of them reading each other's faces before any words. "He settled after two," the nurse murmured, adjusting the pillow to ease the angle of Arthur's neck. "Breathing's lighter. Daughter's on the morning train; transfer in Kingston."

"Okay," Iya said. "We'll keep the room gentle."

They worked together without rush: a roll to the side to check the skin at the sacrum, a small pillow under the knees, a dab of barrier cream where the sheet rubbed. Arthur floated with them, the way some people do when the body is almost done with effort.

When they finished, Iya brushed the blanket smooth again. "I'll be back in a bit," she said. "Lorna's on this morning. She'll come by with the small scandals."

Arthur's eyelids fluttered. "Best... kind," he whispered. The words cost him, and he let his mouth rest.

Iya noted the time on the whiteboard, glancing once more at the narrow stripe of light on the wall, and slipped out, leaving the door ajar so their voices would enter before they did.

The morning moved. She helped Ms. Patel lace her shoes for a walk that would go to the end of the hall and back with ceremony. She found a missing slipper perched like a teacup on a windowsill in 7A. She adjusted Mr. Klein's blinds so the sun wouldn't glare onto the chessboard. Each task was small and exacting; each one returned her to the doorway of 9C where the star on the board meant pay attention.

When she came back, Arthur's eyes were closed. The cedar still hung in the air, thin as thread. She changed his mouth swab for a fresh one, moistened his lips, and waited for him to finish a long breath before touching him again.

He stirred. "Ferry... the horn," he murmured, not a question.

"It still runs," she said. "Sometimes I hear it from the benches by the path."

He let a breath out that might have been approval.

She adjusted the blanket to his collarbone and left the room exactly as quiet as it needed to be.

The Slow Afternoon

By midday, the maple had given up more of itself, its yellow confetti gathering along the curb. The lunch cart rattled down the corridor—metal hard against tile, lids clinking like muted bells.

Lorna leaned into Arthur's doorway with her familiar, opinionated brightness, a teacup balanced on a saucer. "Room service," she announced. "Finest lukewarm tea. Comes with a free rumor."

Arthur opened his eyes a fraction. "...best... kind," he said, the words spaced like fence posts.

"That's right." Lorna set the cup within reach but didn't insist. "Scandal of the day is Doris in 312 flirting with the TV repairman. He's been here twice this week and I ain't seen the busted remote fixed yet."

Arthur's lips tugged, a near smile. "Courtship... of... HDMI," he breathed.

Lorna looked at Iya with mock outrage. "You hear that? He's funnier than half the staff and he's got one lung doing overtime." She shifted her attention back to Arthur, her hand flattening the blanket over his forearm.

He lifted the teacup a few millimeters, hands shaking, then let it settle again. "Smells like... station," he said. "...waiting."

Lorna perched on the mattress edge, careful not to jostle. "If it's waiting," she said, low and sure, "might as well wait with good company."

Iya added, "We're right here with you, Arthur."

He made a small sound—not quite a word, closer to the comfort of agreement.

The nurse slipped in, listened with her stethoscope, and met Iya's eyes. "Comfort measures only," she repeated softly out of earshot, the way you say we're easing now, not fighting. She adjusted the flow of air from the small concentrator to ease the effort of each breath, then left the room to its steady hum.

They kept the ritual simple. Iya dampened his lips with the swab, waited for a breath to finish, turned him a little to his left so the weight on his ribs would change, retucked the draw sheet smooth. Lorna rolled the blinds one finger wider, letting another inch of the day enter without hurry.

"Want the music?" Lorna asked.

Arthur's eyelids fluttered once.

She set a small speaker on the sill and scrolled until an old recording filled the room. "You Are My Sunshine"—the version with the warble that made the radio sound like it had a heart. She kept it low. Arthur's mouth formed the shapes of the words without sound, a muscle memory older than the room. His chest rose, fell, rose again.

Iya watched the way the breath came and went: long in, longer out, the small pause that waited to see what would happen next. She knew the pattern by now. She still counted it with the quiet part of her mind, the part you don't show on your face.

In the early afternoon, a volunteer knocked once and left a small paper bag on the stand—a "comfort cart" offering: tissues, peppermint candies, a tiny jar of hand cream. Lorna held up the cream like she was introducing a celebrity. "This stuff is expensive," she whispered to Arthur. "Don't nobody tell administration I used it on y'all."

She rubbed a little into his hands with her palms, slow circles that smoothed the thin skin and warmed it. "There we go," she said, more to the room than to him. "Hands like a baby."

He drifted in and out, time loosening its grip. Once, he lifted his fingers as if to pinch a tiny screw, turned them in the air, then let the gesture go. Once, he murmured, "Boat... her dress," and the image sat full between them: the photograph on the bedside table—his wife in a bright dress in front of a small boat, hair turned into a flag by the wind.

"The picture's right here," Iya said. "She's got the front seat."

His forehead smoothed, and he slept a while—breathing that soft, shallow rhythm that makes the room lean in.

At two, the phone rang with a number Iya didn't recognize. She picked it up.

"Good afternoon," she said gently.

There was a quick breath on the other end. "Hi, it's me—Arthur's daughter. I'm on the way to the airport. We just left Kingston. I'll be there first thing tomorrow. Please—tell him I'm coming."

"I will," Iya said. "I'm with him now. Would you like me to put you on speaker? He's resting, but he hears."

"Yes please."

She set the phone near his pillow. "Arthur, it's your daughter," she said softly. "She's on the line."

"Hi, Dad," the voice filled the room, thinner now through the small speaker, but still itself. "It's me. I'm on my way. I'm sorry it's taken me so long. I kept thinking I had more time. You used to tell me I'd be late to my own wedding." A small, wet laugh. "You were right about most things."

Arthur's eyelids lifted the width of a fingernail and settled again. His lips moved but no sound formed.

"He hears you," Iya said.

The daughter took a breath that sounded like a person learning to speak gently to a small child. "I'm thinking about the cedar blocks you kept in your drawers. The smell of them would get in the sweaters. I hated it when I was a teenager. It made me smell like the shed." Another soft laugh. "But when I went to university, I took one with me. I didn't tell you. I kept it in my desk, and when I opened it, everything smelled like home. I know you can't talk, Dad. It's okay. Just—take it with you. Take the smell with you."

Arthur's fingers twitched under the blanket, a tiny current running through them.

Lorna leaned on the rail, head bowed, eyes bright. "Keep talking, baby," she whispered toward the phone. "He's here."

"I'm on my way, Dad," she said, and her breath hitched audibly through the line. "We just passed Kingston. The train feels slower than it should, like it knows I should've left yesterday, last week, years ago. I keep staring out the window and all I see are all the times I didn't come. Sundays I could have driven down. Birthdays I let slip with a phone call. Even those nights when I was only an hour away and told myself I was too tired. Too busy. I thought I had more time. I thought you'd always be waiting."

Arthur's lips moved faintly, the smallest shift in his chest as if hearing the weight of it.

Her words stumbled forward, torn between anger at herself and love for him. "You used to tell me work stole too many years from you, and I hated hearing it, because I just wanted you home. And now I'm the one saying it—hiding behind the same excuse. I did to you what you always regretted doing to us." Her voice broke, a sob catching. "I'm so sorry, Dad. I'm so sorry I became the thing you tried to warn me about."

Arthur's forehead smoothed, the smallest ease in his face, and his fingers twitched against the blanket—faint, but enough to answer her.

The daughter's words spilled out in careful order: the garden he'd made from nothing behind their first apartment, the ferry rides when she was little and he would grumble about splinters but take her anyway, the way he tapped the steering wheel to the rhythm of the radio when the light was red. She told him about her own child's new front tooth, about the plant she'd finally kept alive for more than a season, about burning the roast last Sunday and eating cereal with a candle lit out of stubbornness.

Arthur's mouth curved faintly at the roast. It straightened. He slept again, the phone still on, the daughter's breath making a soft weather in the space by his ear.

At three, the nurse returned, checked the angle of his neck and the cushions under his calves, raised the head of the bed a notch to ease the work of each breath. "You're doing good," she murmured, to the room as much as to him.

At four, the light in the sliver of window thinned from bright to the kind of gray that makes people switch lamps on. Lorna moved the blinds another finger. The maple showed off one last time, a little performance to say the day had been.

The tea cooled on the tray, untouched. Iya replaced the swab again, offered a drop of water against his lower lip, withdrew when he closed his mouth. She wiped the corner gently. "That's enough," she said. "We won't ask more of you."

When the playlist slipped from Sunshine to something with a horn that walked instead of ran, the room changed with it. Not heavier. Just closer to the real.

The Night Between

Evening settled over the unit in small steps—televisions dimmed to background noise, trays stacked, call bells coming less often. The halls grew quieter, not because the work was done, but because the rhythm shifted. By night, everything slows into long intervals: medication rounds, whispered checks, the squeak of carts moving soft as breath.

In 9C, the blinds let in only a narrow slice of dusk. Arthur lay still, his chest rising in slow hills and longer valleys, the pauses between breaths stretching wider. His eyes no longer opened fully, just small flickers beneath lids. The kind of flicker that told you he was already elsewhere, drifting toward a place words couldn't follow.

Lorna sat at the foot of the bed, knees together, hands folded, posture steady as a pew-sitter in church. Every so often she glanced at the monitor—not to be informed, but to confirm what her ears and her own chest already knew. Iya sat closer, one hand resting on the blanket near Arthur's wrist, her body leaned forward, refusing to leave him unattended.

The night nurse slipped in and dimmed the lights further, leaving the room in a kind glow. She adjusted the oxygen tubing so it rested gently along his cheek, then smoothed the blanket at his shoulders. "I'll be down the hall," she said softly. "Buzz me for anything."

Time thickened. Staff voices lowered without needing to be

told. The work went on—vitals, bed checks, a tray clatter swallowed by distance—but the whole building seemed to know what hour it was in 9C.

Around one, Arthur murmured. The words barely formed, more sound than speech, but Iya caught them: "boat... wind... dress." She leaned close, answering in a whisper. "We're here, Arthur." His lips stilled.

At two, he turned his head slightly toward the bedside table. The phone sat there, screen glowing with the last message from his daughter: *Tell him we love him. Please hold his hand for me.* Iya laid her palm fully over his hand, as if to let the message pass through her skin into his.

At three, the pauses between breaths widened further, doorways you could stand inside. They tended him in silence: a turn to ease pressure, more swabs to moisten his lips, sheets smoothed without rustle. One would step into the hall for water while the other stayed rooted, then they traded, never leaving him alone for more than a minute.

At four, the nurse reappeared in the doorway, holding a fresh box of tissues. No words, just the offering, then gone again.

By five, another text arrived from his daughter: *Our flight was delayed. We're still stuck in the airport, waiting for the connection. Please... stay with him until I can get there.*

Iya typed a single heart, then added: *We're with him.*

Outside, the unit stirred with the first sounds of morning. A laundry cart sighed around a corner. A night aide laughed once at something on her phone and quickly put it away. Somewhere beyond the window, a bus exhaled at the curb.

Arthur's mouth no longer made shapes. His eyes stayed closed, lids unmoving now. But when the strip of light at the blinds turned from black to gray, his face shifted—not with strain, but release. Like someone hearing their name called softly from another room.

Iya eased the blinds open by one finger. "Morning's trying," she whispered.

"Let it," Lorna said, her voice low, reverent.

There is a quiet that comes only once in a room. Not the hush of night or the lull between call bells, but the stillness that gathers when a life is almost finished. It is not silence, it is presence, spread evenly across the walls, the floor, the air itself.

Arthur's chest lifted one last time, a shallow hill of breath. It lingered at the top, as though waiting for permission. Then it fell—and no breath followed.

Iya kept her hand over his, counting heartbeats in her own chest, waiting for the rise that never came. She lowered her forehead to his knuckles, holding them as if to anchor both of them in the moment.

Lorna smoothed the blanket across his chest and whispered, "Safe journey, Arthur." Her voice caught once, then steadied, because steadiness was the last gift she could give.

The nurse entered, stethoscope ready. She pressed it lightly to his chest, listened, then met Iya's eyes. A small nod, soft words: "Time of death." She said the hour.

On the table, the daughter's last message still glowed: *We're still in the airport. Please stay with him until I can get there.* Iya pressed her palm more firmly against Arthur's hand, as if to let the words keep their promise through her touch.

The window held a new line of daylight now—thin, sure, indifferent. Outside, the maple stood bare in the wind, its branches lifted like open hands.

The Aftermath

They dimmed the lights. The maple at the window had turned to silhouette, branches etched against the new day. The radio had been playing softly; Iya turned it off, then on again, lower this time—as if reminding the room that sound did not need to be afraid of itself.

Lorna returned with a basin of warm water, two towels neatly folded. The nurse signed her name in two places, recorded the hour, and left them in their quiet.

"Ready?" Lorna asked.

"Ready," Iya said.

They began the work that comes after the last breath. Not hurried, not ceremonial, but reverent in its own small way. Warm cloth passed slowly across the forehead, down the cheeks, along the jaw. Eyebrows smoothed with a fingertip until the face looked as though it had simply exhaled into sleep. Hands washed, dried, then crossed carefully at the waist. A touch of cedar oil at the temples—because that is what he asked for, and what he loved.

When they changed him into the clean gown, they moved with the precision of people who had done this many times before and still found a way to make it new. They lifted and folded as if not waking a child, as if carrying a glass filled to the brim.

"I always think of my mother at this part," Lorna whispered, her voice threading just above the radio. "She'd tuck our sheets so tight when we were small. She wanted us to know the bed was ready to hold us."

Iya nodded. "My grandmother too," she said. "You don't forget who taught you how to be gentle."

When the washing and dressing were finished, they gathered his personal things: the glasses, the paperback with its ticket tucked inside, the photograph of the woman by the small boat. Iya held the picture longer than she meant to. "We'll place this on top," she said.

"Of course," Lorna replied. "She gets the front seat."

They called the funeral home. Paperwork stitched the seam between this room and the one he would be carried into. When the attendants arrived—quiet, practiced, respectful— they moved him with the kind of care that makes grief both heavier and easier. Their hands knew the weight of a good life.

Afterward, Iya and Lorna stood at the window, side by side. The maple outside caught the early light, bare branches trembling in the breeze.

"He liked that tree," Lorna said softly.

Iya nodded, watching the wind play through it. "He made it a friend."

CHAPTER 13:

THE SERVICE

The service ended with the soft swell of an old hymn. People rose, chairs scraping gently against the floor. One by one, they filed past the coffin, pausing to touch the polished wood or murmur a farewell. The air was thick with lilies and regret.

At the front, a photograph rested on an easel: Mr. Veylan squinting into sun beside a small boat, a bright dress flowing behind the woman he loved. Next to it, a table of careful artifacts—his glasses, the paperback with its sun-bleached spine, a brass key with no labeled home, and a square of cedar tucked into a dish. The cedar's clean scent tried and failed to cut through the flood of lilies.

Iya stood to the side with Lorna, letting the crowd move. Her hands were folded, eyes steady, face unreadable. The minister's voice, softer now, blessed the family, the friends, the

years. An usher opened the side doors; cool air sidled in and made the flowers shiver.

A small girl in patent shoes tugged at her mother's sleeve near the aisle. "Is grandpa sleeping?" she whispered. The mother bent low, lips to ear; the child's mouth made a round

O of understanding that meant she understood only the shape, not the weight.

On the far side of the room, two men who looked like they belonged to the same chin stood together with identical folded programs pressed flat against their palms. An aunt dabbed at her eyes with a napkin that left lint on her cheek. People greeted one another with the particular energy of reunions at funerals—surprised to see familiar faces dressed in black, sorry it took this to bring them together.

Only when the line thinned, when the crowd pushed toward the foyer, did Iya speak.

She leaned closer to Lorna, her voice low, steady, but with a tremor at the edges. "Look at this hall," she murmured. "Packed. All these people—where were they? He's been with us for years. Not once did I see half these faces at his bedside. Not once."

Lorna exhaled through her nose in agreement.

"They say they're paying respect," Iya went on, voice low but tight, "but respect doesn't sit with a man who can't sleep. Respect doesn't ask about the weather. He wanted someone to talk to. He had stories. And it was us listening—not them."

Her throat worked. She blinked hard, keeping her voice even. "Now they come with flowers, with speeches. Guilt, maybe. But he doesn't know this hall is full. He won't see it."

A woman brushed past them with a bouquet still wrapped in paper, the cellophane making a small storm of sound. Someone laughed too loudly near the guest book, then pressed a hand to their mouth as if to pull the joy back in.

Lorna slipped her arm through Iya's, squeezed gently. "That's why we do it. Because even if no one shows up, we do. That's the job, baby girl. That's care."

They waited for the family to pass, making themselves smaller to give the aisle back to those whose names would be read later at the graveside. Iya watched the daughter—mid-forties, hair pulled back with the practicality of a person who had done too many things in too few days—accept a series of embraces that left her looking both held and bruised. She recognized the voice from the phone, the breath that had filled a small room at dusk so her father wouldn't be left alone.

At the memory table, a man with carpenter's hands picked up the cedar square, lifted it to his nose, and closed his eyes. When he set it down, he pressed his thumb once into the wood as if checking for softness. "Smells like him," he said. "Like his workshop on a Saturday morning."

The line to the family slowed near where Iya and Lorna stood. The daughter looked up and saw them. For a second, confusion flickered—names searching for faces—then recognition changed the shape of her mouth.

"You're from the unit," she said. "You were with him."

"Iya," Iya said quietly. "This is Lorna."

The daughter took both their hands in turn. Her grip was warmer than her face. "Thank you," she said. The words landed heavy, inadequate. "I wanted to come sooner. I kept meaning to. Work was…" She caught herself apologizing to the wrong people and let the sentence fall.

The daughter's grip tightened on Iya's hand. "I know he liked the cedar," she said quickly, then gave a small laugh through tears. "He used to tuck cedar blocks into all his drawers. Said it kept the moths out and made his clothes smell like the woods. That smell was always him."

"He did," Lorna said. "He asked for it every morning. Said it made the day smell like something he could fix."

The daughter's laugh was quick and wet. "That's him." She looked at Iya. "Did he… go okay?"

"He went with someone talking in the room," Iya said. "He waited for you to be on the line."

The daughter nodded. Relief and pain outran each other across her face. She squeezed their hands again. "Thank you for seeing him," she said. "For being there when—" She didn't finish. "If you think of anything I should have, anything that was his…" She gestured toward the display.

"We put his photograph box aside," Iya said. "It's waiting for you at the home. And his book. Instead of admitting it, he would pretend he knew where he left off, flipping pages and continuing as though he hadn't forgotten."

The daughter smiled, the kind that holds and breaks at once. "He always did that," she said. "Starting over to prove he could."

A cousin arrived to tug the daughter into the next embrace. She mouthed thank you again and was carried forward on the tide of condolences. Iya and Lorna stepped back to the wall and let the stream run.

"I don't think it's that people don't care," Lorna said softly, once they were alone again. "It's that they live far away, or they're busy, or they're scared of facing what aging really looks like. Sitting with someone day after day, in their slow routine—that's hard for people. So, they stay away until the end, when there's no more waiting, no more slowness. It's easier for them to show up once, at the funeral, than to sit through all those quiet Tuesdays."

"I know," Iya said. "I know all that. It still feels like arriving at a fire with water after the house is ash."

"It's always going to hurt," Lorna said gently. "That's the

proof your heart's still in this work. If you ever stopped feeling it, that would mean you'd stopped caring."

They moved with the crowd into the foyer. The guest book lay open on a lectern, pages already fat with ink: Great man. Will be missed. We sailed with Art in '92—best storyteller on the lake. I should have called.

Near the doors, ushers stacked programs no one wanted to admit they were taking home. Outside, the day had turned honest—gray sky, a trial of wind, puddles making maps of small feet. People stood in clumps on the steps, coats pulled close, hands wrapped around paper cups.

"Air?" Lorna asked.

"Please," Iya said.

They stepped out into the cold. The smell of lilies lingered behind them; air found its own lungs again. Across the street a woman shook water from an umbrella and startled a flock of small birds into the bare branches of a municipal tree—no maple, but it would do.

Iya closed her eyes and counted a slow breath. "I keep thinking about how he watched the light through the blinds," she said. "We opened them in inches so the day wouldn't rush him."

"That's a kind of respect," Lorna said. "The living kind."

Iya nodded. Her jaw eased, but her chest still ached. She let her gaze drift to the coffin, to the photograph of the woman in the bright dress, wind catching fabric into something like a flag.

Her voice was quiet, almost a confession. "I know it's our job to sit with them. But I always hope their families, their friends, remember to visit too. It makes them feel alive. Value the time while they're still here. Give them respect when they can still see it, when they can still feel it. Not after. Not only when they're already gone."

The thought hung there like incense, heavier than lilies.

And for anyone left behind, that was the question that lingered: How many chances do we waste, waiting until it's too late? An hour a week. A visit. A chair pulled up by a bedside. Not a screen between you, not a distracted nod while your hands scroll a phone. Presence. Real, ordinary presence.

Because when the room finally falls silent, it isn't flowers or speeches that echo—it's the visits that happened, the stories listened to, the moments when we were there.

Iya took a breath, steadying herself, then turned toward the door. Tomorrow, she would care again—because care was presence, not possession.

CHAPTER 14:

CLOSING DOORS

Terms of Engagement

Morning peeled itself open like tape—sticky, reluctant. The apartment was quiet; Maris had left early for a shift swap, her mug still a warm circle on the counter, a comet tail of tea leaves clinging to the porcelain. A single spoon rested on a folded paper towel like a silver line drawn under a sentence.

Iya stood by the window, phone lit in her palm. Ten messages from Leah, stacked like breath held too long.

You make me feel sane.

I can't do "wait."

I'm outside your building. (deleted)

I didn't mean that.

Please don't make me the bad one.

I need you to tell me what to do with this feeling.

I keep thinking about your hands—

Ignore me if you need to.

I hate this silence.

Please.

The deleted one glowed anyway. It always did, like a fingerprint lifted in powder.

Iya's pulse tightened her throat—anger's cousin, vigilance. She wasn't afraid. She was wide awake.

She set the phone on the table, lit screen down, and let her hands move where her mind needed them: kettle on, flame steady; coffee grounds measured like ritual; a slow sweep of crumbs off the counter with the flat of her palm. When the kettle trembled, she turned it off just before the whistle, as if intercepting a thought before it went too far.

Her notebook waited in the bookshelf crease where spines hid it—faded navy, corners blunted by years. She didn't take it out. Not yet. Instead she typed, thumb sure.

If you want to talk, we do it today at 6 p.m., Arcadia Hotel lobby on Meridian. Bright lights, lots of people.

30 minutes.

No touching.

No gifts.

If you can't follow those terms, there's nothing to talk about.

She watched the ellipses bubble, vanish, bubble again, deciding whether to commit.

Okay. I'll be there.

I can behave.

I just want you to hear me.

The kettle ticked as it cooled. She poured. Steam rose in tight threads and loosened her shoulders by increments.

"Presence without possession," she said aloud, testing the words on the air. The sound steadied her hands the way a railing steadies feet.

She added one more thing, not to Leah but to the locked notes in her phone—a safety habit that had saved other women she'd worked with and might, in some small way, save her: location, time, terms, and the person who would check on her after. She typed Lorna for the check-in, then paused, and added Maris as backup. If one missed, the other wouldn't.

Before she left, she wiped the table until it squeaked. It felt good to make one small thing unquestionably clean. She rinsed the sponge, wrung it hard, and laid it to dry with its soft belly up, as if even a sponge deserved to breathe.

On her way out, she slipped the notebook into her bag, just behind her wallet. Not for writing, not yet—just to know it was near.

Flowers at the Front Desk

The facility has the familiar smell of lemon cleaner, oatmeal, and the faint sweetness of hand lotion; if safety had a scent, it would probably be this—a little sterile, a little warm, a little tired. Lorna stood at the whiteboard with a dry-erase marker, her handwriting a quilt of thick motherly letters. Hydration check | 10 a.m. singalong | Patio at 3 if weather permits.

"Morning, Miss Mind-Your-Business," Lorna sang without turning. "They dropped flowers at the desk for you."

"For me?" Iya adjusted her badge—habit, not nerves.

"Little boutique thing. No card. Smells like apology." Lorna capped the marker and gave Iya the sort of look a good aunt saves for a niece she refuses to lose. "You know I love a bouquet, but I don't love a message that pretends not to be a message."

They rounded the corner together. The bouquet sat too prim at the reception counter: clean whites, green veins like delicate maps, and a single red rose cinched like a secret in the center. The paper wrap was slate-gray, tied with a ribbon that knew it was expensive. Water beaded where the stems met their bow, a condensation ring already marking the desk like a claim.

The receptionist shrugged. "Courier dropped it. No name."

Iya didn't touch it. "Please give it to Room 12B," she said. "Mrs. Navarro loves lilies." She met the receptionist's eyes. "Tell her it's from the staff."

The receptionist nodded, relief softening her shoulders. "You got it."

Lorna's eyebrows climbed. "You sure, baby?"

"I'm sure." Iya kept her voice light because the moment

already weighed enough.

They walked back down the hall. A dementia patient near the fish tank hummed the first three notes of a song until they looped back on themselves, a child's lasso of sound. Iya hummed back, off-key on purpose. The woman laughed and forgot to be afraid.

"You good?" Lorna asked finally.

"Yes."

"Cuz good ain't the same as okay. And okay ain't the same as safe."

"I'm safe," Iya said. "I'm... careful."

Lorna squinted. "Careful gets a body home. Just remember —when grown folks turn twelve in their feelings, they'll try to squeeze truth like a tube of toothpaste. It goes everywhere but the brush."

Iya smiled despite herself. "I'll bring the brush."

"Uh-huh. And the floss. Emotional plaque is real." Lorna tapped her temple. "And baby, plaque builds quiet."

By ten, Mrs. Navarro's room glowed with flowers. She pressed a hand to her chest when Iya peeked in. "For me? Look at this! Oh, the white ones smell like weddings."

"They're all yours," Iya said.

"My granddaughter will think I got engaged," Mrs. Navarro giggled. "At my age! Wouldn't that be something."

"It would," Iya agreed, and the yes in her voice let the bouquet be exactly what it had just become: a delight wearing no one's name.

Iya moved on with the day. Room 7 called for help to find a missing slipper that was sitting on the windowsill, upside down like a teacup. Room 2 insisted breakfast toast was a conspiracy; Iya buttered it anyway and told him conspiracies made excellent food. In the common room, Mr. Klein watched the morning news with a frown that belonged to someone who had probably been right about things at the wrong time.

"You're careful," he said without looking away from the TV.

"Always."

"The kind that keeps you safe," he added. "But it also makes you invisible, even when you're standing in plain sight."

"I'm working on being both present and unmissable," she said.

He snorted. "Good luck with that trick."

By lunch, no second delivery came. That, somehow, tightened the quiet. The absence strutted as loudly as a brass band.

In the staff lounge, someone had left half a muffin that had hardened into sculpture. A magnet on the fridge read WASH YOUR OWN DISHES (NO, SERIOUSLY). Iya sat in the steadier chair and texted Lorna for the hundredth time today without sending it. Instead she typed a single word and sent that. 6. Lorna wrote back a thumbs-up and then, after a beat, *I'm your 7:01. If I don't hear from you, I'm the kind of aunt that calls the fire department for a cat in a tree.*

Iya thumbed a heart to that, then tucked her phone away like it had teeth.

At two, she found Mrs. Navarro humming to the white blooms, telling them about a childhood garden as if the lilies were old friends back from a long voyage. That was the kind of re-gifting Iya trusted. The kind that detoxed a gesture, returned it to oxygen.

At three, the patio was all wheelchairs and cardigan corners and sun on thin skin. Someone had queued a playlist from another decade. Lorna told a story about a rooster that used to chase her down a dirt road when she was a girl, and the laughter fell like a blanket over the hard places of the day.

"Iya," Lorna murmured, catching her by the elbow as the song changed. "You ok gurl?"

"I'm good," Iya said again.

Lorna squeezed. "Be whole."

"I'm trying to be."

"Try with your feet, not your teeth." Lorna nodded toward the horizon that was just the top edge of the next building. "Feet get you out. Teeth just break your jaw."

The clock slid toward evening like a plate across a table— slow, inevitable, noiseless unless you were listening for it. Iya sharpened her edges the way some people sharpened pencils.

Lobby with No Corners

At 5:55 p.m., the Arcadia's lobby pressed itself into light.

Brass lamps shaped like flowers burned at a constant, hotel-approved glow. A baby grand piano sat to one side with its mouth closed, lacquer gleaming like a smile rehearsed and withheld. Velvet chairs angled in curated pairs that looked casual until you tried one and realized the arrangement let everyone watch everyone else, as if sightlines were a form of currency.

The floor was cool marble, a surface that asked you to walk like you belonged and punished you with echo if you didn't. Over the bar, a cascade of glass spheres floated in descending constellations—each globe catching the others' light so that illumination became a performance, a chandelier rebranded as a galaxy.

It was the kind of lobby built to make people feel watched, not sheltered.

Iya chose her geography the way a pilot picks sky.

Table against the paneled wall; back protected, view open. From this angle she could see the entrance, the elevators, the revolving door, the concierge's station with its immaculate bowl of too-green apples. She could also see the mirrored column that doubled the room into ghosts—people walking through copies of themselves. It was a good angle if you wanted to know what came for you before it arrived.

She sat. Palms on the table, fingers uncurled, wrists visible. Not a surrender—an outline. Make me boring, her posture said. Let this be furniture, not theater.

Her phone buzzed once. She sent a single word to Lorna: *Here.*

Then, because she could hear Lorna's voice even without the device, she added: *Code stays code.*

A knife emoji appeared almost at once. Then a sun. The combination was Lorna distilled: I will bring light, and if I can't, I will bring something sharp.

Iya allowed herself the smallest breath. She counted two things quietly: her own heartbeat, and the revolving door's patient arithmetic as strangers pushed through and were portioned into the evening.

At 6:02, Leah arrived.

Precisely messy. Hair arranged into whispering disarray. A white shirt you needed money not to wear loudly. A coat draped over one forearm like gravity had decided to be polite. She paused just inside the threshold long enough to be observed—long enough to let eyes find her, to let the lobby place her on its chessboard—then moved with the confidence of someone who believes she improves a room simply by entering it.

The marble accepted her shoes without echo.

"I was going to bring coffee," Leah said as she came into the circle of Iya's table, voice brightening too fast. "But you said no gifts."

"Coffee isn't a gift," Iya said. "It's a tactic." She gestured to the chair across from her. "Sit."

Leah sat. Her hands folded the way a good student does; the set of her shoulders said the kind of student who planned to cheat later.

"You look beautiful," Leah murmured, softer now, like intimacy could be negotiated by tone alone. "Even when you're scolding me."

"This isn't a scolding," Iya said. "It's a conversation with rules."

Leah's laugh popped and vanished, a bubble she killed herself. "Rules. I like rules." The corner of her mouth crept. "You know I'm good at rules when you make them."

"This one is simple." Iya held Leah's gaze as if it were live current and she had decided to ground it. "You crossed my boundaries. You came near my home. You contacted me outside agreed times. You sent flowers to my workplace."

A twitch at Leah's eye like a small electric shock. "They were pretty."

"They were pressure."

"You make everything so clinical," Leah said, smile tightening into wire. "Like feelings are a bad habit."

"Feelings are weather," Iya replied. "Behavior is a choice."

Leah studied her, the wire becoming something thinner, sharper. "Wow. That sounded rehearsed."

"I rehearse what matters," Iya said. "So, I don't improvise where I shouldn't."

A bellhop wheeled a chrome cart past, hat a touch askew; wheels hissed, metal flashed, and the chandelier's descending planets threw light across his face. Behind them, the concierge answered a call with a voice polished enough to sell calm by the pound. Someone at the lounge bar asked for a menu in a hush that still managed to be an order. The lobby thrummed with concealed urgency.

At their table, air tightened.

Leah leaned forward—an inch too far. It was not a reach, it was a measurement: the overlap where breath would meet breath. Then she arrested her own movement and smiled as though she'd found the line and deserved applause for not crossing it.

"I'm not a villain," she said softly. "I just…" She let her breath out in a practiced wreck. "I don't want to go back to the life where I don't feel anything."

"I'm not a rehab," Iya said. "I'm not a cure."

"You're the only place I don't feel invisible."

"That's closer to the truth," Iya said. "But I'm not a place. I'm a person. And my life is not a room you get to live in."

Leah's mouth trembled, then chose to harden. "So, what—" She angled her head, softened her eyes, tried on contrition like a coat. "I should pretend none of it happened? That you did not make me… okay again?"

"I didn't make you anything," Iya said. "I reflected what you already had. Care is not magic. It's a mirror."

"Strength?" The word landed in Leah's mouth like a dare.

"You can stand on what's already yours," Iya said. "You don't need to take mine."

Leah's stare held too long. A shine came into it that wasn't wetness. Something sharpened behind the gaze—a glint the way a blade does when someone tilts it to see if it still catches light.

"If you cross every line you see," Iya added, "you stop being a player. You become the chaos."

"That sounds like fear talking," Leah said.

"No," Iya said. "It's what experience sounds like."

A man in a blazer hovered at the concierge, fingers drumming, deciding whether to flee his own evening. The revolving door performed its fractions and exhaled. A woman in sequins took a photo of herself and found, to her disappointment, the chandelier behind looked better.

Leah sat back a fraction, the fraction read as magnanimity. "You're ending it," she said at last, stacking the words carefully.

"I'm ending the professional relationship," Iya said. She reached into her bag with slow dignity and set a black envelope on the table. Gold letters gleamed without apology. She didn't push it toward Leah. She let gravity argue its case. "I'm returning your last payment."

A wash of red crossed Leah's cheekbones. "That's patronizing."

"It's clean."

Leah's hand hovered over the envelope, a child over a candle. Heat reached her without flame. She didn't touch, but her eyes did. "Why is it so easy for you?"

"You crossed the line," Iya said quietly. "That made this necessary."

Leah's jaw worked—a grind. When she looked back, her voice had become casual, but this was superficial, a wrapper on something jagged. "I found your roommate's account," she said. "Cute apartment. Plants with names."

Her smile thinned into a paper cut. "I didn't just look, Iya. I watched. Do you want to know how easy it was? Your street's cameras don't even blink." She leaned in the way a knife leans —only as much as needed. "I stood there one night, outside your building, and nobody noticed. Not the doorman, not the neighbors. Just me, just you—if you'd looked out."

Iya's pulse thumped once—hard, precise—but her face remained calm. Under the table, her nails pressed crescents into her palm and then released them. She let her next inhale travel all the way down before it returned. When she spoke, her voice would have held a glass steady.

"You're telling me you stalked me?"

Leah's laugh was quick, bright, wrong. Heads turned for a beat and then looked away. "Stalked? No. Protected. There's a difference." She traced the table's edge with her finger as if following a familiar coastline. "You don't get it yet—I see the cracks other people miss. I could keep you safe. From everyone else." Her eyes warmed in a way that chilled the room. "From yourself."

"I don't require protection that removes my freedom," Iya said.

"I know when your lights go out," Leah continued, eyes on her finger's path, voice soft with ownership. "I know your roommate leaves early on Wednesdays. I know you linger at the kitchen window before bed like you are waiting. For me."

For the first time that evening, even the chandelier felt predatory. Each glass sphere reflected a slice of them—Leah's face multiplied into a faceted creature that smiled from five directions at once.

An elevator dinged. Iya didn't move.

"That," she said, thin as thread but steady, "is exactly what you cannot do."

Leah's eyes glassed over and then sharpened like a lens deciding which subject to make important. "I haven't done anything."

"You're standing here telling me you could," Iya said. "That's the difference."

They let the difference sit on the table like a knife. No one touched it, but it made every other object honest by comparison.

Leah reclined by millimeters—an imitation of ease that seemed calculated. "You love control," she said lightly.

"I love consent," Iya said. Her voice dropped; not volume —a register. "If you contact my roommate, my family, my workplace—if you show up anywhere uninvited—there are steps I will take. You won't like the version of me you'll meet if you push past this no."

Leah's smile cracked and showed a tooth. "You make it sound like a crime to love you."

"What I offer you is care. Not love. And what you're asking for now isn't care—it's possession."

Leah's fingers moved faster than she thought. A flick across the table—lightning disguised as a gesture—and the backs of her fingers grazed the soft inside of Iya's wrist. It was brief, deliberate, a thief's demonstration. Iya rotated her arm a degree; Leah touched air. The movement was small. The meaning wasn't.

For the first time in the conversation, Leah's breath stuttered. The laugh that followed belonged to someone who hadn't planned on not getting what she wanted. She studied Iya with something like awe and something like hunger knitting a tight seam. "Do you hate me?" The question sounded like a child asking to be forgiven for breaking a window no one saw smash.

"No," Iya said. "I just refuse to belong to you."

Glass breaking under carpet: quiet, but impossible to ignore. Leah's expression shifted in three steps—hurt, calculation, charm—then she strapped charm to the front like armor.

She reached carefully and pulled the black envelope to her side. No flourish: the motion of a person accepting a verdict not because they agreed but because a courtroom was watching. She slipped it into her bag and drew the zipper closed. The sound was surgical.

Thirty minutes nearly done. Iya glanced at the lobby's oversized clock—the kind that pretends to be timeless by being too big to argue with. "We have four minutes left," she said.

"Can I have a hug?" Leah asked.

"No."

The word landed without spikes. A plain noun, set down on a plain table.

Leah's lips spread a fraction too far. Teeth took the light. "You talk like a therapist who bills in poetry."

"I talk like a woman who won't leave pieces of herself in other people's pockets."

"You don't trust me," Leah said, as if naming a variable she could solve for.

"I don't trust anyone who thinks my life is theirs."

A waiter at the bar rang a small bell by accident; the concierge laughed the laugh of someone paid to be amused; the piano pinged a single note when a passerby brushed it. The lobby gathered all the sounds and arranged them into a frame around the quiet at the table.

Leah stood. The chair's feet made the civilized sigh hotels train their furniture to make. She adjusted her coat on her arm. She did not take her eyes off Iya.

"I wanted to be kind," Leah said, the sentence dressed in sincerity and something else wearing its clothes. "You think I can't be."

"I think you are tired of hearing 'no' from a person who does not explain it in ways you can manipulate," Iya said.

Leah's lashes lowered, lifted. The slow blink of a cat that has never believed in fences. "You'll think about me," she said gently, like promising mercy.

"I'll think about the work," Iya said. "And remind people I'm not theirs to own."

Leah smiled with a fraction more teeth than comfort required. "I hate that you're good at this."

"I hate that you needed me to be."

Then Leah turned and walked.

At the revolving door, she pressed her palm flat to the glass. Didn't move. Testing. Watching the way the door held her pressure. A moment later she looked back over her shoulder, the curve of her mouth thin as a blade hidden in a ribbon.

When she spoke again, her voice was barely there — not

meant for anyone, just the glass and herself.

"You think closing a door makes it over," she said softly. "But some doors remember the hand that touched them. They do not forget. Neither do I."

She stepped forward, slow and deliberate, allowing the door's chamber to take her. The glass carried her away—her reflection, then her profile, then the empty street where rain had decided to turn to mist.

Iya remained seated for the final minute, the way a pilot keeps hands on the controls after landing, waiting for the cabin lights to speak permission. She placed attention on her breath the way you place a weight on a paper to keep it from blowing off the table. In: you did not escalate. Out: you did not fold. In: you said what mattered. Out: you did not give her what she reached for.

She texted one word to Lorna: *Done.*

Then, because the knife needed its daylight, she added: *Sunny.*

Dots appeared. *GOOD*, Lorna replied. *Soup on the stove if you swing by. Also I will personally fight anyone with my church shoes.*

A line eased at the corners of Iya's mouth. *I believe you;* she sent back.

She stood. The chair cooperated. The apples on the concierge desk shone like coins minted from compliance. She nodded at the concierge, who nodded back with professional ignorance. The chandelier kept making galaxies out of strangers.

Outside, the Arcadia's awning exhaled the lobby's captured air into the city. Rain had become the kind of mist that chooses no side and wets everything. Traffic lights washed the pavement in red and green theology. She did not open her umbrella. Water should find skin sometimes; it proved you were still a surface, not a sponge.

Her phone pulsed against her palm. Leah: *Thank you for making me feel seen. I'm angry. I'll get over it. Please don't block me. I won't contact your people.*

Another arrived before doubt could translate itself. *I won't be the chaos.*

Iya typed, deleted, typed again. *Thank you for agreeing to the boundary. Please take care of yourself.*

She left it there. The sentence contained precisely what it contained. No softness she hadn't chosen. No heat she would regret.

Halfway down the block, a hooded figure paused under

an awning and watched her with the specific curiosity of a city that sometimes becomes a person. The hood tilted in assessment and then turned away when the crosswalk chirped permission. Maybe nothing. Maybe something. It did not matter; the plan didn't change.

Her phone lifted its head again. Unknown number: *Nice dress tonight. Didn't suit the way you said goodbye.*

She stopped walking. The mist decided to be rain and then changed its mind. Her screen recorded the sentence without her thumb. The number wasn't Leah's saved thread. Leah was clever enough to buy new numbers the way you buy gum— easy, disposable. If asked, she could shrug: wasn't me. Smoke over smoke.

Iya didn't answer. Not because she lacked words. Because silence was, sometimes, the only accurate vocabulary for a boundary.

She resumed walking, not faster. The ordinary deserved its dignity. On the subway platform, air tasted of brake dust and old coins. A kid practiced kickflips too close to the edge; his mother scolded him in a voice that loved him in public. Posters promised private fixes for public wounds. The train arrived with a sigh.

She stood near the door. The recorded voice said, "Stand clear of the closing doors," and the doors obeyed each other. The window gave her a version of herself she could live with: the woman who holds a hand steady and the woman who removes that hand when it becomes a handle.

Her phone lit again. Lorna: *Soup still on. Parking lot sermon available on request.*

Iya typed: *Soup tomorrow. Sermon always.*

Unknown number: *You didn't block me.*

She didn't type back. Her thumb hovered, then went still. She looked at the reflection in the glass until the glass agreed to be a window again.

The train rose to ground farther north. Rain wrote on the window and then forgot its sentence. Iya pulled her notebook from her bag without planning to. The navy cover knew her hand. She wrote:

There's a line between being wanted and being kept. The danger is how easily one disguises itself as the other. A hand reaching for you can feel the same, whether it means comfort or control. Desire isn't the enemy. The cage is.

Tonight, I felt the difference in my bones.

Wanting can be kind.

Keeping can be prison.

I refuse to live behind someone else's lock.

She underlined lock once. Not twice. Once was a line; twice was a performance.

She closed the notebook. The car had changed in the way rooms change when you decide to leave them. The voice announced the next stop and the doors swiftly opened. She stepped into air that had decided to be honest: damp, unstyled, ordinary.

Outside, the city practiced its indifference with discipline. Signs buzzed. A laundromat glowed lemon and steam. A trumpet on an upper floor tested a scale and looked surprised when beauty almost happened.

At her building door, she chose the correct key on the first try. The lobby plant looked slightly less doomed. On the second landing, she heard Maris laugh through the wall. The sound made her mouth remember how to be kind to itself.

Inside the apartment, one lamp held the room open. A note on the table in Maris's emphatic handwriting: Left you the last slice of galette. Water the dumb fern if I forget (Bertrand is dramatic). Text me if you want me to walk you from the stop. A small heart. An arrow pointing at it labeled not a gift, a habit.

Iya lifted the foil. Apples shone like coins on a map. She ate one bite standing up, then another. Hunger returned as something clean instead of edged. She covered the rest for her tomorrow-self, who would also choose.

Her phone blinked once more. She let it go quiet. She watered Bertrand then washed her hands for longer than a sink demands—not to scrub the night off, but to tell skin the work was over.

At the desk, she opened the notebook again and added:

Close what does not open back.

She did not underline it. She closed the book. She breathed.

Out the window, the street let its neon write harmless poems on puddles. Somewhere a siren blared, and she watched the rain on the window settle into handwriting she could read.

Her phone slept face down on the table. Iya lay down and let quiet do what brains try to steal, waiting for sleep to come.

Before it took her fully, she had one last thought:

Presence without possession. Doors that close from the inside.

The building exhaled. Somewhere—maybe nowhere—another phone glowed. A thumb hovered over a screen, deciding whether to type again. The night didn't vote either way. It offered weather and walls and left people to be their own doors.

And when morning came for its shift, it would find a table wiped, a sponge resting on its soft belly to dry, and a woman who had chosen, and chosen, and chosen.

CHAPTER 15:

COUNTING WHAT REMAINS

Quiet Recalibration

The apartment felt different. Not bigger—but wider somehow, as though someone had cracked a window in a room Iya hadn't realized was sealed.

For three mornings in a row, she woke before her alarm and stayed in bed, letting the early light paint slow-moving shapes across the ceiling. No rush to get up. No buzzing phone dragging her into someone else's storm. Just the rhythm of her own breathing, the slow permission of silence.

Her pillow still carried the faintest trace of Maris's lavender conditioner—comfort in domestic disguise. Iya stared at the ceiling, aware of her body in a way she hadn't been in weeks: the muscles that weren't clenched, the jaw that wasn't locked, the heart that didn't race at phantom texts.

She let the apartment speak first: the lift's groan settling on the far side of the wall; the radiator's reluctant click into warmth; somebody upstairs running water too long, humming a song that never quite found the chorus. A delivery truck was double-parked outside, hydraulics sighing like a tired giant; somewhere, a bottle clinked against another bottle, and the day acknowledged itself.

She remembered other mornings—the ones she'd moved through like a corridor with alarms on both ends. Wake, scan, brace. The way she'd slowly turn over her face-down phone, like defusing a small device; the way she'd ration out silence like a medicine that might run out. Back then, her body didn't rest so much as collapse in between guard shifts.

This morning, she let the quiet sit on the couch with her, uninvited but not unwelcome. She watched dust spiral in the rectangle of light, tiny constellations that only existed when you slowed down enough to see them. She counted them for no reason. That was new too—doing something that didn't prove anything.

When she finally rose, the kitchen greeted her with the smell of frying garlic, sharp and golden, wrapping around her like an old sweater. Maris was at the stove, hair in a messy bun, moving with the unhurried precision of someone who believed breakfast was a kind of art.

"You're moving like a woman who just paid off a big debt," Maris said without turning, flicking the spatula with a practiced wrist.

"Maybe I did," Iya replied, reaching for a mug.

Maris glanced sideways, one brow arched. "Oh? Emotional? Financial? Spiritual?"

"A little of each."

Maris gave her a long look—the kind that measured truth, not tone. "Good. Because you were starting to get that face."

"What face?" Iya asked, amused.

"The one where you're pretending you're fine, but you've already rewritten your will just to spite someone."

Iya laughed—a real one this time, the kind that rose from her chest instead of her throat. "Well... I'm alive. I'm rested. And I'm still me."

"Mm." Maris nodded like a judge ruling in her favor. She plated eggs, slid one toward Iya, then sat across from her with her own. "That's all anyone gets to be. Everything else is just negotiation."

They ate with the easy clink of people who have weathered the same storms. The fork was warm in Iya's hand. She realized she hadn't sat for breakfast in weeks—not without her mind elsewhere, rehearsing the next explanation, the next deflection, the next line she might need to draw. Now, for the first time in what felt like months, she wasn't preparing for an ambush.

Her phone lay face-down on the counter, not buzzing, not a threat. She didn't reach for it. She let the world arrive in normal portions: steam fogging the window; the kettle's soft rattle as it settled; Maris tapping the heel of the loaf against the cutting board to test its stubbornness.

The apartment was ordinary. Which made it precious.

She rinsed her plate and set it in the rack, then wiped the counter out of habit, not fear—a small difference, but she felt it. The sponge squeaked. The air tasted faintly of browned butter and salt. Her hand hovered over the notebook on the sideboard, then rested on the cover—not opening it, she didn't need to, just acknowledging it was there.

"Okay," she said to the room, to herself. Not a declaration. An alignment.

The Measure of Care

Maris leaned back in her chair, coffee mug cradled between both hands like an anchor. She studied Iya the way only someone who lived under the same roof could—with a quiet intimacy that made silence stretch without feeling empty.

"So..." Maris began, drawing the word out as though testing the air. "How's the glamorous world of elder care these days?"

Iya smirked. "Oh, you know. Someone refused their medication, someone else told me the same story about their dog for the eighth time, and I got sneezed on twice before lunch."

Maris chuckled, covering her mouth with her mug. "See? That's what people think caregiving is—just the gross parts. Fluids, complaints, diapers. They don't see the real part of the job."

"They don't want to," Iya said simply. "They think it's all the worst parts of looking after someone, without any of the status. Like it's beneath them."

Maris set her mug down with a small thud. "From what I've seen—even just in my training—people don't value it until they need it. Until it's their parent, their spouse, their kid. Then suddenly it's—" she pitched her voice into an exaggerated wail—Oh my God, I don't know what we'd do without you.'"

The performance made Iya laugh, but the truth in it cut deeper. "And then when the crisis is over, they forget again. Like it never counted."

"Exactly," Maris said, leaning forward, elbows on the table. "It's strange. All these people with big titles and bigger egos, and the moment they can't feed themselves, wash themselves, or remember where they are, the only person who matters is the one willing to care for them."

Iya stirred her eggs absently, appetite half there. "I've seen CEOs cry because they couldn't button their own shirt. Women who've run whole households stop in the hallway because they forgot where the bathroom was. And when you help them, they look at you like you've given them back their life."

Maris's voice dropped. "That's not small work. That's the part of life nobody admits, because if they did, they'd have to change the way they measure worth."

The words sat between them, larger than the plates of food, larger than the kitchen.

Iya swallowed, shook her head. "People still look down on it. Like the only reason you'd do it is because you couldn't do something 'better.'"

Maris's lips pressed into a line. "Then maybe they've never been cared for properly. Because once you have, you know it's not beneath you—it's everything."

Iya breathed out slowly. "Exactly. But try telling the world that."

Maris squinted at her. "You know what your problem is?"

"Only one?"

"You give off this 'museum exhibit' energy," Maris said, wagging a finger. "'Observe respectfully, do not touch, plaque coming soon.'"

Iya snorted. "That's rich coming from the woman who labels the Tupperware like it's a crime scene."

"It is when you eat my leftovers." Maris grinned, then sobered. "But I'm serious. You walk around with that steady face and those calm hands and people think you're indestructible. They don't see the cost because you don't show it."

"I'm not hiding it. I'm choosing where it belongs."

"Which is different," Maris agreed. "But it also makes you look... I don't know—mythic. Like you were built for this."

Iya tilted her head. "Maybe I was built for this."

The sentence struck something in her as soon as she said it. She remembered nights holding trembling hands that had forgotten their own names, mornings brushing tangled hair while someone wept because they thought they were late for a job they hadn't had in thirty years. Those moments weren't glamorous, weren't Instagram-worthy—but they were the line between despair and dignity.

She exhaled slowly. "It's not that I'm always happy doing it. It's... more like it makes sense to me. Some people go back to work after a day off or a vacation and feel that drop—they call it 'back to reality.' I don't feel that. I don't dread it. If anything, I'm better when I'm in it."

The admission felt heavier than the words themselves.

She didn't add the other truth—that it didn't just mean the care home. That in another world, under other lights, with women who whispered their needs like secrets, she was still giving care. Different context. Same spine.

Maris tilted her head, eyes narrowing just a little. "Because it's the one thing that makes sense to you?"

"Maybe." Iya traced the rim of her mug with a fingertip, grounding herself in the circle. "It feels like I'm exactly where I'm supposed to be, doing something that matters."

She paused, and then, almost under her breath, said, "Presence without possession."

Maris caught it. She always did. "You should write that down," she said, smiling. "Before someone else pretends they thought of it first."

Iya gave a small smile back, but her chest was tight. That

phrase was starting to follow her like a shadow—one she needed to believe was her own.

Maris tapped the table twice, like a little gavel. "Also, we're out of garlic."

"That's what you took from that?"

"I can hold two truths at once," Maris said. "You're profound. And we need groceries."

Iya laughed into her mug, and the room lightened a shade.

Work as Anchor

The facility moved in its familiar rhythm, the kind of cadence you only noticed when you stepped into it from the outside world. Walkers tapped the linoleum like slow metronomes. A radio played in the staff lounge, faint through the wall, its station chosen not for taste but for its lack of commercials. Voices carried down the hall, sometimes laughter, sometimes confusion, sometimes the long sigh of someone remembering too much at once.

And always—always—the faint, stubborn scent of lemon cleaner and oatmeal, as if it were holding the building together like plaster.

In Room 8A, Mr. Howard sat by the window, scowling at the plant on the sill. A sturdy pothos, green but slightly wilted at the edges.

"It's looking sad," he said gravely, as if announcing bad news.

"It's not sad," Iya corrected, lifting the watering can. "It's being dramatic. There's a difference."

Mr. Howard squinted, then chuckled. "Like Mrs. Glenn down the hall."

"Exactly. And like you if I forget your coffee."

From the corridor, Lorna's voice rang out. "Miss Iyaaa, you're spoiling that man again! Pretty soon he'll be asking for breakfast in bed."

"As long as he doesn't ask for champagne, we're fine," Iya called back.

"Champagne?" Lorna scoffed, appearing at the doorway with her hand on her hip. "Please. Half these folks could out-drink you. Mr. Howard looks like he's hiding whiskey in his mouthwash."

Mr. Howard raised his voice, so it carried: "Careful, Lorna. If I admit it, half the floor will want a swig."

The three of them laughed, the sound spilling into the hallway and softening the air.

Moments like that always landed differently with Iya. It wasn't just banter—it was proof that care didn't have to be a heavy word. Sometimes it was laughter cracked open in the middle of a shift, or a room that felt warmer when you walked back out of it than when you walked in.

They turned the corner and found Mrs. Glenn humming in her armchair, calling out cheerfully, "Morning, Mary!"—not Iya's name, but one she used often.

"Morning, Mrs. Glenn," Iya replied without correcting her. She crouched, straightening the blanket on the woman's knees.

Mrs. Glenn patted her hand. "You always know how to make a person feel looked aftcr."

"That's the job," Iya said softly.

"No," Mrs. Glenn countered with a sharp shake of her head. "That's the gift."

Iya let the words sit for a beat before standing. She didn't argue. She didn't need to.

At the next door, Ms. Patel was dressed in her good cardigan, purse on her arm, sensible shoes laced with the seriousness of mission. She met Iya with a firm nod. "You're late," she scolded. "If we don't leave now, we'll miss the hymns."

"It's Wednesday," Iya said gently. "Church is on Sunday."

"Don't be silly," Ms. Patel replied, offended at the concept of calendars. "I can hear the choir."

Iya tilted her head. In the hallway, the radio from the lounge drifted—not hymns, but a commercial jingle that could impersonate one if it tried. "Tell you what," Iya said, offering her arm. "Choir's rehearsing today. We'll do a practice run to the end of the hall and back. Full procession."

Ms. Patel's chin lifted with dignity. "Good. And we will not rush. God does not like rushing."

They walked the hallway together—not fast, not slow, just in step. At the end of the corridor, Iya paused, nodded to an invisible congregation, then turned them both around with ceremony. Ms. Patel whispered amen under her breath, satisfied. Back at her door, she released Iya's arm. "You sing poorly," she said, which was true; Iya had hummed off-key on purpose.

"I do," Iya admitted. "But I show up on time."

"Hm." Ms. Patel considered this like a doctrine. "That's something."

By the time they reached the lounge, the TV was blaring the morning news, Mr. Klein shaking his head at headlines he didn't approve of. He didn't look at her when he spoke.

"You've got strong hands," he said suddenly. "Not the kind that break things. The kind that keep things from falling apart. Trouble with hands like those are, people start believing you'll hold everything forever. They forget your arms get tired too."

Iya let the words settle, heavier than his usual commentary. She didn't answer right away. She just flexed her fingers, as if to test whether he was right.

She wiggled her hands in front of her like a magician's trick. "Maybe I'll start dropping things on purpose, just to prove I can."

Klein snorted. "Do it. Watch how fast they notice you were the one holding them up all along."

Iya shook her head, smiling despite herself. "If you keep talking like that, I'll have to add 'resident philosopher' to your chart."

Klein didn't answer—he was already frowning at the news again, as if the anchors had personally offended him.

She moved on, but as she checked Mrs. Navarro's flowers and straightened the stack of board games by the window, her fingers kept remembering his words.

Strong hands.

Hands that carried without complaint.

Hands people too often mistook for permanent.

She flexed them once, quietly.

Still, the work carried her forward. Call lights, medication rounds, helping one patient find a missing slipper and another one find a misplaced memory. She refilled the ice water pitchers, signed for deliveries, adjusted blinds to outwit the afternoon sun. Each task was ordinary and infinite at once, like beads on a rosary. The repetition was not numbing—it was anchoring.

Care wasn't only about what you did. It was how you stayed inside it without letting the tide wash you out.

She caught Lorna at the whiteboard, blocking in the afternoon activities with her thick friendly letters. "You're writing like a coach before a championship," Iya teased.

"Every day is the playoffs," Lorna said. "And I play to win nap time."

They tapped fists—a ritual, a joke, a tiny agreement about the shape of the day. Then the cart squeaked forward, and the building hummed on.

A Quiet Beginning

The afternoon shift change carried its usual noises— clipboards swapping hands, carts squeaking back to the supply room, conversations clipped off mid-sentence by call bells. The rhythm had its own music by now, one that Iya could walk in her sleep.

Luna slid into step beside her, holding a chart like it might steady her hands. Her badge had already dulled at the corners —two months of use giving it the look of someone still new, but no longer raw. There was a nick on the plastic where it had caught on a doorjamb; a thread loose at the pocket seam; clear lip balm, not gloss. A person already adapting.

"I finally figured out the east wing without getting lost," Luna said lightly. "Next goal is remembering where they hide the extra linens before someone yells at me."

"That's the real test," Iya said, initialing a med sheet. "You can't survive here unless you know the shortcuts."

"I'm getting there," Luna smiled, but there was a spark behind it—not nerves, not just gratitude. Something more deliberate, as if she was taking notes on more than linen closets.

They stepped into Room 8A. Mr. Howard was tugging at his blanket, restless as always. Without a word, Iya straightened it, crouching so her eyes met his. His frown softened. The room settled.

Back in the hall, Luna's voice was quiet. "You didn't even ask. You just knew."

"It's not knowing," Iya said. "It's paying attention."

"But you make it look easy."

"Looks lie."

Luna tilted her head, filing that away. "So the trick is learning what to see, not just what to do?"

The way she said it made Iya glance at her twice. Most new staff absorbed tasks. Luna was watching method. Watching her.

They walked. Answered a call bell. Adjusted a footrest. Checked a med time. None of it dramatic, all of it necessary.

As they passed the lounge, Luna asked, "What's the hardest part about this job?"

"Deciding when to step in," Iya said. "And when to step back. Sometimes care is holding. Sometimes it's letting someone wobble."

Luna nodded, thoughtful, as though Iya had given her something more than an answer.

Her gaze lingered—longer than the question needed, longer than simple curiosity. Not admiration, not envy. Something quieter, but heavier. The kind of attention that plants itself and waits for time to grow.

From the lounge, Lorna's voice cut across the hall: "Miss Iyaaa, stop hiding the rookie. Let the rest of us break her in!"

Luna blushed, ducking her head, but her eyes—still fixed on Iya—didn't look away quickly enough.

The rest of the shift passed in the rhythm Iya knew by heart —meals, meds, laughter stitched over the rough patches.

Ordinary work, but steadier now, as though the weight she'd been carrying had found its corner of the room and sat down.

Later that evening, when the halls finally quieted, Iya caught sight of Luna again in the staff lounge. The young woman was laughing at something Lorna had said, shoulders loose, but her gaze flicked toward Iya once more. Not shy exactly —more like she was waiting to be invited into a room that hadn't opened yet.

Lorna clapped her hands together, grinning. "Alright, rookie. You survived two months without quitting, crying, or hiding in the supply closet. That means you're officially ready for the hazing."

Luna blinked, half-laughing. "There's hazing?"

"Of course," Lorna said, solemn as a preacher. "We make you mop the breakroom floor with a toothbrush. Builds character."

Luna threw up her hands. "That's it. I'm filing for early retirement."

"Denied," Lorna said. "You don't vest in your pension until you can find the good pens."

"The good pens?" Luna echoed.

"The ones that don't disappear," Lorna said. "Legend says there are three. Iya knows where two are."

Heads turned toward Iya with theatrical suspicion. Iya lifted her chart like a shield. "Allegedly."

The lounge erupted in chuckles. Someone banged a mug against the table; someone else wheezed. Luna covered her face with her hands, then peeked out between her fingers, smiling, an echo of relief loosening her shoulders.

When she dropped her hands, her eyes strayed back to Iya— just for a beat too long.

Iya held the glance, offered a small nod, then turned back to the chart in her hands. The laughter rolled on around them, but the quiet between their eyes lingered like the last note of a song.

The Widow

The evening had folded itself into that in-between hour when the streets grew quiet but hadn't yet given themselves fully to night. Shopfronts hummed under fading neon, and the air carried the faint warmth of roasted chestnuts from a vendor who worked the corner even in colder months. Iya walked at her usual pace—deliberate, steady, unremarkable. Her hands were free tonight, tucked into the pockets of her coat. She preferred the simplicity of it: nothing to carry, nothing to distract, nothing to explain.

It was then, half a block ahead, that she saw her.

The widow in red.

Except she was not in red anymore. Her coat tonight was a soft gray, cinched lightly at the waist, with a pale scarf wrapped loose at her throat. Her hair fell easier, no longer pinned in defensive neatness. She walked with someone— a man—close enough that his presence looked natural, his hand brushing lightly against her arm as he leaned to say something.

She laughed.

Iya felt the difference immediately. The sound was unpracticed, effortless, alive. Not forced, not polite. It was the kind of laugh that belonged to a woman who had remembered, at last, what it felt like not to guard every breath.

That laugh told Iya more than words could have.

The widow's eyes drifted forward through the crowd, then caught on Iya's. Her step faltered for just a heartbeat before it steadied. A smile rose to her lips, genuine and quiet, and she leaned closer to whisper into the man's ear. He glanced toward Iya, his eyes registering the unspoken request. With a small, respectful nod, he stepped aside.

The widow turned back toward Iya. Her smile deepened, a gentle invitation—the kind that opened space without demanding anything.

She crossed the short distance between them.

"Iya," she said softly, her voice both tentative and sure.

"Good evening," Iya replied, her tone calm, steady.

For a moment, they stood in the hush of recognition, two women bound not by daily life but by one night that had shifted something deep inside one of them. The world continued moving around them—footsteps, passing cars, the faint hiss of a bus brake—but it all seemed to wait outside their circle.

"You look well," Iya said.

"I am," the widow answered. Her smile carried warmth, not performance. She glanced over her shoulder briefly at the man who waited a few paces away, then back at Iya. "Better than I thought I could be."

Her voice softened, thickening with gratitude. "You gave me that... start."

Iya's lips curved into something just shy of a smile. "You gave it to yourself. I only reminded you where to look."

The widow exhaled a laugh, low and genuine. "Always so deliberate. Even now." She paused, words crowding her mouth before settling on the ones she needed to say. "I wanted to thank you. Not just for that night. For reminding me I was still here."

Iya's reply was gentle but certain. "That's all I could hope for. If you have found your own way, then the work is done."

Something inside the widow seemed to soften at those words. She nodded slowly, as though receiving permission she did not know she'd been waiting for. Her eyes shone, and though no tears fell, their brightness betrayed her.

She stepped forward. The embrace that followed was brief, tender, and whole. It wasn't clinging, nor broken, nor desperate. It was the kind of hug that seals something rather than reopens it. Iya allowed herself to return it with equal steadiness, her hand resting lightly against the widow's back before she let go.

When they separated, the widow's voice carried both release and certainty. "Goodbye, Iya."

Iya's smile reached her eyes this time, warm and sincere. "Goodbye."

The widow touched her sleeve once more, then turned back toward the man. He was waiting, patient and calm, his posture respectful. She slipped her hand into his without hesitation. He asked no questions, offered no suspicion, simply gave her hand a reassuring squeeze.

Together, they began to walk away.

She did not look back. She did not need to.

Iya lingered a moment on the sidewalk, watching them fold into the flow of the evening crowd. The widow's laughter reached her again, softer this time, but carrying the same freshness.

Only when they were out of sight did Iya resume her pace. Her steps matched the city again, measured, deliberate. Inside, she felt no ache, no longing, no unfinished thread. What she carried was quieter: completion.

She thought of the black notebook waiting in her drawer, the entry she had written weeks ago:

Client—Widow in red. Post-session prediction: relief will hold. Likely weeks before another call, if ever.

The words had proven true.

And now, so had the unspoken hope behind them.

A breeze tugged at her coat as she passed the chestnut vendor. She didn't stop, but the fragrance lingered, warm and smoky, following her down the street. She let it stay with her for a block or two, a reminder that sometimes care left no souvenirs except the lightness of knowing it had been enough.

Her part was finished.

Later, at home, she set her planner on the table and touched the folded page she'd written:

Will Give | Will Not Give.

They weren't just rules—they were anchors, a way to keep care from turning into surrender.

She added one more line under the last column, less an afterthought than a vow:

Will Not Give—The right for anyone to confuse my presence with possession.

She closed the planner. In the window, her reflection was steady. Not flawless. Not untouchable. Just clear.

Because presence is a choice.

Possession is a claim.

And the difference between the two was the only way her care could stay real.

Presence without possession.

Outside, the city moved as it always did—buses, sirens, laughter, rain turning sidewalks into mirrors. Life wasn't asking her to disappear. It was asking her to stand.

She turned off the lamp. The room did not feel smaller for the dark. It felt exact. Doors had closed where they needed to, and somewhere in the distance, another was beginning to open.

————————

www.ingramcontent.com/pod-product-compliance
Lightning Source LLC
Chambersburg PA
CBHW070753280626

47162CB00016B/211